I0725180

JACOB'S SONG

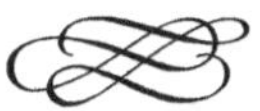

TIFFANY PATTERSON

Copyright © 2019 by TMP Publishing LLC/Tiffany Patterson

All rights reserved.

This is a work of fiction. Names, characters, businesses, places, events and incidents are either the products of the author's imagination or used in a fictitious manner. Any resemblance to actual persons, living or dead, or actual events is purely coincidental.

A special thank you to Melissa at There For You Editing (thereforyou.melissa@gmail.com) for editing.

CHAPTER 1

*G*race

"Hey, heads-up, Dr. Jackass is on a rampage today," Katie, a fellow RN, warned as she rounded the corner of the nurses' station.

I picked my head up, wrinkling my brows at her in confusion. "Dr. Jackass?"

Her warmly tanned cheeks creased as she smiled. "I keep forgetting how new you are around here. It's 'cause you fit in so well, Grace. Dr. Reynolds. Most of us refer to him as Dr. Jackass because … well—"

"He's a jackass," Rachel, the charge nurse, stated before she and Katie giggled. However, Rachel quickly recovered, putting on a stern face. "But we don't say that, do we?" She leveled a look at Katie.

"Not out loud."

I smirked at the banter.

"This will be your first surgery with Dr. J– uh, Reynolds, right, Grace?"

"I believe so," I answered, standing and smoothing out the pants of the electric blue scrubs I wore.

"Okay. Well, good."

I frowned. The pitch in her voice made it sound like it was the opposite of *good*.

"He can't be that bad. He's rated as one of the stars to watch in the city as far as plastic surgeons are concerned." I held up the healthcare magazine I'd been looking through, which featured an article on Dr. Jacob Reynolds. I hadn't actually read the article, having just picked up the magazine from my mailbox that morning on my way into work.

"They're not wrong either. He's one of the cleanest, most precise surgeons I've seen in the OR," Katie complimented. "But he's still a jac—"

She paused when Rachel cleared her throat.

"Well, I don't need to be friends with him to work with him."

"That's true, and thank God for it. Poor Melissa couldn't get along with him."

"Who's Melissa?" I remembered every nurse on our floor in the six weeks I'd been working here at Memorial Hospital and that name did not ring a bell.

"The nurse you replaced," Rachel responded.

My eyes widened. "He didn't—"

"No," Katie started, shaking her head, "her leaving had nothing to do with him. She had her first baby and decided she liked being a mom more than she liked being a nurse."

I nodded in understanding.

"Anyway, just know that Dr. Reynolds is not in a good mood today. This surgery was supposed to happen last week and had to be rescheduled."

"Why?" I stared at Rachel.

Rolling her eyes, she exhaled on an annoyed sigh. "A freaking fourth year med student who was interviewing for the surgical residency program contaminated the sterile field."

All three of us whistled in disbelief.

"Oh I bet the surgical techs had fun with that."

"They were pissed," Rachel answered.

"But none more than Dr. Reynolds."

"I'd imagine so."

Contaminating the sterile field in the OR was not a minor incident. It sometimes required having to entirely reschedule an operation, which was the case with this surgery. Imagine having everything prepped and ready, including the patient, and then someone does something as little as placing their unclean hand on the very instrument that was to be used to cut a patient open.

"A fourth year should've known better," I tutted.

"Absolutely. Ruined his chances of being accepted into the program."

"As it should have."

"Absolutely," Rachel agreed. "Anyway, just be forewarned. We try not to schedule newer nurses with Dr. Reynolds, but you're not a first year, so …" She shrugged.

I slightly inclined my head. A first year I was not. I'd been a practicing nurse for the past four and a half years. So while I was new to Memorial, I wasn't new to this world and I loved my job.

"I'm going to go look at the board and patient charts, and then start prepping," I told the women over my shoulder as I exited the nurses' station.

"Have a good one," Katie wished as she grabbed her purse from the desk. She'd worked the night shift and was headed home for the day, to return later that evening.

Stopping, I looked at the mounted whiteboard with all the scheduled surgeries, operating room numbers, and names of patients and physicians on it. Confirming the time and location of my surgery, I continued down the hallway to the patient's room, pausing to look at the chart in my hands to again confirm I had the right room, patient, and surgery.

"Mrs. Lyons," I greeted with a smile as I lightly tapped the door before entering.

The woman in the bed smiled. "Yes."

"I'm Nurse Young. I'll be the head nurse in the operating room during your surgery today. I just wanted to check on you and introduce myself before you're wheeled out."

"Aren't you a pretty thing," she sighed, her smile growing. The strands of her red hair peeked out of the hair covering that'd been placed over her head. "If I had that body thirty years ago, I wouldn't be having this surgery now."

I lifted an eyebrow, letting my eyes quickly scan the outline of her body, which was covered by the hospital gown she wore.

"Well, thank you, but you look great yourself."

"All it took was having my stomach cut open two years ago."

I nodded, assuming she was referring to the bariatric surgery she had at this very same hospital two years earlier.

"Says here, you've lost a total of a hundred and fifty pounds," I confirmed by reading her chart.

"And that's before this excess skin removal surgery."

"Which we're doing today. You're going to be up and at 'em in no time."

Mrs. Lyons' lips parted for her to respond, but she was cut short by a deep, gruff voice behind me.

"We don't make promises like that around here."

A shiver ran down my spine so quickly, I jumped a half an inch off the ground. Pivoting to look over the new occupant in the room, the first thing I noticed was the black scrubs indicating he was a surgeon. And just in case that wasn't clear enough, emblazoned across the left side of this scrub shirt read 'Dr. Jacob Reynolds.'

Slowly, my gaze rose past the cleft chin, chiseled jaw, pink lips, and aquiline nose to collide with the grey eyes that caught me off guard when I opened that healthcare magazine back at the nurses' station. I'd thought there was no way this guy's eyes were grey in real life, but now here I was, standing face-to-face with him, and sure enough, they were. They were also narrowed and filled with storm clouds that I found intriguing.

Lifting my chin, I stated, "Dr. Reynolds, a pleasure to meet you finally. I'm Nurse Young and will be assisting you with this surgery today."

Slowly, those almost hypnotizing eyes scoured the length of my body before he snorted and moved past me.

I jutted my head back. *The hell?*

"Mrs. Lyons," he said curtly as he moved closer to the patient's bed. "The nurse will finish preparing you for surgery. We should begin in about another thirty minutes. Do you have any questions?" He was focused on the woman as he held out his hand to me.

I suddenly realized he was silently demanding I hand him the patient's chart. I placed it square in the middle of his palm. Rather harshly if the way his sharp gaze rose to meet my eyes was any indication.

I gave him a little smirk in return. Katie and Rachel may have been right about this one. It didn't matter, however. I meant what I said as well. I didn't need him to be anything more than professional as we got this surgery done.

"No, Dr. Reynolds. All of my questions have been answered. I'm just ready for this extra skin to be gone." Mrs. Lyons lifted her left arm, wiggling it, demonstrating the extra skin that sagged against her muscle. A result of her extreme weight loss.

"Very well. Everything looks good here. I'll see you in there." With that, Dr. Reynolds turned and headed out of the room, not even acknowledging me or the two additional staff who just entered the room.

"He's not too friendly but he's a master with a scalpel," Mrs. Lyons stated, smiling.

"Hm."

"He's not too bad to look at either." She wiggled her eyebrows and giggled like a woman half her age with a crush.

"I wouldn't know," I stated as I pulled out my pen and began writing down some notes on Mrs. Lyons' chart.

"Aw c'mon. I may be older than you by about thirty years but I'm not dead!"

My gaze fell to the age on Mrs. Lyons' chart. She wasn't too far off, given her age was fifty-seven. She was about twenty-six years older than my current age.

"You're nowhere near dead, Mrs. Lyons."

"Sure ain't! And I dropped that weight, plus another two hundred pounds once I divorced that good for nothing husband of mine. At fifty-seven, I'm feeling better than I have in the last twenty-years. And as soon as Dr. Reynolds gets rid of these bat wings of mine ..." she paused to lift both her arms, swinging the extra skin hanging from them, "I'm back on the market. This time I'm looking for a younger man."

I giggled along with her. "Okay, Mrs. Lyons. Let's get you into surgery and healed before all of that."

Folding her arms across her abdomen, she nodded. "I wouldn't try anything with Dr. Reynolds though. He's mean. Nice to dream, however."

I shook my head and rolled my eyes. I could tell Mrs. Lyons was enjoying her new life.

The other staff and I spent the next twenty minutes prepping Mrs. Lyons for surgery prior to rolling her out of the room. I headed to the washroom right outside of operating room number two, where this surgery would be taking place. As I pushed through the door, I caught a glance of Dr. Reynolds just before he exited the washroom and entered the threshold of the surgical room. For the slightest moment he hesitated as he stared at me over the mask covering the lower half of his face. He studied me as if trying to figure out a puzzle.

The strangest emotion overcame me. I felt saddened by the fact that I couldn't see those pink lips of his.

"Get yourself together, Grace," I admonished, shaking my head and turning on the fountain to thoroughly scrub my hands. Minutes later, I was entering the operating room, sterile, masked up, cap covering the low bun I'd pulled my curly strands into, and ready for surgery.

"Are we holding you up?"

The entire room fell silent and I felt all eyes on me.

I glanced up to see Dr. Reynolds staring down at me through the clear part of his face mask. Obviously, his snarky question had been directed at me.

I straightened my back and stared at him the same way he was staring at me. "No more than you're holding Mrs. Lyons' surgery up. She's really looking forward to getting rid of those bat wings, so let's get to it, shall we?" I smiled, but since I had on a face mask, no one could actually see it. However, I assumed the narrowing of my eyes from the grin was enough to get my point across.

One of Dr. Reynolds' dark, almost black, eyebrows lifted, as if he was surprised that I'd dared to speak back to him. I got the inclination he wanted to respond but he held himself back.

Snorting, I moved to the side of the operating table, standing behind and to the right of Dr. Reynolds, closest to the table holding the surgical instruments. I peeked over at Mrs. Lyons whose eyes were closed as the oxygen mask covered her face. I glanced up at the head of the table and winked at Dr. Atkins, one of my favorite anesthesiologists at Memorial Hospital.

I caught the wrinkle in the chestnut brown skin around his eyes, his grey beard covered by his mask.

"Let's begin. Nurse, the patient's vitals," Dr. Reynolds stated abruptly, breaking the silence in the room.

Directing my attention to the monitors, I read them loud and clear, for the room to hear. After going through the procedure that was to be taking place, and correctly identifying the parts of the body that were to be operated on, the surgery began.

I carefully kept my eye on the patient's vitals and assisted by providing suctioning for Dr. Reynolds so he could see where he was cutting and stitching. And while he was at times gruff with his direction on telling me where and when to suction, the five-hour surgery went rather smoothly. As Mrs. Lyons was being wheeled out of the operating room, I followed the bed, keeping a close eye on her vitals and then charting them once we made our way into the recovery room.

"Oh, nurse?"

I turned to see a woman who appeared to be about the same age as me with long, red, curly hair coming toward me.

"Were you in there with my mom?"

I lifted an eyebrow. "And your mother would be?"

"Katherine Lyons. I'm her daughter, Jane. How is she? Did the surgery go well?"

I smiled. "I can't discuss the operation in depth. For now, just know that she is resting well. The doctor will be out shortly to—"

"Oh, Dr. Reynolds," the woman called, looking over my shoulder.

I turned to see Dr. Reynolds moving toward us. He glanced at me briefly before his eyes moved to the other woman.

"How's my mother?"

"Surgery went well. As I assume the nurse has—"

"Nurse Young," I interjected.

He paused, looking to me with a wrinkle in his forehead, but I turned back to the woman in front of me.

"Nurse Young should've already told you that your mother is now resting. And as long as she sticks to the recovery plan, I recommend she should do just fine. Is there anything else?"

Even I was jarred by his curt manner.

"N-No. Um, can I see her?"

"No."

"Not yet," I quickly added, giving Dr. Reynolds a sideways look. "You mother needs to spend a little more time in recovery until she can be brought back to her room. It's just a precaution we take with all our patients," I added to smooth out the worry I saw beginning to form on the woman's face. "It should only be another thirty minutes or so. Go have a cup of coffee in the cafeteria, and by the time you get back she should be ready for you."

The woman pushed out a breath and looked between Dr. Reynolds and I before nodding and turning to head toward the elevators.

Folding my arms across my chest, I turned to Dr. Reynolds. "You could've been a little nicer. She was obviously concerned about her mother," I immediately started, not knowing what was prompting me.

"Excuse me?"

"You heard me."

He angled his head. "She didn't need to be concerned. Her mother was in capable hands and it's not the first time she's been through a surgery."

"But every surgery comes with risk, which you are well aware of, and likely, so is she."

"Her mother's fine unless there's something you want to tell me that I don't know." He lifted an eyebrow and folded his arms across his chest, and I couldn't help but notice his muscles as they bunched and bulged.

"No," I stubbornly responded.

"Great. Then Ms. Lyons is expected to be up and on her feet in no time. In the meantime, you should get back in the recovery room to chart her vitals."

"Don't tell me how to do my job."

That retort stopped him in his tracks, and he turned to stare at me. He didn't say anything, just gave me another up and down look before sauntering off down the hallway.

Now I knew why Katie and Rachel referred to him as Dr. Jackass.

* * *

"I'm on my way to the store," I responded into the speakers of my Jeep Cherokee as I talked on the phone with my younger sister, Journey.

"Are you going swimming tonight?"

"Absolutely." I pushed out a hard breath. It was a long day. Not only had I assisted in the surgery with Dr. Reynolds, but after that I was in another trauma surgery that took almost seven hours. The patient had been in a hit and run accident. I often went swimming at the gym I had a membership at after long days. My sister knew this.

"Aren't you tired?"

"Yup, but I have off tomorrow, so I get to sleep in."

"Hey, maybe I can come to Williamsport for a visit soon."

"Maybe," I mumbled, half paying attention to my sister while eyeing the parking spot of a man who was just leaving. As soon as he pulled off, I quickly turned in.

"All right, Journey, I'm here. I'll give you a call later in the week."

"'Kay, don't work too hard."

"Love you."

"Same. Bye."

I disconnected the call and proceeded into the grocery store. It was a little after nine o'clock at night and I just worked a twelve hour shift. Though I was tired, my body had become used to the long hours on my feet so I didn't feel too drained by the day. Instead, I hungered for one of the couscous, salmon, and veggie salads prepared at this grocery store. I loved the lemony dressing they paired the dish with. That for dinner and a few laps in the pool and I'd sleep like a baby.

After I picked up a carton of the pre-made salad, I made my way through the rest of the produce section, picking out a couple of the items I needed for the rest of the week. Due to the time of night, the store only had a handful of other customers and the overhead music could be heard clearly. As soon as Whitney Houston's "I Wanna Dance With Somebody" came on, my shoulders began moving.

My head bobbed as I sang out loud, feeling the music, and wiggling my hips a little. Right before the second round of the chorus came in, I felt myself being watched. My eyes swung to my right and left but no one was there. That was when I spun around and damn near fell backwards when I was met with stormy grey orbs. The very same ones that haunted me earlier in the day. He didn't say anything, just stared.

Feeling defensive, I placed my free hand on my hip while holding the handcart up with my forearm in front of me. "Can I help you?"

"Nurse by day and store clerk by night."

"I didn't mean can I help you with your groceries. I meant—" I sighed, feeling frustrated because I was sure he knew what I meant by my first question. "It's creepy to stare at people in public."

"No more so than to perform to Whitney Houston in the produce aisle."

Point made.

"Good music is to be performed anywhere." I shrugged, unashamed.

"If you say so, Nurse …"

"Young," I added when he didn't finish my name. "Nurse Young. My friends call me Grace, but you …" I stopped, looking him up and down scornfully, "are not a friend so you get to refer to me as Nurse Young."

I gave him one final look before turning on my heels and heading to the cash register to pay for my items.

Minutes later, I found myself eating my dinner in the front seat of my Cherokee, trying hard to get Dr. Reynolds' six foot-three frame out of my mind. Once I finished, I got out of my car, tossed the empty container in the trash, and entered the twenty-four hour gym. Despite the late hour, the gym had a number of patrons roaming about. I waved at a few colleagues I saw. This particular gym offered a special discount for employees of Memorial, which was why it was common to see co-workers here from time to time.

I made a beeline for the locker room and quickly changed into the black one-piece, Speedo bathing suit I kept in my gym bag. Pushing my bag into one of the lockers and then sealing it shut with the lock I carried, I then adjusted my blue swim cap to make sure all of my hair was covered, and affixed the straps of my goggles before exiting the back entrance of the locker room that led to the pool and aquatics area. Thankfully, there was only one other person in the pool, leaving four lanes for me to choose from. Opting for one of the middle lanes, I stretched and did a few warm up exercises before diving in.

I grunted as soon as my body entered the water, getting used to the chilliness of it. The gym said the pool was heated but I was pretty sure they were full of it. However, after a few moments my body adjusted once I did some bobs and a few other exercises to warm up and prepare for a half a mile to a mile of swimming laps, depending on how I felt.

After the first three laps I was feeling good, as if I could continue swimming forever.

And that's when it happened.

One moment I blinked and opened my eyes and swear I saw grey eyes staring back at me underneath the water. Pausing, I blinked and glanced up and around the pool to find only myself and the other swimmer who'd been there before I came in. She was busy minding her own business. Meanwhile, I was envisioning the doctor I helped perform a surgery with earlier that morning.

Try as hard as I might, I couldn't shake the look of those eyes. It wasn't just the color, that was odd and alluring enough. It was the way he appeared as if there was a continuous storm brewing just beneath the surface of those eyes. Like at any moment, one wrong word or occurrence could send him over the edge. And interestingly, I hated to admit, but I also noticed how that look subsided while he was in the operating room. As if whatever troubles he carried seemed to dissipate the moment he took the scalpel into his hand.

No! I yelled to myself in my head. I was *not* even going there. Whatever mess Jacob Reynolds had going on was his and his alone to figure out. I spent enough time carrying the burdens of other people throughout my life. I was not about to seek out the burdens of a grown man. Dr. Reynolds was obviously doing well enough on his own. And if he wasn't, so be it. It was none of my concern.

CHAPTER 2

*J*acob

"You hit like a fucking pussy!" I derided the guy opposite me as we both circled one another inside of the sixteen by sixteen foot ring. Our fists were tightly coiled, and save for the cloth wraps around our knuckles and fingers, there was little protection from the blows we rained on one another. That was the appeal—for me, at least.

"You're fucking crazy, Doc!" Brick yelled in response.

The sardonic smile I'd already been wearing, grew in size.

"I know," I growled before quickly spinning and sweeping Brick's leg. A round of cheers from the onlookers could be heard behind me but I paid them no mind. I didn't give a shit about the people watching this fight between Brick and I. All I cared about was the pain.

The pain of being hit so hard that it took my breath away.

Or the pain of landing the perfect punch against an opponent's bone, so that the sensation bounced back and moved through my knuckles and up my arm, reaching my chest.

It was only once I started feeling that pain that the memories of the day started to fall away. It was only then that I was truly able to relax, a little, at least.

The physical pain was better than the memories.

Today, the memory that I couldn't shake loose was what happened in the OR. I'd been performing a simple breast lift on a patient. A second year resident joined me as part of his training. My first instinct was to kick him out of the wash room when he entered with that stupid, fucking cocky-ass grin on his face. But I opted to let him stay. After all, Memorial is one of the best teaching hospitals in the state. And despite going against my first instincts, I let the resident assist in a delicate process during the procedure. The dumb fucker ended up nicking one of the patient's arteries.

Thus, a surgery that should've been relatively simple and uncomplicated nearly turned deadly. All because I let a fucking resident join in. That was my fuck up. And that is what brought me to the Underground.

"Aw fuck!" Brick grunted when a fist of mine landed in his ribs.

"Feeling a little fleshy, Brick. Been eating good, huh?" I continued to taunt. It was a lie, however. Brick was just as solid as his Underground name indicated. The man was built like a goddamn brick wall. And whereas most guys with his size and build were rather slow, that wasn't the case with Brick. He'd obviously been working on his agility. Which was why in the next second I found myself flat on my back, flailing as his large, six-foot-six nearly two-hundred-and-fifty-pound frame came down on top of me.

Thankfully, I was expecting one of his infamous takedowns, and hurriedly countered his move with one of my own. I managed to wiggle out of his hold and get my legs to wrap around his upper body. I could feel him struggling to get free from the inevitable but it was too late. My legs were soon wrapped tightly around his neck, squeezing the air from him.

He pounded with one fist against my leg but the pain from his punches only invigorated me more. I knew I'd be covered in bruises tomorrow from this fight, but the deep satisfaction I got from the pain was almost intoxicating.

"Let him up!" I heard Buddy yell from the side of the ring.

That's what forced me to release Brick. When I did, I heard the gagging and coughing sounds as he fought inhale normally again.

"Shit!" Brick cursed once he finally got back on his feet. "Anyone ever tell you, you fight like that fucker Luke whatever the hell his name is, from the NFA?" Brick sputtered in between breaths just after he tapped knuckles to signal the end of the fight.

"I don't watch the NFA. I don't know who the fuck that is," I gruffly answered, quickly dismissing his comment and turning to head out of the ring.

"You look like him a little, too," Brick yelled behind me.

Pausing, I turned back to him, my eyes narrowed. I swore I caught something glinting in his eyes. As if he wanted to say more but chose not to.

I spun on my heels and headed for the changing room. I moved through the throng of guys clamoring to pat my back after a fight or angling to convince Buddy to let them in the ring for a fight of their own.

I didn't stay to find out who was entering the ring next. I got what I came here for. Relief.

That was all I ever sought most nights in this place that to the outside world looked like an abandoned building. But to the men who gathered here two to three nights out of the week, we knew it was more. It was a place where most of us chose to let our demons out so we wouldn't unleash them on the rest of the world.

"Good fight, Reynolds," I heard from behind me as I redressed in the pair of dark jeans and T-shirt I'd worn to the Underground that night.

I rose to my full six-foot-two height, which still caused me to be about three inches shorter than the man standing opposite me.

"Connor." I nodded but didn't bother to reply to his initial comment. He never called me by my Underground name—which was Doc—for obvious reasons. Most of the men down here were professionals with our own careers or businesses. But like I said, everyone needed some sort of outlet to release the bullshit of the day.

"You get what you needed?"

I nodded while also throwing the strap of my gym bag over my shoulder. "I always do," I answered as I moved past him and through the door of the changing room to take me out into the main area again. I could feel Connor's eyes on my back but he didn't say anything else. As the co-organizer of this underground fighting ring, he was sort of the Godfather of the guys down here, I supposed. But not mine. I didn't need a fucking father figure or anyone else to oversee me.

After exiting through the main door, I hopped into my dark-colored Range Rover to make the twenty-minute drive back to my condo. However, once I arrived and pulled into my parking spot in the enclosed garage, I wasn't ready to head upstairs just yet.

I still had the energy from the fight coursing through my veins and that did not make for a good night's sleep. Thus, instead of heading toward the elevator to the twelfth floor of my building, I headed for the stairs that led to the open sidewalk. Walking aimlessly for a while, I ended up approximately ten blocks from where I started—on a street lined with bars and a few restaurants that converted to lounges this late in the evening.

Most of the doors of the nightclubs and bars were open, seeking to lure people through their doors. The giggles and cheers of the patrons in each of the bars turned my fucking stomach. I didn't like being in large groups of people. Hell, I didn't like most people in general. So, I opted to keep walking, with no intentions of stopping at any of the clubs. There was a bar at the end of this street that was usually pretty quiet. Every time I came to this establishment, there were only a handful of other patrons; I wondered how they stayed open. Nevertheless, the beers were cold and that's all I needed.

Just as I was passing one of the newer lounges on the street, my feet stopped moving. All on their own. I found myself turning to look inside the lounge. Of course, the lights were low, making it difficult to fully see around, but the sound coming from the center stage was what pulled me closer.

Before I could tell what was happening, I entered the lounge as if I was being pulled in. The smooth, soft sound of the voice coming from the front of the room held the entire audience captive. She wasn't belting out the song, but the way her vocal cords wrapped around every single note, as if they were her own little playthings to dance over, held all of our rapt attention. And I hadn't even seen her face yet. Once I did, it was as if someone punched me in the gut.

"Grace," I whispered, saying her name for the first time.

She was no longer dressed in those electric blue scrubs all the nurses wore. This Grace was dressed in a skintight, black mini dress that stopped inches above her knees. The dress was sleeveless and the lights on the stage perfectly reflected off the tawny brown skin of hers. Those hickory eyes were enhanced by the dark eyeshadow she wore, and her heart-shaped lips were lined in a blood red color. This wasn't Nurse Young on stage.

This was a woman singing on stage, begging her lover not to judge her. Her voice was cooing in a way that wasn't a turnoff, which I didn't understand how that was even possible. She swayed her perfect hips in time with the music, slowly and hauntingly. The heels on her feet gave an additional four inches to her five-foot-six height. I took every inch of her body in. From the top of her head, noting the bouncy curls hanging around her shoulders, to the smooth tops of her perfectly formed shoulders, over her collarbones, down to her adequately sized breasts which were outlined by the tight dress. The way her small waist gave way to her hips reminded me of the images patients would often bring to my office asking if I could make them look like this model or that one.

This woman had a body my patients paid thousands of dollars for. And I would bet dollars to donuts she hadn't spent any time on a surgeon's table to earn it.

Somehow, I found myself much closer to the stage than I'd anticipated. Luckily, I was able to get ahold of myself within seconds of her finishing the song. I backed away from the stage, not wanting to take my eyes off of her until the very last moment. She didn't see me due to the fact that she was busy bowing and receiving hugs from some of the band members on the stage. I took that opportunity to slip out the same door that'd allowed me entrance.

I shook my head as I turned and reversed my steps to carry myself back to my home. I don't know how long it took to get back because I was too busy replaying every second of Grace's performance in my head. Whenever I came to the end, it was almost like I'd hit the rewind button and replayed the tape all over again. I did that over and over until I arrived home, making it behind closed doors.

Pressing my back against the door, I closed my eyes, and again she was there, crooning her fucking heart out. She'd kept me hypnotized —so much so that the surgery from earlier, the Underground, and everything else fell away. However, she'd held my attention from the first moment I laid eyes on her. It was the way she looked at me. She didn't show the signs of fear that other women did. Even women who I dated in the past tried to get me to open up to them, but I refused because I could see the fear in their eyes. They'd never say as much, but I saw it. The storm clouds I often found staring me back in the mirror in my eyes, the emotions that sent me to the Underground to fight, and my off-putting demeanor struck fear in them.

But not Grace.

I found myself smirking as I remembered the stubborn way she lifted her chin at me in defiance. How she mouthed back when I put her on the spot in the OR. She wasn't afraid of me, and that pulled me to her just as much as her siren voice drew me to the stage in that lounge.

"Fucking pull it together," I growled at myself, starting to feel pissed off. I took a walk to work out the energy from fighting only to return with a different type of energy moving through me.

I huffed some more as I pulled my shirt over my head, tossing it into the grey laundry bin I kept right next to the door of my master bedroom. Moving to the bathroom across the hall, I took a long, steamy shower, hoping that would help. It did, but just enough to wash away most of the events of the day.

Once I dried off, put on a pair of running shorts, and climbed onto my empty mattress, save for one uncovered pillow, I was almost ready for sleep. My final act of the night was to reach for the remote I kept on the far nightstand and turn on the large flat screen mounted on the wall directly across from me. I pressed a couple of buttons, pleased to find that the NFA fight I scheduled to be recorded earlier that night was saved.

As usual, I'd already looked up the result of the fight but wanted to see the actual fight for myself. I sped through all the commentator talk and other bullshit that didn't hold my attention, to get to the actual fight. I stated at the screen as one of the top NFA fighters, Luke McConnell, took on another, much less skilled opponent. I kept the fight on mute because the voices of the fucking commentators had my fingers inching to get them in the ring. All of the shit they talked, asking whether or not Luke was passed his prime, washed up, or just lazy pissed me off.

Once I saw him place his adversary in a very similar leg chokehold I put on Brick a few hours earlier, I knew it was over. I pressed the power button, turning off the TV before the official bell rang. Like I said, I already knew the results.

Tossing the remote back onto the nightstand and turning over on my side, I closed my eyes and let the exhaustion of the day do the rest.

* * *

GRACE

"That was a great set tonight, Grace."

I inhaled deeply, forcing myself not to roll my eyes. Plastering a big smile on my face, I spun around and thanked Jackson for his compliment. And I silently prayed that that's where he would leave it. Unfortunately, he just couldn't.

"We make a pretty good team on stage, don't we?"

I couldn't help the ballooning of my eyes that was caused by that statement, but again, I relaxed my face and nodded.

"Yeah, sure."

We had just gotten off the stage together. While Jackson was a very good saxophone player, he also had a nice voice. And sure, it did match well with mine when we sang H.E.R's "Best Part". But that was where it ended … for me, at least.

"So, I was thinking our union didn't need to end once we got off the stage."

Lifting an eyebrow, I cocked my head to the side, and suddenly a burst of laughter fell from my lips. "I wasn't expecting that," I snorted.

"Come on? You weren't expecting me to ask you out?" he retorted good-naturedly.

Shaking my head, I held my hand up. "No, I mean, yes. I was expecting you to ask me out but not with that type of pick-up line." Though a saxophone player, Jackson came across as actually pretty shy where women were concerned. At about six-foot, caramel-colored, smooth skin, and a bald head, he wasn't a bad looking guy either. You'd think women were falling over themselves to get to him, and yet he seemed to be unaware of his good looks and charisma afforded to him by his career.

"Ron told me that one. He suggested I give it a try." He smirked.

"Lesson number one, don't take dating advice from Ron. Of all people." Ron was a notorious serial monogamist. The man would meet a woman one night, by the following week she was living with him, they were in love and getting married, and a month later it was all over. In the last year I'd been singing at Rocket, I counted at least five supposedly serious relationships Ron had been in.

"Noted. So about the da—"

"No." I shook my head.

Jackson's shoulder's instantly deflated, and I ignored the little voice telling me I was being too harsh.

"Listen, it's not you. It's me. And I totally know that's a thing people say when really it's not them, it's the other person. But in this case ... it totally is me."

Jackson's forehead wrinkled as he gave me a confused look. "That doesn't make any sense. How do you—"

"Look, do you want kids? A home? A woman to build a family with?"

"Sure, of course. Doesn't everyone?"

"Not me. I mean not in the practical sense. I spent much of my life raising and caring for my little sister and my m— uh, others from a young age." I shook my head, refusing to divulge more information. "It's not going to work," I stated firmly.

I watched as the hope drained from Jackson's eyes. The twinge of guilt I felt was ignored as I raised my chin. "We can still be friends."

With that, a grin opened up on Jackson's face until his lips spread wider, allowing a deep chuckle to emerge. "Now *that* line is the kiss of death if ever I've heard one."

Lowering my face, I laughed to myself. He was right.

"It's cool," he finally stated, shrugging.

I refrained from telling him another one of those cheesy lines you hear to let someone down gently. *There're other fish in the sea* or whatever. Truth was, Jackson had other options. He was good looking with an appealing career. He'd be fine.

"I'm heading out for the night. You have a good one," I said, grabbing my purse off the back of the chair and turning to head out, not even waiting for his response. I wasn't a particularly cold woman, nor was I immune to a man's charm. At the moment, I didn't feel the need for romantic entanglements in my life. I just started my job at Memorial, and though I wasn't new to nursing, taking on a new position anywhere came with its own amount of stress. Add to that I was considering going back to school at some point, and the timing simply wasn't right for romance.

CHAPTER 3

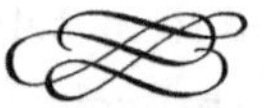

*G*race

"You're assisting Reynolds again," Stephanie, the scheduling nurse for my morning shift, informed me as soon as I placed my bag under the desk of the nurses' station.

I stood up to my full five-foot-five height with a raised eyebrow.

Stephanie shrugged. "You work well with him. And Janice is afraid of him." She whispered the last part.

I glanced over Stephanie's shoulder to Janice, whose back was to us as she typed something into the computer. I knew what Stephanie said was true. Janice was afraid of Dr. Reynolds. She would turn a corner and go the opposite direction whenever he walked in her direction. I'd seen it happen.

I shook my head. The day I let a man, or anyone for that matter, make me cower in fear like that was the day I'd take my last breath on this Earth. I'd been through and seen too much to let any one person put that kind of fear into me. *Even if that person is a six-foot-two, broadly built, chiseled jaw man with grey irises, and an impressively skilled surgeon to boot. So what that he—*

"Did you hear me, Grace?"

Shaking my mind free of run away thoughts, I looked down at Stephanie. "Huh?"

"I said, you two have a scheduled boob job this morning."

I blinked. "Boob job?"

Why the question came out as me not knowing what in the world she was talking about, I couldn't explain.

"Yeah, it was scheduled for last week but the patient had to put it off. Family drama or something. Seems her kids don't think a woman in her mid-fifties needs her boobs done, but ..." Stephanie trailed off, shrugging.

"Okay," I said slowly, gathering my thoughts. "I'm going to go check in with the patient, run her vitals, and make sure everything's on the up and up."

Stephanie nodded and then her gaze dipped back to the computer screen as she began moving on to her next task of the day.

All the way down the hall, I managed to keep my thoughts from straying to the fact that I would be working with Dr. Reynolds. He was just a man. Nothing more, nothing less.

"Hello, Mrs. Churchill," I greeted, knocking lightly on the door to the room of the patient being operated on.

"Hello," a woman who appeared to be in her early to mid-fifties smiled and greeted from the bed.

"Looks like we'll be performing a surgery on you today," I joked.

"I sure hope so."

Smiling, I peered down at the chart I'd grabbed from the wall-mounted box, right outside of the patient's door. I checked over Mrs. Churchill's vitals and recorded them, satisfied that everything looked great.

"Dr. Reynolds should be in soon to go over any last minute questions you might have about the surgery, and then we'll begin prepping you, all right?"

"How long will my mom's recovery time be?"

I blinked, looking across the room at the man who'd just abruptly interjected. I noticed him when I first walked in the room, as he frowned from the corner. I kept my smirk to myself. I'd seen similar scenarios before, where a patient's family member, namely their child, found it appalling that their parent would want any type of cosmetic surgery.

"I'm sure Dr. Reynolds will be better able to answer those types of questions for you, Mr ..."

"Churchill. Same as my mother's."

"Mr. Churchill."

"Well, where is he? I've heard he's supposed to be one of the best. Tuh," he tutted, and pushed out a breath, his face looking doubtful. "Hard to believe he's that good and not working in private practice—"

"Not every physician worth their weight in gold desires to open a private practice." The words slipped from my lips before I knew what was happening. "I've worked with Dr. Reynolds and he's one of the most skilled surgeons I've ever seen in the OR." Again, the compliment flowed freely, without any hesitation. And the worst part was, it was the honest to God truth.

At that precise moment, the hairs on the back of my neck stood up. My back was to the door as I spoke to the patient and her son, but I knew as soon as I turned around, he would be standing there.

Against my better judgment, I turned around, and as I'd predicted, there he was, staring at me through narrowed eyelids. The same look that'd covered his face in the grocery store the previous week as he watched me sing and dance to Whitney Houston, was on his face now.

"Thank you for the compliments, Nurse Grace."

I could've sworn I felt the slightest belly shiver at hearing my name coming from his mouth.

Clearing my throat, I looked down at the chart in my hands and back to the machines at the right side of Mrs. Churchill's bed.

"As she said, I am one of if not *the* most highly skilled surgeons in this hospital. Possibly the city, but I'll let others debate that. And no, I'm not in private practice, and yes, that is by choice. Do you have any other questions, Mr. Churchill, or shall I tend to your mother's inquiries?"

Daaamn.

I bit my bottom lip to keep the smirk off my face. He didn't have to put the son in his place like that. The confidence in his voice was so evident it silenced any other lingering doubts, I'm certain. Even if I hadn't been in the OR with this doctor before, I would've been half convinced of his abilities by his statement alone. But I had worked with him, and I knew he wasn't just fluff. The man lived for the OR.

He was cocky, yes, like most surgeons. They're the bad asses, the jocks of the hospital, but he wasn't all bravado. He walked the walk as much as he talked the talk.

"Everything looks good, Mrs. Churchill. I'll see you in there." Reynolds nodded, and I watched as his gaze moved from the patient over to me.

I was expecting him to remind me of what my responsibility to prep the patient was, but he didn't. For whatever reason, his eyes lingered on me for a second longer than necessary before he nodded and turned for the door. I didn't have time to give it much thought as a couple more staff members piled into the room to help ready Mrs. Churchill for surgery.

About forty minutes later, as I stood over Mrs. Churchill in the OR, Dr. Reynolds entered the room, with the customary hands in the air after having just thoroughly scrubbed. His gaze caught mine as his gown was tied behind his back and his mask tied in place.

I cast my gaze lower, onto Mrs. Churchill as Dr. Reynolds made his way over to her.

"It's time for you to go to sleep now, Mrs. Churchill," he stated.

"I'll have the breasts I've wanted for a long time when I wake up." She smiled.

Reynolds didn't comment on that. Instead, he lifted his head and nodded at the anesthesiologist, who then inserted the medication that would send Mrs. Churchill off into a dream world while we operated on her.

"Scalpel."

After placing the scalpel in Dr. Reynolds hand as ordered, I carefully observed Mrs. Churchill's vitals as he began to make his first incision. When my gaze lowered to the table, I swallowed at the sight of her scars, from a previous surgery.

"Is there much scar tissue?" I questioned without thinking.

Dr. Reynolds briefly looked over his shoulder and then back to the patient. "Nothing more than I can handle."

I nodded and watched, transfixed as Dr. Reynolds first did away with the scar tissue that had accumulated over the years in preparation for putting in the breast implants. I thought about Mrs. Churchill's son, now out in the waiting room with his wife who'd arrived right as we were wheeling his mother down the hall.

What he didn't know, because his mother hadn't wanted him to, was that this wasn't Mrs. Churchill's first surgery on her breast. Nearly two decades ago, she lost her right breast to cancer and had worn a prosthesis ever since. She and her husband opted to keep the cancer a secret from their then teenage son. How the hell they managed to pull such a thing off, I'll never know, but they had. Since then, Mrs. Churchill's husband passed away from liver cancer himself, and Mrs. Churchill spent years debating on whether or not to get this surgery, until finally making a decision. She just had never let her son in on the full reason why she wanted it.

"You're not using the textured breast implants for this operation?" a voice called from the back of the room.

Dr. Reynolds didn't even bother to pick his head up to look from what he was doing. He shook his head. "No."

"Why not?"

I couldn't see the bottom half of his face, as it was covered by his surgical mask, but I imagined his lips pulling back into an irritated frown. "Do you think it would be a wise decision to place a product into a patient that has the potential to increase their chances of anaplastic large cell lymphoma? Especially, when that patient has a history of breast cancer? Does that seem like a logical thing to do, Dr. Holland?" Reynolds' eyes remained on his patient as he asked.

A clearing of someone's throat could be heard from the corner of the room where Dr. Holland, a second-year resident, stood. "N-No, I don't believe it would make sense."

"Glad you approve of my decision." Sarcasm dripped from every word of his retort.

"Perhaps, Dr. Holland would like to move a little closer to get a better view of what's happening on the table," I suggested. It wasn't a secret that since a second-year resident nicked a patient's artery in one of Dr. Reynolds' surgeries the previous week, he would barely let a resident come near his operating table. Let alone assist in the actual surgery.

"This is a teaching hospital," I finished.

For the first time since he started, Dr. Reynolds did take his eyes off the patient, to look over his left shoulder, down at me.

"Suggestions on how I should run my OR, Nurse Grace?"

I wanted to roll my eyes so badly but chose not to. "I wouldn't dream of it, Dr. Reynolds. But as I said, this *is* a teaching hospital."

"Dr. Holland, are you learning from your position?" He asked the resident the question but his eyes held mine.

"Um, I could actually—"

"What was that?"

"Yeah, I'm great over here. Learning a lot."

I frowned.

"See, Dr. Holland is learning a lot, Nurse Grace. Memorial's teaching program remains intact."

It seemed since our little exchange at the grocer, Dr. Reynolds enjoyed using my name every chance he got.

"Whatever," I mumbled.

"Maybe you could sing to us, Nurse Grace, to keep us all entertained."

My head popped up at his suggestion, stunned. He hadn't said it loud. In fact, he said it low enough for only me to hear. That was when I remembered he'd spotted me at the grocer singing Whitney Houston. Maybe he was just referring to that.

"No thanks. Singing in the OR isn't my typical style. I like to keep my act contained to the produce section of our local grocer," I joked.

"That, among other places."

Again the hairs on the back of my neck stood up. It wasn't only the words but the way in which he said them. As if he knew a secret nobody else knew. I quickly flipped through my mental rolodex, trying to recall if I ever shared with my coworkers that I performed at a local night club, bi-weekly.

I hadn't. The conversation never came up, and as I was still in the stage of feeling my coworkers out, I thought it best to keep my private life to myself. Besides, singing was something I did all for myself. I didn't have the desire to share that with anyone else. But Dr. Reynolds knew. At least he implied that he did.

And when I glanced up at him to find his stormy eyes staring back at me for the briefest of moments, he conveyed in that span of silence that he knew.

"Shit!" I cursed as the suctioning instrument I'd been holding in my hand slipped. Thankfully, I moved swiftly enough that it didn't fall to the floor but the mistake revealed how rattled I'd become.

"Everything all right, Nurse Grace?"

"Fine, Doctor," I responded through gritted teeth. I could hear the superior tone in his question. He enjoyed knowing my secret and likely enjoyed even more that it obviously, threw me off.

"We're almost finished up here. Nurse Grace, would you go out with Dr. Holland to tell Mrs. Churchill's son we're almost completed and everything went well."

"Sure thing." I practically sprinted out of that operating room, only feeling like I could take a normal breath once I was on the opposite side of the wall as Dr. Reynolds.

Dr. Holland followed me out of the washroom connected to the OR. "I can't believe he won't even let me hold a damn scalpel in there," the doctor in his late twenties muttered, the frustration evident as he pushed through the double doors that opened up to the rest of the floor.

"His OR, his rules." The words slipped out of my mouth again but hadn't been meant as a defense. Why the hell would I feel the need to defend Dr. Reynolds of all people? I guessed Dr. Holland didn't see it that way.

"How am I supposed to learn anything if I can't actually partici-pate? That's what residency is all about," he stated, whirling on me.

"Dr. Holland, I get you're upset, but the best way to get in the game is not by venting like a spoiled child once you're out of earshot of Dr. Reynolds. It's to prove to him that you are worth him taking his time to invest in your education."

"How am I supposed to do that if he won't even give me a chance?"

I shrugged. "You were smart enough to get into medical school, pass your classes, and get into one of the best residency programs in the state." I patted Dr. Holland's shoulder. "Figure it out."

I stepped around him and proceeded to the waiting room where I found Mrs. Churchill's son and daughter-in-law waiting.

* * *

Jacob

I rounded the corner from the nurses' station and logged into one of the computers to double check the vitals of all my patients before heading to the change room, to retrieve my belongings and call it quits for the day. I had two surgeries that day, but two other patients of mine remained in the hospital for observation purposes. One was being discharged the following morning, and the other, later that day.

"Thanks for checking on that patient for me, Grace."

The sound of her name had my head moving upward from the computer screen. I looked around the station until my eyes landed on her smiling face. I admired the dimples that formed in her cheeks as she did so, noticing them not for the first time. Of course, it was a rarity for her to smile in my presence. Which was why the only time I caught those dimples was when she was smiling at someone else. That pissed me off. So much so, that a frown formed on my lips.

That was when her eyes darted to mine and her smile faded, taking the dimples with it. Her eyelids narrowed to slits.

Why that caused me to smirk, I don't know. Wait, that's a lie. I did know. The fact that I was able to cause her any emotion revealed to me that she wasn't immune to me. That did have me feeling better since I'd long discerned that I wasn't immune to her.

Without a word, I logged out of the computer system, stood, and started to head for my office and changing room, down the end of the hall.

As I strode, I heard footsteps behind me, and soon knew who they belonged to.

"What was that comment about me singing in the OR this morning?" Grace demanded, with her hand on her hip as she cut me off in the middle of the hallway.

My answer wasn't immediate. I let my eyes drift down the length of her body, landing on the fingers resting against her hip bone. Her fingers weren't covered by gloves, as they were in the OR. I could see them clearly. I took the time to take in the delicate bone structure of her long fingers. I imagined their softness. Not like a surgeon's hands.

I looked back up to her, my body going slightly rigid as I took in her heart-shaped mouth. Lips that were full and coated in a clear gloss of some kind.

"That's what you're good at, isn't it?" I finally stated with a raised eyebrow.

"I'm good at a lot of things, Dr. Reynolds."

Before I knew it, I found myself chest to chest with this woman, my arm moving around her waist. I was certain she hadn't even meant for her words to be a challenge in the way I took them, but I also found very little resistance on her part as I pulled her body to mine. The fact that we were both in the middle of the hallway, albeit a semi-private wing of our floor, made little difference to either one of us, it seemed.

My lips hovered above hers right when my pager's alarm went off. I immediately dropped my hand and unclipped my pager from my hip, checking it.

"911 in the ED."

Grace was moving even before I was, as we rounded the corner to find the rest of the OR staff moving quickly.

"It's all hands on deck in the ED. There was a major pile up on the freeway and they're already understaffed. Grace, can you—"

"I'm on my way," Grace answered her charge nurse before she could even get the full request out.

I surmised as much from the page I'd gotten, and was hot on Grace's heels as we took the stairs down to the emergency department.

"Dr. Reynolds, you're going to assist in the ER?" one of the newer technicians asked as I entered the ED.

"I'm also a general surgeon seeing as how my specialty required five years of general surgery practice before two years of specialized training. I think that qualifies me to be here, don't you?" I didn't bother awaiting his response as I grabbed a gown to put on, along with a pair of gloves, and proceeded to head toward the double doors for the ambulance arrivals.

To my left I found Grace, tying her own gown and anxiously looking toward the parking lot entrance where the ambulances were beginning to pull in. A handful of minutes later, the ED was a madhouse as gurney after gurney began being rolled off the emergency vehicles, and the paramedics expeditiously read off the conditions, vitals, and what procedures they performed in the field on each patient.

"Grace, with me!" I ordered as I was handed off one of the most critical patients. I stared down at the body of a little boy who'd been in the backseat of his parents SUV, which was struck head-on. At least, that was the quick overview of the situation I was given by the medic.

"Heart rate dropping," Grace called out as we wheeled him into one of the open rooms of the ED.

"Mooom," the boy managed to croak out, in obvious pain.

"Your mom's being taken care of, sweetie," Grace consoled, and I—not for the first time—was relieved that she was the one in here assisting me.

"Severe burns over at least forty percent of his body," I analyzed out loud. "Burns may be compressing his airway."

Grace looked at me with sympathy and fear in her eyes. She already knew what we would have to do. It was almost as if words weren't needed. A minute later, we were joined by Dr. Holland, who assisted with bagging the young boy, who had fallen into unconsciousness. That was probably for the best. Briefly, I almost wished that he would be able to remain in this state for the next six months to a year. I knew the type of pain these injuries would cause him. And that was *if* he survived.

But I wasn't a wishing man.

"OR three is open," a staff member called out as he pushed through the curtain that'd been pulled shut as we worked.

"Book it. Let's go," I insisted, knowing the sooner we acted, the better.

Grace continued to compress the airbag rhythmically, ensuring that enough oxygen was reaching the boy's lungs and rest of his body.

I doled out orders as we entered the elevator while Grace continued to call out his vitals. We seemed to bounce off one another naturally, and while I'd worked and trained with some of the best operating room nurses there were, not one of them seemed to have this natural ease with me that she had.

Grace scrubbed and dressed first to enter the OR and establish that the patient remained stable enough for surgery.

I watched her fluid movements through the window from the washroom. She was confident, assured, and ready to do what needed to be done. And even though ninety-nine percent of my thoughts remained on the young boy on the table, my eyes kept straying to Grace.

"There's likely some internal bleeding, and more scar tissue forming than we're aware of," I said to Dr. Holland, who stood beside me, scrubbing as well.

"You're letting me assist, right?"

I looked at him briefly, a scowl on my face. "Don't fuck up," was all I said before hitting the sink's nozzle with my elbow to turn the water off and exiting the washroom to enter the OR. I was masked and gowned, scalpel in hand, within ten minutes.

The surgery wasn't one of the longer ones I'd had but it was grueling as I was forced to remove a great deal of dead skin from the boy's body as a result of the burns he sustained in the accident. There was some good news, however. The only internal bleeding we found was from his spleen, which I was able to stitch up without having to completely take out. But he would need a great deal more surgeries to his body to help it heal.

"We're going to have to wait a few days to do the skin graft," I stated as we completed the first surgery. "Is there anyone in the waiting room for him?" My question hadn't been to anyone in particular, since my gaze was still trained on the stitching job I was doing.

"Both his parents were in the accident. His mother's been rolled into surgery herself but it's not looking good. His father is still in the ED," a nurse from the corner of the room replied.

I nodded. "I'll speak with his father once we're finished here." I sighed, hating that particular aspect of my job.

"I'll go with you."

My eyes bounced to the other side of the table. Grace, who was standing next to Dr. Holland, peered up at me, with eyes full of sympathy. That look unnerved me more than the prospect of cutting someone open. I didn't acknowledge her statement at all, my focus moving back to the table and task at hand.

A little bit over a half an hour later, as the boy was being rolled into one of the burn unit rooms, Grace was right by my side while I moved down the stairs to retrace the same steps we'd taken hours earlier, to the emergency department. The ED was still swarming with injured patients who had to wait to be treated after the most serious cases were taken care of.

"We're looking for the father of Johnny Westbrook," I told the nurse behind the station.

She looked up at me, blinking, taking a second to recall who I was referring to.

"The little boy who was burned in the accident," Grace cleared up.

"Oh, oh, right. Uhhh, he's in ED3."

I nodded and headed to room number three of the emergency department.

"Mr. Westbrook?"

A man with a greying beard and red-rimmed eyes stared back at me from the bed he laid in. I noticed his right arm had been strapped in a sling indicating a possible fracture. The right side of his face was swollen and bruised, and his left leg was propped up on pillows in another sling. He'd obviously been through the wringer himself.

"I'm Dr. Reynolds and this is Nurse Grace. We took care of your son, Johnny."

He immediately tried to sit up. "H-How is he? I've been tr-trying to g-get information—"

"Shshsh, don't try to speak, Mr. Westbrook," Grace consoled, seeing the man in obvious pain, both physically and mentally.

Swallowing, I averted my gaze. Again, this was the aspect of my job that was my least favorite.

"Johnny is stable for now. The good news is he did not have as much internal damage as we originally believed." I paused, letting Mr. Westbrook brace himself for the obvious bad news. "His burns were extensive. He has third and fourth degree burns over fifty percent of his body. And while he is stable now, he's going to have a long road ahead of him for recovery. We will have to operate in a day or two to begin the process of skin grafting to help regenerate new skin to grow where he was burned."

Mr. Westbrook swallowed, obviously confused, pained, and in deep anguish. "B-But he's alive."

"Yes, he's alive and resting in our burn unit, Mr. Westbrook," Grace added, reassuring.

Again, I was glad she was there.

We spent a little more time with Mr. Westbrook, discussing his son's condition until an orthopedic surgeon and nurse came in to tend to Mr. Westbrook's fractured limbs.

"Are you hungry?" Grace suddenly turned to me asking once we exited the ED.

"I am," came my quick reply. It was almost nine o'clock at night, well past the three p.m. hour I was scheduled to leave.

"The cafeteria's a short walk a—"

"Let's do it." I didn't need her to finish her suggestion.

CHAPTER 4

*G*race

"Oh man," I blurted out before sighing and sitting down at the square, wooden table next to the large window in the hospital's cafeteria. "I'm exhausted."

Dr. Reynolds didn't say anything but his heavy movements as he plopped down across from me gave away the extent of his tiredness as well.

"And you didn't have to pay for my food," I added quickly, frowning at him.

"I don't have to do a lot of things I choose to do." His words were followed by him shoving a forkful of steamed broccoli into his mouth.

I forced my eyes to keep off of his lips as he chewed but it was a struggle. His statement reminded me of my own retort earlier in the day, right before he was paged to the ED. In that moment, I could have sworn he was going to kiss me. And I needed to ask myself if I would've let him. I certainly hadn't even thought of pulling away when I felt his arm around my waist.

I looked up again, shoving aside that little memory, to realize Dr. Reynolds was still staring at me.

"You don't talk much, do you?" I inquired.

He made a movement with his shoulders. "I speak when I have something to say."

"Like telling me to sing in the OR."

"Like telling you to sing in the operating room. The staff would've enjoyed it. You have a beautiful voice."

My eyes widened at the unexpected compliment. I didn't know if I'd been offended or surprised at his suggestion earlier. But hearing the sincerity in his voice now, a warm feeling started in my stomach.

Instead of responding, I took a forkful of my quinoa and salmon salad into my mouth and chewed. After swallowing, I took a sip of the coffee I ordered. That's when I noticed Dr. Reynolds' eyes fall to the hand with my cup.

He frowned. "Coffee at nine thirty at night?"

I shrugged. "It won't keep me up too long. I need some energy for my swim once I leave here."

"Swim?"

I averted my gaze, deciding how much of my personal affairs I cared to divulge to this somewhat strange but tempting man.

"I work out at a local gym, most of the time swimming laps."

He nodded and then cut into the chicken he ordered. That time I did allow myself to watch the movement of his mouth while he ate.

"We make a pretty good team."

At first I didn't know if it was he or I who made that statement. But when my brain began functioning again, once I pulled my attention from his lips, I recognized that he said it. The second time a man has said those exact words to me in the span of the past five days. But this time, I didn't have the same internal reaction as when Jackson said them.

"Strangely enough," I agreed.

"I don't do teams." He said it as a threat and a challenge. A challenge to what, I had no clue, but it was one nonetheless.

"I'm not one for teams myself," I reiterated, honestly.

"Then that makes two of us."

"You're a strange man, Dr. Reynolds."

"Jacob."

I blinked. "What was that?"

"My name's Jacob."

"Is that an invite to call you by your first name?" It would seem obvious, but I wanted to be sure. Most doctors expected nurses and most hospital staff to use their professional name.

"I don't give most people my first name for reference. Not out loud anyway," he finished, glancing down at his name embroidered on the black scrubs he still wore.

"Jacob," I stated just loud enough for me to hear, but when I looked across the table I was surprised to see his nostrils flared, and the typical storm that raged in his eyes stilled for the briefest of seconds. A song with his name in it immediately came to mind, and right there on the spot, I decided to add it to my next set, the following weekend at Rocket.

"You're getting that far-off look you have onstage."

That comment pulled me back to the present moment.

"Is that what you were thinking about? Performing again?"

He was way too close to the truth and far too observant. It pissed me off.

Abruptly standing up from the table, I grabbed my tray. "Thanks for dinner. Have a good night, Dr. Reynolds." I attempted to storm off with my head held high but my left wrist was soon locked in his strong hand. I looked down at his hand holding me in place and then to his face.

"Jacob."

I clenched my teeth. The demand that he release me was on the tip of my tongue but I couldn't force it out to save my life.

"Jacob," I finally said instead. It was only then that his hand loosened until it fell completely away from my wrist. The coldness I felt at his release was startling. But I wasn't going to stand there and ponder it with his gaze still trained on me.

Free to move, I did so, carrying my tray over to the garbage to discard my half-eaten plate, and then I hightailed it out of the cafeteria, doing my best not to look back to see if *Jacob's* eyes were following me.

* * *

ALL THROUGHOUT MY swim and up until the moment I crawled into bed and passed out the night before, I'd thought of him. Luckily, I was so tired my sleep was dreamless, but I'd be damned if he wasn't the first thought on my mind when I woke up that morning.

I did everything I could to dissuade my obviously broken brain from going back to the feeling of his hand covering my wrist. Surgeons had strong hands, they had to. While all physicians needed to have an obvious level of intelligence and mental acumen, surgeons depended on their physical bodies as well to be able to perform the delicate cuts, stitches, and movements required to perform their jobs. Jacob was no different. However, there was something very different about the feel of his skin on mine that I hadn't anticipated, nor wanted, but couldn't ignore.

I did everything I could to stop thinking about that moment in the cafeteria as I showered, washed, and then conditioned my hair. I sung songs, tried to think of a new outfit to perform in. Reminded myself of the patients that I saw the day before and what it was I needed to be cognizant of when I went into work that day. But of course, thoughts of work immediately went to thoughts of *him.* I couldn't win.

I finally gave up on even trying anymore when a loud banging came from my door, as soon as I stepped out of the shower.

"Just a minute!" I called while tying my black, fuzzy robe around my body, before tightening the belt and slipping my feet into a pair of slippers to head to the door.

"I'm coming!" I called to the impatient knocker. It couldn't be a delivery man this damn insistent. Glancing through the peephole, a smile touched my lips. I couldn't get my door opened fast enough.

"Journey!" I flung the door wide, arms outstretched, excited to see my sister standing there on the other side of my threshold.

"What took you so damn long?" she questioned loudly as she pulled me into a tight hug.

"First of all, watch your tone when talking to me, little girl," I warned just after ushering her in and closing the door. In spite of my not wanting or intending to, I couldn't help but treat my younger sister as if she was my child instead of my sibling.

"And second of all, I was in the shower. Had you told me you were coming, I would've known to be expecting you."

"Never mind that. Do you have anything to eat?"

Before I could even answer her question, Journey zigzagged through the furniture of my living room and made a beeline for my kitchen, dropping the lime green backpack she wore onto one of my grey and white stools at the bar in the center of the kitchen.

Since my home had an open floor plan, I could easily see her from my position in the living room. First, she raided the cabinets, frowning until she found a jar of peanut butter and the large box of animal crackers, which were her favorite.

"See! You knew I was coming." She grinned, holding up the box and shaking it.

I didn't need to admit that wherever I lived I kept a box of her favorite treat on hand just because.

"When's the last time you've eaten?" I questioned, moving to the kitchen and staring as she voraciously scooped what looked like a full tablespoon of peanut butter onto one of the crackers before shoving it into her mouth. My sister still ate like a teenager, but by looking at her you would never know. Her five-foot-six frame appeared as if she barely weighed more than a hundred twenty pounds.

"Uh, what's today?" The question was muffled due to the food in her mouth. "Anyway, I've been traveling all day."

"All day? It's barely eight o'clock in the morning." I frowned, a funny feeling rising in my belly.

Journey's dark-hazel eyes couldn't seem to focus on one thing for too long. "All night, I guess."

"Why all night?" I asked as I took in the tie-dye T-shirt she wore with the ripped jeans. The outfit looked to be in style for someone her age, but her appearance seemed as if she'd been wearing the clothing for more than a night. "The flight here from home is only about two hours."

Journey lived in the next state over, and there were frequent flights to and from Williamsport and the hometown we grew up in.

"Oh, I didn't come from home. I took the bus from Chicago."

My eyes bulged. "*Chicago*? The bus? Why?"

Shrugging, she placed the still open box of animal crackers on my marble countertop, spilling crumbs onto the shiny black counter.

"I need some water." She hurriedly moved to my double door refrigerator, yanking the doors open and taking it all in.

"You only have vegetables in here." Her voice was disgusted as she slammed both doors closed.

"I get the water from there." Using my head, I gestured to the water and ice dispenser on the door. I moved from the bar to a cabinet over the sink, opening it and removing a glass to hand her to fill with water.

"What's this for?" she asked, confused, staring at the glass in my hand.

"You just said you wanted some water."

"Oh," she waved me off with her hand, "that was a long time ago. Let me tell you about this guy I met." She pulled me back into the living room by the hands.

"The one that had you in Chicago?" I guessed.

"Yes. How'd you know?" Her expression was one of shock.

"Wild guess."

"You're good. Anyway, his name is Keith and he's an artist. That's why he's in Chicago. He lives there but came to Williamsport for work. He flew down two days ago and I—"

"So he flew down and he had you take the bus?"

Journey bit her bottom lip, running my words through her head. "Yeah." She nodded happily. "Anyway, he's great. I'm going to meet his kids today, and w—"

"His kids?" The knot in my stomach continued to grow the more she talked. The glossy look in her eyes, her exaggerated and excited movements along with the rambling were like stepping back in time. A period of my life I desperately wanted to escape.

"I have to go," Journey finally announced.

"Wait, go? Where?"

"I just told you. I can stay here with you, right, Grace? Cool, cool," she said answering her own question and heading for the door.

"Journey, wait. Let me at least make you a real breakfast. I've got eggs and everything to make your favorite omelet."

She was shaking her head before I could finish. "No time. Maybe tomorrow. Or the next day. Whenever. I've got to meet Keith. Bye, sis. Love you." She ran back across the room, plopped a wet kiss on my cheek, and was out the front door in no time.

I made it to the door, opening it to see Journey climbing into the back of a yellow cab and pulling off. *Was the cab driver waiting out there the whole time?* I didn't want to think of the cost for him to wait. The bad feeling began to rise in my belly even more.

Despite my need to get ready for work, I ran down the hallway of my one story house, retrieving my cell phone, which was still attached to the charger, and dialed my father's number.

"Dad," I screeched as soon as I heard his baritone on the other end of the line.

"Grace, good morning. Everything okay?" he questioned, knowing I never made calls this early; primarily because I was either sleeping in from a night shift or getting ready to go into work.

"No. Journey just left here."

"Oh." There was dread in his voice.

"Oh? What do you mean '*Oh*'? She was almost frantic, eating animal crackers for breakfast and saying she took the bus all night from Chicago. I just spoke with her last week and she was home."

"Yeah, she met some man named—"

"Keith."

"I'm pretty sure that's his name." He sounded doubtful.

"*Pretty sure.* As in you just can't remember his name because it's so early in the morning and you're too tired to think clearly? Or, you can't recall because she's in love with a different guy every other week?"

There was a pause on the other end of the phone. My shoulders sank and my eyelids slowly closed because the conclusions my mind were coming up with scared the living daylights out of me.

"Don't go making assumptions, Grace. Journey is young and—"

"She's twenty-five."

"Right. Twenty-five is young, and she's still figuring things out—"

"Twenty-five is typically the age the illness is diagnosed."

More silence.

"You know what this means, right? Have you even bothered to have her tested? To speak with her?"

"I think you're jumping to conclusions. She's not Victory."

"You're going to ignore these obvious red flags just like you did with my mother and leave me again to—" I cut myself off. This was an old argument with my father. One that I thought I'd let go of and forgiven him for. His abandonment in my and Journey's childhood hurt terribly, only made much worse because we were left alone with my mother and her untreated mental illness.

"I'm sorry," I quickly amended. "I have to go to work."

"Okay," was all my father said but I could hear the hurt in his voice. It pained me to hear it but the thought of my sister showing obvious signs of bipolar disorder, just as my mother had, and my father choosing to ignore it once again hurt even more. I disconnected the call.

I tried to call Journey as I put on my work scrubs but both of my calls went straight to voicemail. I chose to send her a text informing her of what time I'd be home and that I wanted to speak with her. As I closed and locked my door behind me, to head to work, I sent up a silent prayer that she would be okay.

CHAPTER 5

*G*race

In spite of my hectic morning, I managed to make it into work a few minutes early, which was good since I wanted to check on the young boy from the accident the day before. After stashing my purse underneath the nurses' station, I took the stairs up one floor to the burn unit where he was recuperating. Aside from oncology, the burn unit had to be one of the most difficult units to work on. Caring for burn victims wasn't an easy task by any means. The recovery process was beyond painful. And some of the stories of how patients ended up here in the first place were even worse to deal with. There, of course, were the usual accidents or mishaps that couldn't be helped. But I've had patients in the past who were intentionally set on fire by someone. How anyone could do that to another human being was beyond my comprehension.

My body shivered at those thoughts when I rounded the last corner of the unit. As I quietly slid in the doorway of the room, I caught the image of a male figure in the corner of the room, by the window. He was silently watching the young boy. For a nanosecond I thought it might be the boy's father, but then I remembered his father had a severely broken leg and arm. There was no way he would be standing. And if that realization hadn't hit me, the fact that the hairs on my arms raised, along with goosebumps as my body warmed from just catching a glimpse of the man, told me this wasn't Johnny's father.

"Jacob," I stated just above a whisper as he pushed away from the windowsill, striding closer to me.

"Morning," he responded, his eyes raking over my body.

God, why does his voice sound so deep and good this early in the morning? I looked away from him, to the small figure in the bed. Out of the corner of my eye I saw Jacob's head turn to the bed as well.

"He's stable. Been that way all night."

I turned back to Jacob. "You've been here the whole night?"

He shook his head. "Few hours. Nurses updated me on his condition throughout the night."

There was a pause.

"His mother died around midnight."

My shoulders sank and my heart ached for the little boy currently resting in the bed. The only things saving him from yelling out in severe pain at the moment, were the heavy doses of drugs that kept him unconscious. The poor thing was in for a world of hurt when he woke up, both physical and emotional.

"She was probably a good mom." I don't know what prompted me to make such a comment.

"How do you know that?"

It wasn't the question but the sharpness in Jacob's tone that had my gaze flying back to his in confusion and feeling like I needed to defend my statement.

"The way he called out for her yesterday."

"That doesn't mean she was a good mother."

"It does indicate that when he was scared, in pain and confused, and surrounded by strangers, the person he looked to for help was his mother. Which likely means he felt safe with her."

Jacob's lips tightened but he didn't say anything further. He simply gave Johnny one final look before turning and heading for the door. I followed him out just as quietly as I'd come in. Our discussion had been held in hushed tones, so I hoped that Johnny couldn't hear what was said.

"Here."

I blinked at the cup of coffee that was suddenly thrust in my face. I had briefly registered the cup Jacob was holding firmly in his hand but thought it was his.

"Oh." The surprised gasp slipped from my lips when upon taking the warm cup from his hand, my fingers brushed against his. It was as if a light switch had been turned on throughout my entire body from the small connection. The same feeling I felt the night before when his large hand encircled my wrist.

Ignoring the fact that he was carefully watching me the way he often did, I lifted the coffee cup to my nose, inhaling the vanilla scent. My taste buds instantly watered and I moved fast, taking my first sip. It was perfect. Made just the way I like it. Sweetened with vanilla creamer and one packet of stevia.

"That's good," I pushed out, already feeling the effects of the warming liquid as it moved through my body.

And just that quickly my eyes popped open and I stared curiously at Jacob, who, of course, continued to watch me.

"How did you know how I take my coffee?"

"I guessed."

"Bullshit." My short retort fell from my lips with ease. I hadn't thought about it or its effects. But something I couldn't have ever imagined occurred from my snarky response. A smile actually crested on Jacob's lips, and it pulled a sound from his throat that had me stumbling backwards a couple of steps.

Jacob's smile and deep chuckle were the stuff miracles were made of. His usual deep, brooding, and stormy gaze were irresistible. But his smile and slight laughter made me want to follow him around for all of eternity just to get a glimpse of it again.

"Thanks ... for the coffee," I managed to say, holding up the cup as if he didn't know what I was referring to. "I need to go clock in for my shift."

There was no looking back, no second guessing, and no hesitation.

I needed space. I needed to get the hell out of that hallway and as far from Jacob Reynolds as possible ... for the time being. He had my damn senses all out of whack and I had no idea what to do about it. *No one* had ever thrown me off so much from his laughter alone.

* * *

Jacob

The sound of my own laughter was foreign to my ears. I found myself just as surprised as she obviously was when I laughed at her quick comeback. I wasn't one for laughing much. Didn't see too much in this world that was a laughing matter. But Grace had pulled it out of me without even trying. And that turned me on.

So, as I watched Grace scurry down the hallway of the burn unit, away from me, with her coffee cup in hand, I knew that I wasn't going to let her get away so easily. She felt it, too. All of it.

From the moment I put my hand on her the night before, I couldn't stop thinking about her. When she finally said my first name something inside of me turned on and wanted more. I memorized the coffee order she made the previous night in the cafeteria, without really even trying, and it was the first thing I ordered once I entered the cafeteria this morning. After a couple of hours sitting by Johnny's bedside, I headed downstairs to get coffee for both Grace and I. It was even a thought or consideration. It just felt natural.

Just as Grace rounded the corner, the pager resting at my hip went off. Pulling the pager off my scrub bottoms and reading it, I recognized a colleague of mine was requesting a consult. On my way down to the consult, I stopped by the nurses' station of the surgical floor.

"I'll need Nurse Grace to assist in today's surgery," I firmly stated, barely glancing at the charge nurse who was positioned at the computer.

"Oh, I was going to have—"

"Grace. With me, assisting with the scar removal surgery. And Johnny Westbrook should be ready for the skin graft surgery tomorrow. I will need Grace in that surgery as well."

I glanced downward, again plucking my beeping pager from my hip and frowning at the interruption. Noticing I hadn't heard a confirmation from the nurse, I peeled my eyes away from my pager and placed them on the woman who was staring at me, stunned, mouth wide.

"Is there a problem?"

She shook her head. "Not at all, Dr. Reynolds. I will have Nurse Young assist in both surgeries. She'll begin prepping your patient just as soon as she completes her rounds."

I nodded and headed off in the direction of the colleague's office who requested the consult.

"You requested me," Grace stated in a hushed tone as we emerged from the hospital room of a patient who would be rolled off to surgery soon.

I glanced down at her face, which was covered in a quizzical expression. "I did."

"Why?"

I paused before answering that question because the immediate response I wanted to give was that I enjoyed having her in the operating room with me. That for some unknown reason I felt calmer and more stable with her standing next to me or across the table in the OR. And I wasn't a man who ever felt *unconfident* in the OR. It was my home. The one place on this planet I know I was born to be.

"I only request the best in my OR," I simply answered.

The surprise on her face quickly turned to wariness, as if she was trying to discern what my angle was.

My anger flared. I didn't need to grant anyone access to my surgeries to get in their pants, if that's what she was thinking.

"Grace, I've told you before I believe you're one of the best surgical nurses I've ever worked with, and I've worked with many. Do you think I need to dole out compliments as a means to get access to what's between your legs?"

Her sudden intake of air almost had me reeling. The gasp of surprise wasn't a put on, and when she quickly firmed her lips shut, trying to conceal her reaction to my words, not for the first time my cock stirred in my damn scrubs.

"Prepare the patient for surgery. I will see you in the OR." I turned my back on her and proceeded down the hallway to calm my bullshit hormones before surgery. I hadn't even kissed this woman yet and she was beginning to drive me fucking crazy.

Who was I fooling?

She was way past beginning. The inevitable was becoming more and more obvious.

* * *

"Nurse Young, would you please prep the surgical area," I requested while my gown was being tied in the back by another staff member, just inside of the doors of the operating room.

"Sure thing, Dr. Reynolds."

I frowned behind the surgical mask I wore. I understood and respected the need for professionalism among our colleagues. That didn't mean I enjoyed hearing Grace refer to me as anything other than my first name. That in and of itself should've told me this woman had me where no one else had.

I strode over to the table where the patient laid unconscious after having been put under by the anesthesiologist.

"Another boob job, huh, Dr. Reynolds? You ever get tired of doing these?"

I paused with the scalpel in my right hand, a half an inch above the patient's body, and glared across the table at the third-year resident.

"Tired of doing my job, Dr. Wu?"

Eyes widening, his lips parted and then closed again. His dark brown eyes darted from me to Grace, to other staff members.

"Do me a favor, Dr. Wu?"

"What's that, sir, um, Dr. Reynolds?"

"Don't ever speak before I've made the first cut." By the time I've made the first incision I can drown out the stupidity of the residents and their questions but not before.

I proceeded with the operation, again noticing how well Grace and I worked together. Even before I called for suctioning she was there, with the tool, aiding my ability to see the field clearly. And whereas I'd had to tamp down on my anger because I often felt suffocated by the nearness of other surgical nurses who were merely doing their job, Grace was different. I couldn't get enough of her closeness. In fact, my body felt cold when she moved away.

"We are almost done here," I stated about two hours later.

"I'll go—"

"No. Dr. Wu can go and tell the husband how his wife is doing. Dr. Wu." I looked to him across the table expectantly. I could see in his eyes that he preferred to stay but that would've meant sending Grace out in his stead to talk with the family while I did the final stitches on the patient. That just wasn't going to happen.

"No problem, Dr. Reynolds."

I nodded and kept stitching. A half a minute later I heard the door of the operating room open and close as Dr. Wu exited.

"What are your career goals, Nurse Young?" I suddenly found myself asking a question that'd been on my mind for a while.

"Excuse me?"

"Do I need to speak louder? Is my mask making it difficult for you to hear me accurately?"

I didn't bother looking over my shoulder to see her reaction to that snark. I could feel the daggers her eyes were throwing my way. My lips cracked into yet another smile behind the mask I wore.

"What are your career ambitions?" I questioned again when there was no immediate response.

"What would make you ask that?"

"Because a nurse of your caliber doesn't stay in one position for long without itching to move up or seek out more education. At least, not in my experience."

There was a long silence as I continued the delicate stitching process that would complete this surgery. I could hear other conversations around the room. To my far right, a surgical tech was going over the different tools that were used throughout the surgery to a third-year medical student. A nurse across the table, farther back from where Dr. Wu had been standing, was explaining OR procedures to a nursing student. But to my immediate right, there was silence.

I parted my mouth to ask the question again when I finally heard, "I've been thinking of going back to school to complete my licensure to become a nurse anesthetist."

That answer didn't surprise me at all. Of course that was her career goal.

"Trying to take my job, huh?" Dr. Graham, the anesthesiologist for this surgery, joked from his position at the head of the table.

Grace laughed. "You're irreplaceable, Dr. Graham."

Lifting my gaze, I scowled at the man. No one fucking invited him to be a part of this conversation.

"Why haven't you completed your education for the position?"

I saw Grace's head turn to me. She shrugged. "Life got in the way for a little bit."

That was a coded way of saying some shit occurred that she didn't want to talk about. I knew all about not wanting to discuss one's past. Typically, I didn't give a shit enough to find out about anyone else's life, but again, Grace wasn't like anyone else.

"But you're back to considering it?"

"Yes."

"What's keeping you from just taking the plunge? A husband? Kids at home?" And because I wanted to see her face when she answered those questions, I pulled my gaze from the patient, after making the final stitch.

Those brown eyes were wide. "No." She shook her head. "God, no," she responded, as if the idea of a husband or children at home waiting for her was the last thing she wanted or needed.

Good.

That damn sure made two of us.

"Let's go talk to this patient's husband, shall we?" I said as I dropped the surgical tools in my hands into the metal dish another nurse held out for me. I turned to the anesthesiologist. "Dr. Graham?"

"Everything looks good."

I nodded and gave some final instructions to wheel the patient out to the recovery room prior to discarding my surgical mask, gloves, and robe, depositing them in the waste before exiting the OR. Grace was right next to me doing the same. It was almost uncanny how natural our flow felt.

CHAPTER 6

*J*acob

It was a Saturday night. I had the entire day off and wasn't scheduled to be back at the hospital until Monday. Typically, that meant my weekend nights were spent down at the Underground looking for a fight to get into, or at the very least, to watch. But tonight was different.

I entered the darkly lit lounge and my gaze immediately went to the woman on the stage. I frowned. It wasn't Grace.

Lifting my wrist in front of me, I noted the time was just about nine-thirty. I still had some time before Grace hit the stage. I made it a point after my last shift on Friday to look up the schedule to see the next time she was performing. It was tonight. I could've asked her but I didn't want to give her the opportunity to skip out on performing because she knew I would be here. I liked the element of surprise.

Pausing at the bar to the left, I ordered whatever the best beer they had on tap was. I was limiting myself to one beer for the evening so I might as well make it a good one. As I eased my way past the other patrons, I spotted an empty table directly in front of the stage. Just as I arrived at the table, another guy started to pull out the chair on the opposite side of the table.

"This one's taken," I growled.

His peered up at me, mouth opening as if he was about to challenge me, but right before he said anything, he must've thought better of it. He soon released the chair and headed to another open table.

I released the breath I was holding, realizing that I'd been completely willing to get into a full-on fight with a random stranger over a table so I could have a front row view of the woman I came to see. And worse than that, I was completely okay with it.

Placing the glass holding my beer down at the center of the able, I pulled out the black wooden chair, sitting down and crossing one jean-covered leg over the other. I folded my arms across my broad chest, frowning at the woman on stage, wishing she would instantly disappear and make room for the real star of tonight's lineup.

The wait felt like forever, although it was less than ten minutes before the woman, whose name I didn't bother listening for, exited the stage. I uncrossed my leg and sat upright in my chair, bending at the waist to prop my elbows on my thighs. I felt my body gearing up in anticipation. It was almost the same exhilaration I felt right before surgery. As a doctor I knew the signs of an adrenaline rush. My brain was redirecting blood from my internal organs to my muscles in preparation for fight or flight. But neither of those were an option at this moment. No way was I about get up and miss Grace on stage.

Closing my eyes, I inhaled deeply and let the breath move out of my body with ease, calming me down. It was a practice I learned early on in my surgical career whenever I got jittery. I hadn't had to practice it in a long time since I no longer got nervous before surgery. But sitting here, in an audience of about fifty to sixty other people, with no one's attention on me, I felt anxious.

"Ladies and gentlemen, please welcome to the stage Grace Young!" the host, or whoever the hell she was, yelled into the microphone. The room swelled with cheers and applause from the audience. I kept my body rigid. I didn't want to miss a second of Grace from the time she emerged from behind the curtain.

"Thank you," she crooned into the microphone, smiling.

The dimples in her cheeks were evident, causing my gut to clench as if I'd been sucker punched. And when she slowly closed her eyes and began humming the notes of whatever song she was preparing to sing, I knew I was indeed sucker punched.

She inhaled, her lips parting, and she began singing.

I obviously wasn't familiar with the song but that didn't matter because she held my rapt attention. This was a different type of song than the first time I saw her perform. That one had a jazzy feel to it. This one was a pop song. But her delivery of the song gave it the backbone it needed so that it didn't go too far into thoughtless pop territory. My more reasonable mind tried to persuade me that I might be just a tad bit biased in my assessment of her delivery of the song, but as I heard the cheers and singing along from some of the audience members, I knew that was bullshit. She was as every bit enthralling as I thought she was the first time. Hell, even when I spotted her shaking her hips to Whitney Houston in the produce aisle, she held my complete attention. And she wasn't doing it for anyone on a stage then. She was just enjoying herself.

She belted out the lyrics of a woman telling her love not to try to satisfy her with empty platitudes. And at the height of the song, our eyes collided for the first time of this performance.

Her shock when she realized I was sitting there, blatantly ogling her as she did her thing on stage, filled me with a surge of energy. And just like the pro she was, she quickly recovered and continued with the rest of the song without missing a beat.

I found myself clapping as loudly … no, louder than anyone else in the room.

"Thank you. That was a little Fifth Harmony for those of you who aren't familiar with the song." Her eyes dipped to meet mine and I knew she was speaking directly to me. I didn't give a damn about the name of the original artists who sang the song. As far as I was concerned, once Grace performed it, it was hers.

A second later I heard the distinct sounds of a string instrument playing from behind Grace. Again, she began humming before opening her lips to sing. The words coming from her were covered in some sort of magic because I slipped into an enigmatic trance that I didn't want to escape from. It was almost like an out-of-body experience watching her on stage as she closed her eyes for the parts you could tell she was really feeling.

And just when I thought I couldn't sink any further into this spell she had wrapped me in, a dark figure emerged from the corner of the stage. A deeper voice began to meld with hers as a man dressed in a dark pair of jeans and black T-shirt, holding a microphone, started harmonizing with Grace, filling out the male part of the song.

I recognized him.

He'd been on stage since I arrived, playing the saxophone for the other songs. His nearness to Grace pissed me off. My body rebelled against the way she turned to him as they sung the lyrics in unison, bouncing off one another. I remained in my seat, though it proved difficult. More difficult than it should've been for a woman whose lips I'd still yet to feel on mine.

I released the breath I was holding as the song ended and Grace turned away from the man, smiling toward the audience. She pressed a kiss to the tips of her fingers and blew on them toward the audience, taking in their applause. Her smile dropped a little when her eyes landed on me again. There was a smoldering gaze behind those hickory irises of hers and I was certain it mirrored the gleam in my own eyes.

"Thank you, everyone! Please enjoy the rest of your evening," Grace said into the microphone before waving and placing it back into the stand.

I was on my feet before I even had a chance to think too much about it. My hand extended toward her, to help her down and off the stage. She looked at me, hesitating for a moment before placing that delicate hand of hers into mine, allowing me to assist her. Instinctively, my free hand went to her waist. She was wearing a semi-long, puffy skirt that held her waist firm as the cream-colored bodysuit she wore outlined the top half of her body.

"Do you want a drink?" were the first words that came to me so I went with them. I was also well aware that I still held onto her hand even though we'd left the stage behind. She didn't need my assistance to walk, but releasing her hand wasn't an option. Nor did she try to pull away.

"I shouldn't." Her voice was soft, not like the confident nurse who could run circles around all the residents and most of the attendings in the OR.

"You're not on call and you don't have to go to work tomorrow," I said as we moved closer to the bar. I paused to turn and stare at her. Her hair, which was normally kept in a neat bun at the back of her head while at work, was down again, flowing freely around her shoulders. I had the strongest urge to reach out and finger one of the tightly coiled curls to see if it would bounce back in place.

That was an odd feeling for me. I wasn't a touchy feely guy. In fact, I didn't like to be touched at all. So when I glanced down and still found Grace's hand in mine as if that was where it belonged, I remained baffled.

"How do you know my schedule?"

"I looked it up," I stated honestly. It wasn't exactly difficult to find out the nursing staff's schedule if I wanted to. However, I had never wanted to in the past.

"One drink."

I nodded. "What'll it be?"

"Margarita."

"Salt on the brim?"

"Of course."

Hiding my grin, I turned toward the bar to order her drink. Reluctantly, I released her hand as I took the margarita to hand it to her. But not so cautiously, I watched as she took her first sip of her drink. Her eyelids fluttered, I assumed from the tartness of the drink, but soon she released a deep sigh of satisfaction.

"That's good." She took another sip before peering up at me. "You're not having a drink?"

"I had one already." I jutted my head toward the table I had vacated, indicating that I left my drink over there. I didn't bother telling her that I barely got more than two sips of it before she hit the stage. And that once she had, I forgot all about the beer.

"Thank you for this." She held up her glass.

"Welcome." I paused, and then something I'd been wondering since the first song she sang came to mind. "How come you don't date but always sing love songs?"

She stopped and cocked her head to the side in a way that let me know my question had flared something in her.

"First of all, how do you know I don't date? And second, I don't *always* sing love songs." She finished the rest of her margarita. Plucking the empty glass from her hands, I placed it on the bar.

"Because when I questioned whether you had a husband or children at home you looked like you were about to have a conniption at the idea."

"That doesn't mean I don't date. And how do you know my face wasn't just a result of you asking such a private question in the middle of a surgery?"

"It was the end of a surgery, and I was drawing a reasonable conclusion based on the facts that I had in front of me. Simple analysis."

"Like the scientist you are."

"Yes."

"What if your conclusion is wrong?"

"It's not."

"How do you know?"

I stepped closer to her, crowding her space, leaving her nowhere to move since there was a couple standing directly behind her.

"Because the way he was looking at you on stage …" I stopped and jutted my head toward the saxophone player who was still onstage setting up for his next set. Pushing her hair behind her ear, I lowered my lips. "I can tell he wants you, and my guess is that he's even tried but you've turned him down." My voice was low as I said the words directly into her ear.

"You're right," came her whispered reply.

I looked down, my eyes landing on those full lips of hers. I had every mind to run my tongue along the seam of them, prying them open and capturing her every moan until she begged me for more.

"Dance with me." Pulling back, I waited for her response.

When she nodded, I took her by the hand again and led her to the center of the dance floor, before bringing her into the circle of my arms. I didn't even recognize the notes of the song that began playing, but I appreciated that it was a slow song because there was no way I was about to let her go from my embrace.

"Sam Smith." She sounded pleased.

"You know this one?" I questioned, looking down on her.

My jaw tightened at the smile that appeared as she nodded. "'Say it First' is the name of the song."

I could've asked her to sing but I chose not to. I wanted to just be with her in this moment, for whatever reason. Maybe I could steal memories of tonight, with her in my arms, for the long nights alone. Possibly.

Grace must've felt the same way because soon enough she melted against my body, into my arms. Her free arm stretched up and over my shoulder to wrap around my upper back. She laid her head to rest against my shoulder and began stroking my back with her hand. I stiffened, waiting for the usual discomfort I felt whenever women got too close to well up in me. Typically, I could hold a position like this for maybe a minute or two before it got too uncomfortable and I needed out. But the feeling never arose. It was the oddest and best feeling I'd ever felt.

I let my arms tighten around her body, pulling her into me even more as I intently sought to listen to the lyrics of the song. The singer was revealing to his lover his vulnerabilities and asking that she tell him first. The *it* was obvious. He was asking that she love him and tell him so. I wasn't one for music, let alone love songs, but listening to the words of this song hit me deeper than any song had in a very long time, if ever.

I moved back from Grace; the hand that had been resting at her hip rose, cupping her neck and cheek, angling her head upwards. And without hesitation, I lowered my lips to hers. The need to know what her lips felt like had finally won out.

The tiny gasp of surprise she let out pushed me further, filling me with need. She soon relented and gave into the kiss, opening her mouth, granting me entrance to just one of the many places on her body that I sought to explore.

My entire body lit up, and felt like I was spinning around at a dizzying pace. But instead of wanting the spinning to stop, I began to ache for more. I attempted to deepen the kiss but it was at that moment that Grace pulled away from me. A bewildered look in those brown eyes stared back at me. Her eyes searched mine for something as she heaved, trying to regain control of her breathing.

Just when I thought she was going to completely move away from me, she lunged back into the kiss full force, this time pulling my face to meet hers. My hands went to both sides of her face, cupping it to regain control of the kiss. When she surrendered to me, to my controlling the tempo of the kiss, that ache began to well up in me again. My tongue flicked against the corner of her mouth and she let out a dangerous moan. So much so, that I knew it was time to end the kiss, although my cock squarely disagreed.

When I pulled back, with her face still in my hands, we both were breathing heavily, staring at one another. I don't believe either one of us expected the kiss to be that damn intense or that damn fulfilling.

"This is just the beginning."

Her eyes widened at my declaration, but I wouldn't elaborate or take it back. Because the truth was, I had no fucking clue what this was the beginning *of*. And the expression on Grace's face told me she was just as lost. But in that moment, I determined that being lost with her was a hell of a lot better than being safe and sound with anyone else.

"You should get home."

Where I would've expected a protest from Grace, she dipped her head and said, "Yeah."

I allowed my hands to drop away from her face and silently watched as she turned and headed out the back door of the club. My lower self was telling me that I should follow her to make sure she got home safely but I refrained. I had a feeling that there was going to be plenty of nights of me following her home in the near future.

* * *

I COULD'VE GONE to the Underground that night to fight after I watched Grace leave the club. Any other night when I felt any sort of tension running through my veins, it was almost as if muscle memory took over and I found myself in the boxing ring burning off the excess energy that had become a familiar foe throughout my life.

But I hadn't gone to fight after Grace left. Instead, I pivoted and headed out the front door and walked the few blocks to the building where I lived, back up to my condo. And on that night, once the door closed behind me, the sense of shutting the world out that often came wasn't there. Instead, it reminded me that I was alone again. Typically, that was the way I liked it, the way I wanted it, but obviously not tonight.

Feeling frustrated and full of sexual tension that my cock was reminding me still needed to be released, I ripped the T-shirt I wore over my head and tossed it into the laundry bin by the bathroom door, before undoing my belt buckle and the button of my jeans, peeling out of them.

Turning on the water of my waterfall shower, I let the water run for a while until the stall became steamy, just the way I liked it. The hot water was a shock to my system as I stepped in, almost causing me to flinch back in pain, but I gritted my teeth and beared it. Eventually my skin and muscles surrendered to the feeling and adjusted to the temperature. However, the sexual tension flowing through me refused to ebb.

That was when, with one hand pressed against the black and silver tiles of my shower wall, I leaned my head against my forearm while my free hand went to my erect cock. As soon as it did, images of Grace as she sang onstage came flooding back. I gritted my teeth again as my hand tightened around my shaft and the memory of the fucking kiss on the dance floor had me stroking my cock like I was digging for gold.

My hips began moving on their own as the water continued to pelt against my back. My sweat began to mix with the water from the shower, and the grunting sounds coming from my mouth drowned out everything else. I rarely masturbated—I hated hand jobs from women even more—but I needed this release more than I needed my next breath.

I ran my thumb along the tip of my cock, feeling the droplets that were coming from it. And an image of having Grace bent over in this very shower while I pounded into her from behind, all while she screamed my name was what sent me over the edge. I tossed my head backward and let out an unfamiliar sound as the muscles of my ass tightened due to the orgasm coursing through my body. Semen spilled out of me onto the shower floor, only to be swept away down the drain. I stood, sagging against the wall until the last droplets fell from my body. Only then did my knees buckle and I fell to the granite bench in the shower to catch my breath.

I remained seated there for a long while, allowing the water that was starting to cool off, run over me. I waited for that sickening feeling I always got after orgasming to overtake me. Instead, my mind filled with Grace's dimples as she smiled. It was the very opposite of disgust that filled me. It was that moment, I stood up and turned off the water.

Stepping out of the shower, I grabbed my navy blue towel from the wall mount, wrapped it around my body, and padded my way across the hall to my bedroom.

I stared at my bare mattress and plopped down on the edge of the bed after grabbing the remote from the nightstand. Turning on the TV, I pressed the button that would take me to the fight I recorded the previous night.

"Luke, what were your thoughts before going into this fight?" the commentator asked before thrusting the microphone in the fighter's face.

He frowned, obviously annoyed by having to do one of these interviews right after a fight.

"To fucking win," he grumbled.

"Yes, and some say that you weren't looking as good as we've seen you in the past, in your practices for this match. What do you have to say to that?"

"Who the hell said that? My training's private."

I shook my head. Luke McConnell was obviously a hothead who didn't like to be challenged.

Sounds like someone else I know, my mind quipped. I paid it no attention as I rewound the recording to watch the fight from the beginning. Luke had won this fight but it was close. Closer than it should've been. In fact, the fight was so close that during the third round I just cut the damn thing off. He had won, I guessed that was good enough. I didn't need to watch him struggle through the fight to get the W.

I tossed the remote back on the nightstand and stood, removing the towel and pulling on a pair of boxer briefs to sleep in for the night. Turning on my back, I spread wide over the bed, feeling comforted by the fact that there was no bedding on the mattress. The kiss of the wind on my skin from the ceiling fan above me, aided in cooling me off just enough that I was able to drift off into a dreamless slumber.

CHAPTER 7

*J*acob

I felt lighter as my steps quickened through the front doors of the hospital toward the elevator bank. I thoroughly enjoyed my job but I was *never* cheery to get to it. However, as I pressed the button to the fifth floor, a sensation that might be described as pleasant overcame my mood. It had nothing to do with the two surgeries I had lined up for the day either. One was a rhinoplasty that I was assisting another plastic surgeon on to learn more about the procedure. And the first was the skin graft on Johnny Westbrook.

My disposition had everything to do with the woman I made sure would be in the OR for both of them, however.

"Morning, Dr. Reynolds," a female voice purred from behind the desk.

I glowered at the smiling brunette. I couldn't place her and I was familiar with all of the nurses on this floor. They all knew not to speak directly to me until I've had my morning coffee, which was still very much full in my right hand.

"And you are?"

Her smile dropped a smidgen but it picked right back up in no time. "I'm Suzanne, but my friends call me Sue." Her brown eyes sparkled with the suggestive tone of her voice.

A familiar queasy feeling arose in my stomach. I didn't say anything in response to the woman. Giving her a final glare, I quickly scanned the rest of the nurses' station and was disappointed to see Grace wasn't behind it. My head dipped and I checked the time on my watch. It was two minutes until nine o'clock. Grace was always early. I wondered what was holding her up.

"I see you're performing two surgeries today, Dr. Reynolds," that pesky female from behind the nurses' station called.

I didn't bother acknowledging her comment, as I pressed onward toward the whiteboard that hung on the wall, listing off all the scheduled surgeries for the day. Seeing Grace's name listed by mine for the Westbrook surgery but not for the rhinoplasty, I frowned.

"Looks like I'll be assisting you in your second surgery of the day."

I glanced over my shoulder, looked the woman straight in the eye, saying nothing at all before tucking one of the cups of coffee under my right arm and turning back to the whiteboard, lifting the dry eraser to erase her name, and then writing in Nurse Young as the OR nurse assisting on the surgery.

"Doesn't look that way anymore," I retorted before taking my first sip of my coffee and then sauntering off toward my office. I shared my office with one other plastic surgeon but we often had opposite shifts so we rarely saw one another. I placed my bag on the black leather loveseat that I'd spent more than one night sleeping on just so I wouldn't have to go home after a long surgery. I didn't even bother firing up the desktop computer on my desk. Any information I needed to update could be done later. Right then my two objectives were to check-in on Johnny Westbrook and ensure everything was ready for his surgery, and to find Grace, and not necessarily in that order.

I adorned the coveted white coat over my black scrubs, threw my stethoscope around the back of my neck, and headed out the door, two cups of coffee in hand.

Taking the stairs up to the fifth floor, I entered the burn unit and strode down the hallway, constantly keeping an eye out. Before I even hit Johnny's room, the sound of feminine laughter stopped me in my tracks. It moved right through my chest as if it was made to grab ahold of something deep in my soul ... if I had one.

I moved closer until I reached the doorway, and there I found her, exactly where I figured she would be. By the patient's bedside.

"Morning," I interrupted, and didn't miss the way Grace's dimples flashed as she turned to face me. I didn't miss the way her smile grew either, before it quickly disappeared, and she cleared her throat.

"Good morning, Dr. Reynolds," she responded in a professional tone. "Mr. Westbrook and his family were told it was okay to spend a little bit of time with Johnny before he goes in for his surgery this morning."

I scanned the room, noticing Mr. Westbrook sitting at the side of his son's bed, in a wheelchair, along with two other men, one woman, and a teenage girl.

"Yeah, hope you don't mind, Doctor. These are my brothers, Mark and Charles, this is Charles' wife, Gail, and their daughter, Anna."

My gaze dropped to Mr. Westbrook. "It's not a problem at all. I don't think a few minutes of family time will hurt."

That wasn't entirely true. As a burn victim, Johnny was highly susceptible to infection, thus making it important to keep the number of visitors down. But everyone was wearing a hospital-issued gown and mask over their face, obviously taking precaution.

I moved past Grace toward the bed of the one person I hadn't actually spoken to or acknowledged yet.

"Hello, Johnny. I'm Dr. Reynolds," I introduced. "Do you remember me?"

"N-No." He tried to shake his head but the pain it caused was apparent.

"That's okay. Try not to move too much. I took care of you when you first came into the hospital, along with Nurse Young." Turning to Grace ... and found it difficult to look away from her once I did. "We'll be taking care of you again today."

"Will it st-stop hurting?"

Shoving my fisted hands into my pockets, I swallowed. "We'll try to give you something to help with the pain. But you'll be asleep during the surgery, which will help with your healing." It was the only assurance I could give the young boy. The fact was, the pain would last for a while and the scars were something he'd be dealing with for the rest of his life. But he, nor anyone else in the room, needed to hear that at the moment.

"Nurse Young—"

"Johnny's vitals look good," she stated as she handed me the chart, already knowing what I was going to ask.

I checked over the numbers she wrote down this morning and nodded in agreement. By the looks of it, Johnny's body should be able to withstand this surgery.

"Nurse Young and the surgical staff will prep Johnny for surgery, and I'll be waiting for him in the OR. The surgery will take a few hours, given the section of Johnny's body we're working on today," I said, looking across the bed at the boy's father.

He smiled but I saw the fear and hesitation in his hazel eyes.

"Excuse me," a voice interrupted as he knocked.

Turning toward the door, I frowned at the sight of a priest, Bible in hand, entering the room.

"Father Donald," Mr. Westbrook started, sounding hopeful, "you came."

"Of course I came, Mitchell. I would've been here sooner but traffic got the better of me. Is it okay if I come in?"

"We're trying to keep the chance of infection low," I stated in a monotone voice.

"Please," Mr. Westbrook insisted. "Father Donald is our priest and we wanted him here to pray over Johnny before he goes into surgery. Janice would've insisted on you being here." The man's voice cracked and I knew the Janice he spoke of was his deceased wife.

"It won't hurt for a minute. Please, enter," Grace allowed.

Biting my tongue, I stepped away from the bed to make room for the priest to do whatever it was he was there to do. I started for the door.

"Dr. Reynolds and Nurse Young, would you please join us in the prayer?" Mr. Westbrook questioned.

My gaze immediately dropped to Grace, who gave the man a sympathetic smile before nodding enthusiastically and moving closer to the bed.

All eyes around the room fell to me as I remained close to the door. I looked back to the boy in the bed and pivoted away from the door, closer to his bed, giving a slight nod.

"Dear Heavenly Father ..." the priest began.

I didn't hear the next words as revulsion and resentment coiled inside of me while this family prayed to something that wasn't there. My disturbance got the better of me and I soon found myself turning and exiting the room before the prayer and words from the priest were completed. Johnny would be better off if I was getting scrubbed and ready for this delicate surgery, instead of me standing there as whatever gibberish was spoken.

* * *

GRACE

"Aww man," I groaned as I stretched my neck to one side and then the other, working my tired muscles after exiting the operating room. Johnny's surgery took longer than initially thought due to the extensive nature of his burns. There was more scar tissue on his abdomen and arms which made for a tricky surgery.

"You were great in there," the compliment spilled from my lips with ease as I peered up at Jacob who walked beside me.

His eyes shone with something before he blinked and it was gone. "As were you. But he's still got a long road ahead of him." He sighed in anguish.

My heart tugged at his forlorn expression. "You have a soft side, Dr. Reynolds," I joked.

He surprised me by rounding in front of me, stopping us both right before we turned the corner to the main hallway. He didn't say anything at first, waiting until a few of the last remaining staff members who'd assisted in the surgery passed by us.

"I don't have a soft side."

I smirked. "You do. It doesn't like to make an appearance too often but you've shown your hand with Johnny Westbrook. You were almost as delicate talking to him in his room, as you are when making those perfect butterfly stitches." I giggled at my own joke.

Jacob's lips formed a frown but his eyes sparkled, telling me he wasn't actually pissed at what I was saying.

"You even tried to stay in the room as the priest prayed for him," I blurted out. I saw the way his face changed to one of caution and distrust once the priest showed up. He hesitated when the family asked him to remain for the prayer, and although he acquiesced, he left the room before it was over.

"You saw that, huh?"

I nodded. "Not one for organized religion?"

"Organized or unorganized."

"You're an atheist."

The lower half of his jaw worked as he clenched his teeth.

"That make me some sort of leper to you?" he asked, as if my answer truly mattered.

I shrugged. "You're not the first physician I've encountered who was an atheist. Far be it from me to judge anyone on their spiritual beliefs, or lack thereof, as in your case."

He moved closer and my body warmed. I looked down to see his left hand covering my arm, his thumb tracing the inside of my forearm.

"This isn't an episode of *Grey's Anatomy*, Dr. Reynolds."

"Call me Dr. Reynolds again when it's just the two of us and I'll have your ass sore and you screaming my name in a fashion even Shonda Rhimes couldn't be creative enough to write."

My inner thighs tightened and my entire body was jolted by his words and the gleam in his eyes as he said them. The hairs on my arms stood at attention, as if daring me to try him just so he could follow through on his threat. Or was it a promise?

Looking up into Jacob's eyes, I knew that it was a promise.

"Have dinner with me."

My eyebrows spiked. "Where?"

"That's for me to discern. All you have to do is say yes."

"Yes."

The lack of hesitation should've surprised me. But after the kiss we shared over the weekend, I knew Jacob Reynolds had an uncanny way of getting me to step out of my comfort zone.

A half smile touched his lips, and I knew it wouldn't be long before I was saying *yes* to a lot more than a dinner invitation. A nervous pang ran through my belly.

"Let's go tell the Westbrook family how Johnny's surgery went."

I hated when he let his hand fall away from me, knowing that he needed to. We were at work, and contrary to popular belief due to shows such as *Grey's Anatomy,* all the doctors and nurses weren't screwing each other in the on-call rooms.

"I'm with you, Dr. Re—" I stopped myself when warning flashed in those grey irises. "Jacob."

Satisfied, he nodded before continuing down the hall to the waiting room.

CHAPTER 8

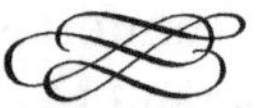

Jacob

Holy shit, was the first coherent thought I had after Grace opened the door of her home. I ogled her as she stood there in heels that had to be six inches off the ground. The golden-colored heels were matched with a wine-colored, sleeveless bandage dress that stopped just above her knees. The dress also had some sort of a chiffon cape that elegantly swayed whenever Grace moved even the slightest bit.

She made the dress look amazing, not the other way around. She'd done her makeup lightly, just enough to give her usually caramel cheeks a rose-pink color and her eyelids a golden tone. My first thought upon seeing her glossed lips was, *I definitely plan to ungloss them with my own mouth.*

"You look …" I started but couldn't finish because nothing seemed to fit. Ravishing, astonishing, beautiful were all too dull to describe how fucking good she appeared. "You straightened your hair," I finally said as I reached up with my free hand, touching a few of the sleek strands.

Her smile dropped a bit.

"It's great."

70

I would've never thought Grace was the type of woman to thrive off of or seek out compliments, but the way her smile illumined told me I was wrong.

"Thank you. The humidity decided to calm down a little at the end of summer so I thought straightening it would be a nice change."

I nodded, not knowing what humidity had to do with straightening one's hair or not but whatever.

"This is for you."

She glanced down at the light pink gift box in my hand. "You got me a gift?"

"Open it," I insisted. I didn't normally pick out gifts for anyone and I wanted to see her reaction to what I chose. I suspected that flowers for a first date were a little played out, and this felt perfect when I saw it.

Tucking the golden clutch in her right hand underneath her left arm, she took the box from my hand, opening it.

"Wow." Giggling, she lifted the silver keychain from the box. "She believed she could so she did," she read the quote on the pendant, which hung from a chain, out loud. Alongside the pendant hung the caduceus symbol with the letters RN inscribed in between it.

"The quote reminded me of you."

Her eyes lifted and she moved closer, pressing her palm to my chest and lifting up to kiss my cheek. "Thank you."

She started to move back but I caught her hand and leaned in, planting a kiss to her lips. I thought it was only going to be a quick grazing of her lips. *That's all I need*, I told myself, *before we get this night started*. But I'd fooled myself yet again, because the kiss deepened on its own. I soon found myself wrapping Grace up in my embrace, pulling her body toward mine because no matter how close we were she never seemed close enough. It was almost as if she was a blanket that warmed my cold soul … and I didn't even use blankets.

Somehow, I reeled it in and pushed back enough to let us both catch our breaths. "We should go have dinner now," I said against her lips.

Her lips pressed together as she nodded.

I stepped backward, giving her enough room to close and lock the door to her home. Once she moved to my side again, my hand went to take hers, leading her around my white Range Rover to the passenger side, and opening the door for her. My gaze lingered on her legs for a few seconds before shutting the door and rounding the car to the driver's side.

"You're okay with eating Ethiopian food, right?" I asked if she had any food allergies or if there was any style of food she didn't like already but I wanted to make sure.

"I've only had it once before, but I liked it."

"We're heading to the new restaurant that opened down on the Mainline."

"Great."

The drive was about twenty minutes from her house to the other end of the city of Williamsport. We didn't talk much in the car, but it was a comfortable silence, which I enjoyed.

"Thank you," she said as I helped her out of the car just before passing my key to the valet to park.

I slid my hand down her back to her waist as we walked through the doors that were held open for entrance.

"Reynolds," I told the hostess. I made a reservation since I'd heard this restaurant gets pretty packed on weekend nights.

"Right this way." She grabbed two menus and left us to follow. I allowed Grace to step in front of me, following the hostess, not only to be polite but so I could also watch and enjoy her movements from this angle. Sliding my hand into the pocket of my black pants, I warned my cock to chill the fuck out as I continued to stare at the sway of Grace's hips while she walked. The heels, the dress, and even the cape all displayed the fact that this was a woman who took care of her body. I'd seen it before, of course, while she was on stage performing, but knowing she dressed up for me tonight made it that much more enticing.

"Here you are," our hostess announced.

I looked at the table and then around the restaurant and frowned.

"We'll sit here," I insisted. The table was right next to the one the hostess placed us at, but this one was better.

"Oh, um, okay." She put the menus down and smiled.

Pulling out a chair, I inclined my head toward Grace. Once she sat, I trailed my fingers over her bare shoulders before moving around the table and taking my seat. Quickly scanning the room, I felt satisfied with the positioning of this table.

"What was that about?"

I lifted an eyebrow.

"The table thing."

"I don't sit with my back facing the exits."

Grace turned to look over her shoulder, and then back at the table which remained empty a few feet from us.

"No matter where you sit at that table, you can't see all the exits. Here I can."

Her forehead wrinkled; a new expression I'd never seen before but immediately found just as appealing as the rest of the faces she made.

"Were you in the military?"

I shook my head. "What makes you ask that?"

"That's a very military thing to do. I had a patient a year ago, at my old job, who told me that he never sat with his back to a door anywhere."

"I was never in the military," I reiterated without explaining myself any further.

She glanced around, taking in the decor. "It's beautiful in here."

For the first time since sitting down, I took my eyes off of her and looked around the restaurant. The hardwood floors were matched by a similar glossy wood of the walls, aligned with what I assumed to be Ethiopian artwork. The dining space was illuminated by overhead hanging lanterns that were outlined in colorful wicker designs.

"It's not bad." I turned back to her, enjoying this view much more.

"What made you want to be a doctor?" she asked as our waitress brought out two glasses of water.

I paused, allowing the waitress to place our waters down and take our orders. Grace opted for the eggplant vegetable medley with injera while I chose the chicken tibs, also with injera.

"I wanted to help people," I responded to her earlier question. I pushed back in my chair when she immediately started giggling. Her laughter actually tugged a smile from my own lips.

"That's the kind of bullshit answer you give in an interview. What's the real reason you became a doctor?"

Quickly sobering up, I planted my elbows on the table, leaning in. "I was forced to." Those four words, or rather the weight of them, seemed to sober Grace up as well.

She frowned and tilted her head, questioningly.

I shrugged. "In my family you were either one of two things, a doctor or a lawyer." I looked down and unfolded the napkin into my lap, avoiding eye contact for a handful of seconds before lifting my gaze again.

"What stopped you from completing your licensure to become a nurse anesthetist?"

Grace avoided my gaze in a similar way I had earlier. "Life got in the way." Her eyes darted to the corner of the room.

"Life? What does that mean?"

She looked me in the eye. "You don't know how to take a hint, huh?"

I leaned in farther. "I know how, I'm just choosing to ignore it." It was obvious she didn't want to tell me the full reasoning behind her career delay but I didn't care about her not wanting to share. I wanted to know more and more about her with each passing day.

"All you need to—"

"Jacob?"

I was instantly annoyed by the interruption as I was forced to look away from Grace to the couple who approached our table. I reminded myself I shouldn't be too annoyed seeing as how the man inching closer to our table was the main reason I was able to get on the reservation list for this restaurant in the first place.

"Joshua," I greeted. "Kayla." I nodded at his wife. Joshua Townsend knew me better as "Doc" from the Underground, but in public we used one another's names.

"Sorry for the interruption, I just wasn't expecting to see you tonight." Joshua smiled as I stood to shake his hand.

"No problem," I lied, and the small smirk that crossed his face told me he knew I was lying.

"This is Grace. Grace, this is Joshua Townsend and his wife, Kayla."

"Hello—"

"No, please don't stand. We don't mean to interrupt your dinner. Joshua just wanted to say hello to an old friend," Kayla insisted to Grace.

"Yes, we'll be on our way. Enjoy your meal," Joshua stated before wrapping his arm around Kayla's waist and heading off.

"Wow. I had no idea you knew *the* Joshua Townsend."

Before I could say anything, Grace smacked her forehead in a silly way and said, "What am I talking about? You're a plastic surgeon, and people like the Townsends probably know every surgeon in your field from here to the East Coast."

Shaking my head, I grunted. "Something like that." Joshua, nor anyone in his family, had ever been a patient of mine but that wasn't for me to bring up.

We made idle conversation for the next few minutes until our food arrived. Once it did, I derived a distinct pleasure in watching Grace enjoy her food. So much so, that my plate was only halfway eaten when she took her final bite. For the duration of our meal, I only had one main thought: *I'm going to fuck her so hard.*

* * *

GRACE

Jacob had gotten quiet during dinner. It would've made me uncomfortable if I hadn't already felt safe with him. When that happened, I had no idea. It was as if he'd snuck up on me entirely and his charm, or lack thereof, was no match for the walls I'd built up around me.

"Let's go for a walk," I suggested as the valet pulled his car up in front of the restaurant. "The Riverwalk's not too far from here."

Jacob nodded as he closed the passenger door and then rounded in front to climb into the driver's seat.

I slid comfortably into the leather seats and sighed as I relaxed into the seat. I couldn't remember the last time I felt this comfortable in my own skin, especially with a man.

The drive to the Riverwalk was only about ten minutes, and Jacob pulled into one of the parking lots along the road, paying for parking. Minutes later we were strolling down the paved walkway that followed the Williamsport River which snaked through the city.

Before long, my body warmed as Jacob pulled me into his side, draping his long arm over my shoulders.

"Are you warm enough?"

I peered up, nodded, and just stared at him. He was so damn handsome, gorgeous even. And either he didn't know it or didn't care.

"Do you enjoy being a doctor?"

He pulled back to look down at me with shock but didn't completely remove his hand from my shoulder. "Yeah," he finally answered. "At first I thought of it as something I *had* to do. Even when I … stopped listening to my parents, I continued with med school because I'd never even thought of doing anything else. But during my first round of rotations as a med student, I knew. When I stepped into an operating room for the first time and watched an actual surgery being performed, there was no other option for me."

I sighed because his words were so genuine. He didn't need to say them. I'd instinctively picked up on everything he said just be watching him in the OR. The man got a natural high from performing surgery.

"It's the same with you." He suddenly stopped, pivoting his body so that my back was pressed against the railing that outlined the river. His hands went to either sides of my body as he brought our bodies to touch. "I don't know what the hell you've done to me, and maybe I don't want to know, but there is no option of me ignoring what's building between us," he growled just before dipping his head and taking my lips in a soul-awakening kiss.

I gave into the kiss almost immediately—because not doing so hadn't even occurred to me. His lips, his tongue, and even the tiny hairs of the his five o'clock shadow all singed my skin with a burning desire. His large hands cupped my face, pulling me to him even closer. It felt like he was attempting to suck my soul directly out of my body. And if it continued to feel this damn good, I would let him without a second thought.

His capable hands trailed down the sides of my neck to the tops of my shoulders, leaving a trail of goosebumps behind them. I sighed into his mouth, feeling freer than I had in a very long time. But when his hands moved underneath my breasts, I was quickly brought back to reality. Without breaking the kiss, I guided his hands lower, to my waist. Only when they were fully planted on my hips was I comfortable enough to fully enjoy the kiss again.

And as I got into it, Jacob pulled back. His eyes were dark. I didn't know if that was due to the lack of lighting where we stood or if it was something else.

"Let me take you home," his deep voice insisted slightly above a whisper. He wasn't requesting just to drop me off at my house after our date. This was his way of requesting that I let him inside once we got there.

I swallowed, and against my better judgment, nodded in agreement.

Wordlessly, we retraced our steps back to the parking lot where Jacob had parked, and after he closed the passenger side door for me and climbed in, we were headed in the direction of my house. Jacob's right hand rested on my left knee and his thumb traced little circles on the flesh there, sending tiny electrical current throughout my body for the duration of our drive.

I wanted to tell him to hurry up and slow down at the same time. This was moving so quickly, I felt as if I couldn't catch my breath. But when I turned and stared at his profile, as he focused on the road, any hesitation I had subsided.

Unfortunately, I wouldn't get the opportunity to say anything because as soon as we turned into my driveway, Jacob's headlights shone on a figure lying on the concrete step that led to my front door.

"Who is that?" I questioned, my hand going to the latch to open the door.

"Wait!" Jacob insisted sharply, freezing me in my tracks. "Don't jump out when you don't know who or what that is." His voice was angry sounding.

Just then the figure moved and I recognized my sister's face immediately, thanks to the light's from Jacob's Range Rover.

"Journey!" I called, moving to get out of the car.

I ran around the front of his car before stopping and squatting in front of Journey's slouched over body. "Journey, what's wrong?" I pleaded, taking her hand in mine. Instinctively, my hand moved to her neck to feel her pulse. I sighed in relief when I found it beating normally.

"H-He dumped m-me!" She struggled to get the three words out before slumping over.

Her eyes were glossy, and in the darkness of the night I couldn't figure out if it was the result of tears or something else.

"You know her?"

Turning to Jacob, I told him, "She's my sister."

His eyes widened and he stooped by my side as well. "We should get her inside."

I nodded and stood, hoping Journey could stand on her own power. But then Jacob did something that had me sucking in air in surprise.

He leaned forward, and without a word, placed his arms underneath my sister, lifting her from the step. "Open the door."

I took his direction easily, the same way as when we were in the operating room. Finally managing to find the key in my clutch, I used it to open the door.

"Put her on the couch," I instructed, pointing in the direction of the long, grey couch that could be seen around the wall separating the living room from the entrance area.

I closed the door behind us, locking it, and went over, kneeling by my sister's side. She had immediately coiled up into the fetal position facing me, but her eyes were blank and staring out into nothing.

"Journey." My voice was low as I pushed the long braids she wore behind her ear to get a better view of her face. "Are you hurt?"

She squeezed her eyes tightly and started crying … sobbing.

I lowered my head because this was starting to feel too familiar. Hearing a noise behind me, I remembered that Jacob was there watching all of this.

Standing, I turned. "I'm sorry—"

He shook his head, cutting off my apology. "Don't apologize. What do you need?"

It wasn't a question I was expecting but one I appreciated greatly.

"The linen closet is down the hall on the left. Could you bring me a blanket out of there?"

His face darkened but he nodded and turned to retrieve the blanket.

I knelt down next to Journey again who continued to cry and hiccup. I began stroking her arm, feeling desperate to do anything to help her through this.

A shadow fell over me when Jacob returned a minute later, holding out the blanket to me. I took it, barely looking over my shoulder, and unfolded it, covering Journey's body. Her crying decreased to whimpering but the tears kept streaming down her face.

"I have to go."

I heard the words that sounded like they were from halfway across the room. And before I could turn around fully, I heard my front door opening and slamming shut. My heart sank. Obviously, Jacob didn't want any part of this mess. Sighing, I turned back to my sister.

"Journey …" I called, but that only served to increase her crying spell, it seemed. I started doing the only thing I could think of. I began singing. The first song that came to mind was Sam Smith's "Pray".

Journey's body ceased shivering from how hard she was, crying with each line of the song. The sounds coming from her throat became less anguished. And while the tears continued to flow, she calmed down.

Just as my mom had done when I was a child and she was too sick to get out of bed, begging for me to sing to her until she felt better. I would sing to her for hours by her bedside.

I continued to sing. One song moved into the next because that was the only thing I could do right then for my sister.

CHAPTER 9

*J*acob

"Don't fucking touch me!" I yelled at Buddy, who'd put his arm over my shoulder as I entered the ring.

His greying eyebrows rose in surprise but there wasn't any fear in his brown eyes. "Oh, we're having one of those nights, huh? Okay." Nodding, he moved farther away from me, toward the guy I was fighting as soon as he got his ass out of the way.

Buddy was the organizer, coach, trainer, and whatever else was needed for these fights. While Connor and Joshua financed the operation, it was on Buddy's word whether or not a fighter got into the ring of the Underground. I met Buddy about ten years ago after I joined a local boxing gym he owned, during residency. Eventually, he told me about this underground fighting ring he ran and asked if I was interested. I'd been coming ever since.

"Let's go!" I growled, anxious to hit something as the memory of Grace laying the blanket over her sister flashed before me. That memory began to melt with other memories I'd worked long and hard to bury.

"Keep ya' shirt on, we're coming!" Buddy snickered at his stupid ass joke since I wasn't wearing a shirt.

"All right, gentlemen, you know the rules. No hitting in the face, and I hope you're both wearing your cups. Everything else is a go!" With that, Buddy lowered his hand and stepped out of the way, allowing my opponent and myself to circle one another.

I stared into the dark eyes of my opponent. I wasn't familiar with this fighter. He was new but I really didn't give a shit whether I'd fought him before or not. He was about to get his ass beat if my mood was any indication.

We circled one another a couple of times before I finally had enough and lunged in his direction, aiming for his kidneys.

"Fuck!" he bellowed at the direct hit.

"Kidneys," I growled. "Might want to protect those." I lunged again as he opened his mouth to respond and landed a right hook to his abdomen. But I was feeling too good with the direct blow because he was able to quickly recover and land a punch to my ribs.

I grunted at the hit, but also felt a renewed sense of calm from the pain that shot through me. I slowed down my movements, and that's when another blow from my opponent landed to the other side of my ribs. And before I had the chance to recover from that blow, another punch to my belly stole my breath, nearly collapsing me to the floor. Stumbling, I managed to keep on my feet, even when he tried to side swipe my leg. A move I was typically known for in this particular circle.

Fortunately, I didn't fall to the ground and was able to avoid being taken down by the leg sweep, but the burning from the hits I'd taken continued to sting and reverberate throughout my entire body.

"I was told you were tough shit, Doc. Guess everyone fucking lie—"

I hated the sound of his fucking voice, and made it known that his talking wasn't appreciated as I landed a spin kick to his side, causing him to stumble backwards. I didn't wait for him to recover, when I did a leg sweep of my own and then pounced on his body with my legs around the top half of his body. I hurriedly draped his neck in a choke hold and patiently waited for him to realize he had no other choice but to tap the fuck out or pass out. Either one was fine with me.

"Let him up!" I heard Buddy yell from the corner of the ring.

At the same time, I felt a tapping against my leg, alerting me to the fact that he surrendered, conceding my win of this fight.

Satisfied, I pushed out a breath and released him, moving to stand. I didn't bother to stick around for the cheering or lifting of hands. I won, obviously, and not once did I ever enter into a fight for the purpose of accolades or applause.

Stepping out of the ring, I made a beeline for the changing room where I'd left my bag. As I pushed through the door, the idea of staying for yet another fight appealed to me.

"What the hell was that?"

I spun around as Connor's angry question was hurled in my direction. Apparently, he'd entered the changing room right behind me. I was so focused on the feeling of satisfaction that came from the pain still coursing through my knuckles and ribs that I hadn't even noticed.

I narrowed my eyes and tossed him the same angry glare he was giving me. "What the fuck was what?" I didn't bother waiting for his response as I yanked the wooden locker I'd placed my belongings into open. I quickly jumped back when Connor pushed it shut again, slamming it, nearly catching my goddamned hand in it.

"You know what I'm talking about. You let that fucker almost beat you."

"He didn't beat me though, did he?" I growled.

"He came a hell of a lot closer than he should've. You purposely let him get those hits in."

I shook my head. "I don't know what you're talking about." I yanked my locker open, forcing Connor to step back or be slammed in the face by it.

"You're full of shit."

"I'm not the only one."

Connor's eyes narrowed.

"You think I don't know guys like Josh and Damon take it easy on me in the ring?" I declared.

His face didn't even register shock.

"That's why you request newbies."

"They don't softball me."

"That's what you think they're doing?"

"*Think?* I fucking know! Slow ass punches and leg sweeps they do in the ring with me," I grumbled the last part as I stuck my head through the grey T-shirt I was changing into.

I ferociously commenced to unwrapping my hands, grunting at the tenderness I felt on my knuckles.

"They're saving you."

Pausing, I glared at Connor. "Fucking how?"

"You're a goddamned surgeon. You get injured in there, your hand gets broken or twists the wrong way and your whole fucking career is over. You may have a cracked rib as it is from that damn hit you took."

"And what concern is that of yours or anyone else's?" I was fuming as I slammed the locker shut, ignoring the sharp pain that ran through my side, as if confirming Connor's diagnosis.

"We're not a bunch of fucking animals down here."

"Maybe that's what the hell I need. A fighting league where there's actual fights and not a bunch of fucking pussies worrying about day jobs!" I didn't waste my time putting on the jeans I carried in my bag as I shoved past Connor and headed out the door of the changing room, into the main fighting area. There was already another fight underway, but I didn't give a flying fuck. I was too pissed off to just stand around and watch.

I got in my car and slammed the door shut. It was well after midnight but I couldn't go home. I was too keyed up for that. After a fight, I usually felt calmed down and ready to shower and sleep for the night but that wasn't the case. Connor had pissed me off with his fucking inquiries into my private life. If I wanted to fight every fucker from here to the East Coast that was my business. I could manage my own damned career.

Turning the car on, I began driving with no particular destination in mind. Somehow after taking turns and streets I barely knew, I found myself sitting outside of Grace's small home. All of the lights were off, and as I turned the lights and the ignition of my car off, I wondered if she was still perched at the side of her couch, trying to console her sister.

I didn't let myself get too deeply into that wondering because it would lead to me remembering what it was that pushed me out of the house and into the ring in the first place. Instead, I took in the view of Grace's home, all the while stroking my tender ribs at my side.

* * *

"THEY'RE NOT BROKEN but there is some bruising to the muscle and cartilage," Graham Avery grimly stated, frowning as I carefully slipped my scrub top over my head.

I sighed in relief. Bruises I could work through the pain, but a broken or cracked rib would take more time to heal.

"Want to tell me how it happened?"

I paused, looking across the room at Graham. He and I first met during residency and we both ended up at the surgical unit at Memorial, although he was an orthopedic surgeon.

"No."

He shook his head with a half smile on his damn face. "What happened? Got a little too restless in bed last night?"

"What the fuck did you just say?" I growled, standing so quickly that pain from my bruised ribs shot through me. But my anger was greater than the pain, and I ignored it as I moved across the examination room.

"Hey, chill out," he demanded with his hands in the air. "I was just joking."

"Do I look like I'm in a joking mood?"

"Do you ever?"

"Then why the hell would you think now would be an appropriate time to make such an asinine comment?"

I was pissed but held my composure. I'd known Graham for a number of years, and while he wasn't a friend, I knew he often made off-hand comments and jokes. Most people just laughed it off. I, for the most part, ignored it. Though his comments were unnecessary and rather juvenile, he was a very skilled surgeon, having assisted me a number of times in the OR.

But this last joke had dug deeper than even Graham realized, sparking my impatience.

"You'll probably want to reschedule any surgeries you have for the next week, at least," he continued, filling the silence as I continued to glare at him.

Blinking, I tore my gaze from him, remembering that I was at work and he was a colleague.

I shook my head. "A week is too damn long to be out of the OR. Not happening."

"Jacob, just because your ribs aren't broken doesn't mean this injury isn't a serious one. You'll be in a lot of pain over the next few days. Bruising to the muscle and cartilage around your ribs can greatly restrict you—"

"I went to medical school just like you. I don't need to specialize in ortho to know the difference between a bruise and a fucking fracture." My voice was heavy with sarcasm.

Graham shook his head. "At least take the next few days off; the pain may subside by then. I can write you a script for the pain after that."

"No meds." I shook my head. I could live with the pain. I became a master at hiding pain very early on in life. It was a skill that's served me well.

"I'll reschedule today and tomorrow's surgery, and I have the next two days off. Four days should be enough."

Graham shrugged. "Suit yourself."

Grabbing my white coat from the exam table, I slid my arms in either side before putting my stethoscope around my neck and heading for the door.

"You let me know if the pain gets any worse. And try not to overdo it."

I looked over my shoulder and nodded wordlessly at Graham before turning and exiting the room while rolling my eyes.

"Glorified carpenters," I grumbled as I left.

"I heard that!" Graham yelled from behind me.

"You were meant to," I retorted, but had to grab my side because the expansion of my lungs and chest movement of raising my voice even slightly caused my ribs to rebel.

Instead of taking the stairs back up to the surgical floor, I opted for the elevator to save myself the discomfort. I avoided the nurses' station since Grace wasn't in yet anyway. I'd purposely come in early to seek out Graham for him to do an X-ray and diagnosis of my ribs, before coming into work for the day. Heading into my office, I flicked on the light and tossed my stuff on the sofa, and immediately fired up my computer to make the rearrangements to my schedule. I tried to convince myself it wasn't a terrible thing to be out of the OR for the next few days since I did have a huge amount of paperwork that I'd been avoiding, which I needed to catch up on.

But the thought of Grace being in surgery, standing next to a surgeon in the OR, and that surgeon not being me, began to play around in my head. The jealousy I started to feel was unlike anything I'd experienced before. I didn't get jealous, not over a woman anyway. Another surgeon getting a coveted surgery, sure. A fighter at the Underground besting me in the ring, hell yes. But a woman causing me to feel envy that I couldn't be next to her at all times? The feeling was completely foreign, yet here I was experiencing it.

CHAPTER 10

*G*race

"I heard he fights in a secret fighting league or something."

"Really?"

I heard the whispered words of the two nurses as I entered behind the desk of the nurses' station, placing my bag underneath, in its usual position. I recognized the voice of Angela. It wasn't unusual to hear her gossiping about any of the hospital's employees. If someone had personal business they didn't want known, it was best to stay far away from Angela. The woman was a great nurse, but couldn't keep her mouth from moving. The second voice I heard was less familiar, but I recognized it as coming from Suzanne. She was also a newer nurse to this floor, though she'd been at Memorial for a few months before I started. I hadn't worked directly with her just yet, but from the first time I met her, something about her eyes gave me pause. She always seemed to be scheming on something or someone.

"Good morning," I interrupted, hoping this would end the gossip fest.

"Morning, Grace. How are you? Did you hear Dr. Reynolds rescheduled his surgeries for the next couple of days?"

That had me spinning around so quickly I nearly lost my balance. Recovering, I smoothed my palms down the sides of my scrubs. "No. Is he going to be out of town?"

I pulled my lips inward and mentally scolded myself for being so damned obvious. But Jacob wasn't one to reschedule his surgeries without a good reason, as far as I knew. My gaze fell on Angela for an answer.

"You don't know?"

That question had come from behind Angela. It was Suzanne who was peering at me with her arms folded as if she knew something that I wasn't aware of.

"No, I don't." I tried to make my voice come out as even as possible.

"He'll be in town as far as I know. No real reason was given. In the system the surgeries are just posted as rescheduled," Angela continued, obviously not picking up on the tension between Suzanne and I.

"Well, I heard he fights in some sort of secret fighting club. Probably got hurt fighting," Suzanne stated poignantly, staring at me.

"What kind of a doctor gets involved in underground fighting? A *surgeon* no less," Angela wondered out loud, while staring at the computer.

"I don't know but that's what I've heard. You wouldn't know, would you, Grace?"

Blinking, I took in Angela's superior grin. I couldn't tell if she was happy that she believed she knew information I didn't or if she was just excited to be aiding in the spreading of gossip about yet another doctor.

"I wouldn't know. And trust me, even if I did, I wouldn't be standing here spreading rumors about the people I work with behind their back." I spun around while rolling my eyes and rounded the corner of the nurses' station to check the board for the day. Sure enough, the schedule that I was supposed to be working with Jacob was off the board. I had another surgery scheduled for ten o'clock that morning with a different surgeon. Looking over at the clock high on the wall, I saw that it gave me enough time to go and check in on Johnny Westbrook before I needed to prep the patient for surgery.

All the while, as I walked to Johnny's room, I kept glancing over my shoulder, wondering if I'd see Jacob, and if so, what I would say. The previous night didn't end how I anticipated—nor he, I would assume.

I ran my hand down my face at the heavy feeling that settled over my heart at the thought of my sister, still curled up on the couch this morning. She only got up twice—once to go to the bathroom and the second time to eat a little bit of soup that I'd defrosted. And that was only after I begged her to eat. She wasn't home alone, however. That morning, I went over to my retired neighbor's home, who had also been a nurse, and asked if she would check-in on my sister throughout the day. Mrs. Walters readily agreed.

"Hey," I greeted, surprised when I entered Johnny's room and saw Jacob standing there.

"Morning, Grace."

My knees wobbled slightly at the sound of my name from his mouth, and my eyes traveled to his lips.

Soon, a smile crested my face as he thrust a cup of coffee in my direction.

"Two pumps of vanilla creamer and a packet of stevia."

I took the cup from his hand, not surprised by the electric current that ran through me at the touch of our fingers. I'd gotten used to that feeling by now.

"How'd you know?" I let my gaze linger on him over the lid of the coffee cup as I took my first sip. It was good but not as good as the taste of his kiss.

"You always come check on him before starting your shift."

I nodded and let out a small laugh. He was right. Checking on the young boy had become a routine of mine.

"How's he doing?"

Jacob turned at the same time my eyes went to the bed.

"He's resting now. The skin graft is healing well. We'll have to perform another on his legs early next week."

"He'll be ready for it," I said just above a whisper as I moved closer, my gaze lifting to the monitors displaying his vitals. "He's a tough cookie." I peered down at the nine-year-old little boy and smiled. However, it faded as I looked over the bandages covering his body.

"His father was discharged yesterday."

"I know. He should be in soon, though." I had the feeling Johnny's father wouldn't stay away from the hospital for too long given that his son was still here.

"He has to prepare for his wife's funeral."

Sighing, I stepped back from the bed.

"Pain is a part of life. He'll get used to it sooner or later."

Jacob's heavy words caught me by surprise. My gaze was drawn to him, and I saw that stormy look in his eyes as he stared down at the young patient.

"Let's go."

I nodded and followed Jacob out of the room, exiting just as quietly as I entered. We passed the boy's aunt and uncle who informed us they were going to sit with Johnny for a few hours while his father couldn't be there.

"Good thing he has a loving family." I sighed as I watched the aunt and uncle enter the room. "Not everyone has that."

Jacob snorted.

I turned to him; something dark passed through his eyes and he glanced away for a second.

"Speaking of family, how's your sister?"

Swallowing, I shrugged. "The same," I admitted. "I have a neighbor checking on her so she's not alone all day."

He nodded, and suddenly I felt the need to defend my sister.

"She's not on drugs."

"I didn't think she was. You don't seem like the type who would care for someone who was on drugs."

I shook my head. "I'm not. Addiction is an illness and all of that. I understand. Nevertheless, I couldn't give safe harbor to someone who was intentionally harming themselves in that way." I hesitated, biting my bottom lip. "She's sick."

"Mental illness?"

I nodded. "Bipolar … I think … just like our mother." That was the first time I'd said the words out loud to someone outside of my family in … ever.

"Think?"

I shrugged, holding my hands out in an *I don't know* manner. "She hasn't been diagnosed with it officially. But the symptoms, the signs … they've all been there for some time. I grew up watching it happen. I know what's going on even if no one else wants to admit it."

"She refuses to get help?"

"No one has made her get help. My father ignores it and thinks it'll all go away just like—" I cut myself off, feeling the anger and frustration rise in my belly. "I'm working on it."

I folded one arm around my body while bringing the coffee cup to my lips for another sip, feeling completely exposed. I avoided Jacob's gaze.

"I found this for you."

I wrinkled my forehead as Jacob pulled out some folded papers from the pocket of his lab coat.

He unfolded the papers and handed them to me.

I took them in my free hand and read them over while continuing to sip my coffee.

My eyes rolled up to meet Jacob's. "Requirements for getting into Williamsport University's Nurse Anesthetist program?" It came out as a question, but it was obvious what I'd been reading.

"They have one of the best programs in the city and it can be tailored to your experience and education level. Also, this is one of the few programs that allows you to continue to work full-time and go to school part-time … if that's what you want."

My mood instantly shifted from one of gloom, when thinking of my sister, to one of pure happiness that he would've taken the time to read up, study, and print out this information for me.

One second I was just standing there, and the next, my arms were around his, pulling him into a tight hug. It felt even better when the warmth of his strong arms wrapped around my body tightly.

I started to pull back but caught Jacob's face wince in pain.

"What happened?" I questioned. The minor movement he just performed shouldn't have been painful. We embraced much more tightly than this the night before and I hadn't spotted one ounce of pain in his face.

"Nothing."

"Is this why you had to cancel your surgeries for the next few days?"

"They're not canceled."

"Rescheduled."

He shook his head. "I was asked to consult on a patient in the ER. He was belligerent and kicked me in the ribs. No big deal."

Stepping back, I glared at him. "That lie came out way too easily."

"Gr—" He was cut off by the buzzing of the pager on his hip.

"I need to go anyway and prep a patient for surgery." I abruptly moved around him and headed in the opposite direction down to the surgical floor to begin my work for the day. Stuffing the papers he gave me into the pocket of my scrubs, I pushed aside the fact that Jacob just blatantly lied to my face, after I revealed things about my past that I hadn't shared with anyone else.

* * *

Jacob

She's ignoring me.

I was reminded yet again as she swiftly passed me on her way to assist another doctor. We were both down in the ED, helping out due to the fact that there had been call outs. Today was supposed to be my day off, but when I couldn't get Grace on the phone for the past two days, I chose to bring my ass down to the hospital where I knew she was working the night shift. That was when I was asked to stay and pitch in due to a number of car accidents as a result of stormy weather earlier in the day.

"Dr. Reynolds, can you take this one? He just needs stitches to the wound on his forehead."

Without thinking, I snatched the X-rays from the head nurse of the ED and looked them over, evaluating whether her statement was correct or not. I quickly concluded that she was.

"Yeah, I'll need an assist from …" At that moment, Grace emerged from behind the curtain of another room. "Nurse Young," I said loud enough for her to hear me.

"You got it," the ED nurse agreed. "Nurse Young, you're assisting Dr. Reynolds with this patient with a head wound."

"But I'm already helping with the ortho patient. He's getting ready to go up for surgery."

I narrowed my gaze at her obvious desire to continue to avoid me.

"Dr. Graham is competent enough to complete the surgery without your assistance, I assure you."

Her eyes threw daggers my way but she gave no more protest as she passed me, through the curtain of the patient I'd be stitching up. Truth was, I didn't need her assistance for some stitches. Graham probably could've used her help more but screw him. He could find another surgical nurse.

"Hello, Mr. …" she looked down at the patient's chart. "Odeski. This is Dr. Reynolds and I'm Nurse Young. We'll be stitching up that wound for you."

"It hurts like hell," the fifty-seven-year-old man grumbled, in obvious discomfort.

"We'll try to give you something for that. Doctor?" She gave me her most professional, stiff smile.

"Mr. Odeski." I nodded and quickly prepared to stitch this patient up and send him on his way. He was lucky that aside from a sizable gash he hadn't sustained any other injuries in the accident. Apparently, he was cleaning the gutters of his home, and slipped from the ladder, hitting his head.

"Next time I'm going to leave cleaning the gutters to my damned son, like my wife suggested."

Grace giggled, as she wiped the area of his wound, disinfecting it. "I think that would be a good idea, Mr. Odeski."

I didn't say much as I slipped my hands into gloves and picked up the tools I'd need, which had been neatly laid out by Grace on the table. I gave the man something to numb the area and waited a few minutes for it to kick in. After checking to ensure he was fully numbed, I worked to stitch up the gash.

"Is this going to leave a scar?"

I frowned. "A faint one, possibly."

"Oh drats!"

Grace's eyes widened, "You want a scar, Mr. Odeski?"

"Hell yeah," he stated firmly.

I looked to Grace, whose confused expression mirrored mine. "Why?"

"I've gone almost fifty-eight years without any battle scars or serious wounds. I wanted people to look at my scar and wonder why type of melee I was in that caused it." He chuckled deeply.

Rolling my eyes, I shook my head. "Just your luck you got one of the best plastic surgeons in the state to do your stitches," I affirmed right as I clipped off the end of the final stitch, placing the tools into the bin, and standing, looking over my work, feeling satisfied.

"And humble, too," Grace mumbled sarcastically.

"You sound sure of yourself, young man."

"Piece of advice, Mr. Odeski?"

He nodded.

"Don't ever let a surgeon that *isn't* this damn confident cut into you." I snatched off the gloves I wore and tossed them into the hazardous waste bin. "You should be able to go home after about an hour of observation. Enjoy the rest of your day."

I waited and followed Grace out of the room, feeling pissed off all over again when she didn't even spare me a passing glance.

"Let's talk," I growled, taking her by the arm and leading her in the opposite direction of the main area of the ED. Grabbing the door to the first room I saw, I twisted the knob, feeling satisfied when it opened. I practically shoved Grace inside of the closet before slamming the door behind us.

"Are you serious right now? We're at work!" she whisper-yelled.

"We wouldn't need to do this at work if you hadn't been ignoring my calls."

Folding her arms across her chest, she lifted her chin defiantly. "I've been busy."

"Doing what?"

"None of your damn b—"

I couldn't take it any longer. Between the past three days of barely a word from her and seeing her laughing and talking with other nurses and doctors, I lost myself. I crushed my lips to hers, ignoring the stabbing pain in my side that resulted from my sudden movement. Feeling my lips covering hers again for the first time in four damn days was worth the discomfort.

Before I could take the kiss too far, I pulled back with my hand at the nape of her neck. I wanted more than anything to undo the tight bun she wore and run my hands through those bouncy curls of hers.

"If you say what you do is none of my business, I promise you I will make it my business to have you ass naked, bouncing on my cock as you scream my name loud enough for the entire emergency department to hear," I growled through gritted teeth.

Grace's lips curled in anger, and my cock twitched from the fire in her eyes. "If I didn't know you had bruised ribs, I'd punch you for this damn caveman act." She moved away from me, taking a step backwards.

"You haven't seen anything yet."

The vein at the side of her neck pulsed, obviously turned on.

"I need to get back to work."

Her forward propulsion was stopped by my arm around her waist.

"Jacob—"

"What time does your shift end?"

She didn't respond immediately. Finally, she said, "Ten."

"Let me take you somewhere."

"Where?" The look she gave me was hopeful and filled with curiosity.

"The truth. To find out where I got this injury from."

Her lips firmed shut. The warring going on inside of her was obvious to see in those maple irises.

"Okay," she finally agreed, and I let out the breath I'd been holding.

Only then did I release her from my grasp. She gave me one final glance before turning and pulling the door open, exiting the tiny closet I tugged her into.

I revealed something to her that I hadn't shared with any other person in my life. At least, not anyone in my work life, which was most of my life.

CHAPTER 11

Jacob

Why the hell was I nervous? I don't get nervous. I could stand in front of the head of surgery or the head of this multi-billion dollar healthcare facility I worked for and not bat an eye. But the knowledge of where I was taking Grace that night caused me to pace like a first-year resident waiting to hear back on whether or not he passed his boards. I hadn't been nervous for that either.

"Okay, I'm all set. Should I go home and change or is this okay?" she questioned as we stood outside of the front entrance of Memorial Hospital, holding her arms out. She was wearing a pair of skin-tight jeans, black wedge booties, and a flowy black top with a leather jacket folded over her arm in case it got colder out.

"How did you change?" I was expecting her to come down in the pair of scrubs she wore all day. And I wouldn't have had any problem with that either. She looked damn good in anything.

"I always keep some extra clothes in my locker just in case I need to stop somewhere unexpectedly after work. Don't doctors do that, too?"

I grunted. "I don't do unexpected stops." At least I hadn't until I met this woman. She had me doing things I hadn't anticipated on doing quite often.

Grace gave me a look but didn't say anything else. "I'm parked over here." I took her hand in mine and led us to my car, holding the passenger door open for her.

I circled the car and climbed in, preparing myself for whatever happened at the end of this twenty-minute drive.

"How was the rest of your shift?" I asked, wanting to break the silence. I listened as Grace went on to describe the rest of her time in the ED, and then the trauma surgery she assisted on. A pedestrian on a bicycle was involved in a hit and run, and sustained massive injuries.

"The police are still looking for the driver, last I heard," she finished.

"How's your sister?"

Out of the corner of my eye, I saw her head turn in my direction. "She's a little better. She was actually up to going out to dinner with some friends she has here in Williamsport. She told me she was planning on staying the night with one of them." She sighed, obviously feeling concerned.

"She'll be all right," I stated, reaching out my right hand to cover the hand resting in her lap. I truly didn't know if her sister would be okay, but I knew that Grace was worried and I loathed the fear that entered her eyes whenever she thought about her sister.

"I've been looking out for her since before she could walk. I'm more of a mother to her than a sister, oddly enough."

I swallowed the lump in my throat, identifying with what she was feeling but not saying anything. Removing my hand from hers, I placed it back on the wheel.

"Where are we?" Grace finally questioned glancing around.

"Don't worry. It's not as bad as it appears." I was well aware that the empty looking building we were pulling up to could be intimidating to someone who didn't know what to expect.

"Are you taking me to an abandoned building?"

I shook my head. "It's not abandoned. Just looks that way from the outside. See ..." I jutted my head forward for Grace to peer ahead, "there're other cars around." Parking behind a black BMW, I immediately recognized whose car it was.

I hopped out of my Range Rover and cursed, my right hand going to my ribcage. I kept forgetting that damn injury and how fast movements were painful, and likely would be for at least another week.

"So this is the place where you got that injury?" Grace questioned with a lifted eyebrow as she folded her arms across her chest.

"You didn't wait for me to open the door for you," I countered.

"I was afraid you were too busy keeling over and needed CPR."

I chuckled in spite of the pain but the grimace on my face must've been obvious.

Moving closer, Grace stroked my chest with her hand. "You probably should be home resting."

"I'm fine." I slid my right arm over her shoulders and guided us toward the metal door, where I gave the signature knock—two knocks, a pause, followed by three knocks in rapid succession.

"Who is it?" a gruff voice questioned from the other side through the rectangular hole that he slid open.

"Doc."

The hole slammed shut. Grace looked up at me, confused.

A second passed by before the door was pulled open.

"Get in here, Doc."

I allowed Grace to step inside before me. Nodding in the direction of the door's guard, I wrapped my arm around Grace again for comfort. I could tell by the wide-eyed expression on her face, she didn't know what was going on.

"What is this place?"

"You'll see," I answered, and guided her to a second door that wasn't guarded but did reveal what we came here to see.

As soon as we crossed over the threshold, loud cheers and clapping could be heard. I peered up ahead and spotted two guys in the ring dueling it out, while Buddy moved around them, carefully watching and refereeing the fight.

"Is this ..." pausing, Grace took in the scene before her, "an underground fighting league?" Those hickory eyes turned to me.

"We don't exactly call ourselves a *league.*"

"*We?* So you take part in these fights also? You're not just a spectator?"

I shook my head and took her by the hand, guiding her closer to the front of the guys standing around. Upon closer inspection, I could see the two guys in the ring were Brick and Damon.

"Doc, didn't expect to see you here."

I turned to my left and see Joshua Townsend, smiling at me, before his eyes drop to my right side, at the same time Grace moved into his line of sight.

A small gasp escaped her lips.

"Grace, right? We met the other night."

"Yes, Joshua Townsend."

He chuckled. "Just Joshua down here."

"I call him something else but that's between the two of us," a female voice stated.

I looked to his left to find Kayla grinning as her eyes moved, glancing between Grace and I.

"Nice to see you again … especially in a place like this," Kayla snorted. "This guy doesn't let me come down here too often, but considering how sensitive and hormonal I've been lately, he wised up and agreed to let me watch him tonight." Kayla's hand went to her rounded belly.

"Congratulations." Grace smiled at Kayla.

Seeing the excitement on her face as she stared at Kayla, my heart began racing with tension. I wondered if that was what she wanted. I had to turn away. Wondering if a woman ever wanted children had never even occurred to me before. Because it never mattered in the past.

"Thank you. We're hoping for a boy this time," Kayla gushed while holding her belly. "Though if we have one, there's no way he's ending up down here." Smirking, she faced her husband.

Joshua simply grunted and kissed his wife's forehead.

"You fighting tonight, Doc?" he turned to me, asking.

"He better not be."

A half smile touched my lips at the concern I heard in Grace's voice. It beckoned me, and I leaned down to press a kiss to her lips before turning back to Joshua.

"We're just here to watch."

Grace sighed in relief.

After a few more words, Joshua and Kayla headed off toward the ring. I watched as Joshua guided his wife around the ring to a chair that was separated from everyone else but could still be seen from anywhere in the fighting square.

"They seem nice. I still don't understand any of this."

The way her face wrinkled in confusion and worry was so damn captivating to me that I took her face between my hands and kissed the shit out of her because it was the only way I could convey everything that I was feeling.

"You're done ignoring me now, right?" I questioned against her moist lips.

I groaned inwardly at the same time my cock came alive in my jeans when she sucked in her bottom lip, thinking before she answered me.

"Maybe."

She giggled when I let out a growl.

Her gaze circled the room, though her head was unable to move due to the fact that I was still holding firmly to her face.

"This is where you got those busted ribs?"

I frowned, my brow furrowing. "They're not busted, just bruised slightly."

Her eyes slanted. "Slightly? You rescheduled two days worth of surgeries and you've been limping and grimacing around all damn day."

"You're sexy as hell when you curse."

"Don't try to sweet talk me." She pushed out of my hold and I let my hands fall to my side. "Which one of these guys was it?"

"Which one what?" I knew what she was asking, but I was having fun staring at her as she looked around the room, searching out the source of my bruised body.

"Who put a hurting on you so bad you had to reschedule your surgeries? I wanna see him?" Her lips were poked out angrily.

I pulled her to me. "Why? You want to get in the ring with him?"

"I just might." Her arms folded over her chest, she lifted her chin in that way that *always* had me thinking of getting my dick wet.

"You are amazing." Placing my forehead to hers, I let my hands move to her waist, pulling her body into mine.

"You can't compliment me while I'm still mad at you."

"You're not still mad at me."

"You lied to me."

Sighing, I pulled back. "And now I've told you the truth." I looked around the room. It certainly wasn't the entirety of my truth but it would have to suffice for now.

"Why do you do this?"

I peered down at her again.

"You're a surgeon, Jacob. You have to know how dangerous something like this is for your career. I mean, aside from some bruised ribs, you more than anyone in here have the potential to lose everything you've worked years to earn. And for what?"

"For the rush of it all."

Her expression turned quizzical as she grew silent, waiting for me to continue.

"Because sometimes getting hit feels better than being in the OR."

She gasped.

Hell, my comment stole my own breath for a minute. Because it was true.

I lowered my forehead to hers again. "I can't explain it all to you …" Maybe I could but just didn't want to. "It's how I release. How we all do." I gestured to the crowd, including the rest of the guys around me in my explanation solely because I didn't want the focus to be on me. I didn't fight alone down here. I wasn't the only abnormal professional guy who needed more than a night out at a bar to blow off some steam. I needed something hard, risky, and yes, painful to take the edge off.

And when I couldn't find any more words to explain it to Grace, I stopped trying. It was too fucking jumbled up in my own head to make sense. I let my lips do the talking when I captured hers in a kiss. I could feel the warring inside of her. She wanted to know more, for me to explain it to her until it made sense. But eventually she gave into the moment and accepted the kiss. Not only did she accept it, she caved into it, allowing me to move my hand to the back of her head, pulling it back to angle myself better to deepen the kiss. She moaned into my mouth, and the cheers around us felt as if they were miles away.

"Your exploration of the Underground is over for tonight, Grace." My voice had deepened considerably.

"Is that an invitation to somewhere else?"

"Yes." Taking her by the hand, I led us out the same way we'd come in, only twenty minutes earlier. She hadn't even been able to see an entire fight. But as I glanced over at her while driving, I realized she didn't seem too disturbed by that.

* * *

Grace

I want this, I had to remind myself over and over to calm my jittery nerves as Jacob pulled into my driveway. The sexual tension that'd filled his car since we left the fighting group, or club, or whatever it was, was enough to choke a damn bear. My palms were sweaty, and I couldn't stop adjusting myself in the seat, mainly because I was so damn horny I couldn't sit still. Especially not with Jacob's hand damn near burning a hole through my jeans as he caressed my thigh.

"Your sister's out for the night, right?"

I swallowed and turned to Jacob. "Right."

His gaze dropped to my lips, and all the muscles in my belly tightened at the way his eyes seemed to come alive. That stormy, dreadful look that often filled his eyes fell away, replaced by one that was all-consuming and filled with passion. To be at the center of that gaze felt like being in the middle of a whirlwind.

Jacob extended his right hand, taking my chin in between his thumb and forefinger, pulling me closer to him. Our lips collided somewhere in the middle, and for the shortest while all of my concerns, fears, and anxieties fell away. There was no thinking, just being. With him, in this moment. This perfect moment.

His agile fingers traced a line down my neck that was followed by a trail of his kisses.

"Jacob," I whispered his name helplessly when his teeth gently scraped across the skin of my neck.

That area wasn't even my typical soft spot but the usual rules obviously didn't apply where Jacob Reynolds was concerned.

"Tonight, I'm going to write my name all over this pussy, Grace," he whispered in my ear while his hand slid down to cup me at the space where my thighs met, over my jeans. "Will you let me do that?"

God yes!

I was tongue tied so all I could do was nod. But that was enough. Jacob released me and got out of the car, going around it to open the door for me. His chivalry was also a major turn on.

I scanned the front of my home once again, making sure I didn't see any signs of my sister. I'd been worried about her ever since she told me she was leaving for the evening, but she was an adult and I had to let her be. Besides, I also had my own needs. One of which was the man standing behind me, with his body pressing against my backside, allowing me to feel his erection through his jeans while I fumbled trying to get my key into the lock.

Sighing in relief as the knob finally turned, I shoved it open, moving inside. Jacob was faster than I was when he pulled the door from my hold, closing and locking it, and pressing my body against the wall. His lips were covering mine again. My hands reached up and pulled at the T-shirt he was wearing, bringing his body closer to mine. I needed to feel surrounded by his warmth.

"Where's your bedroom?" he asked impatiently.

"Down the hall to the left." Not for the first time, I was thoroughly grateful for my small home. In this case, it meant less time between here and my bed.

Jacob charged down the hall, his long legs eating up the space between the front door and my bedroom—so much so, I found myself having to nearly run behind him lest I be dragged by the tight grip he had on my hand.

As soon as he entered the bedroom, he flicked on the light switch as if he'd been here before.

"I need to see all of you."

My stomach dropped and fear seized me. Thankfully, Jacob didn't pick up on my fear in that moment because his hands bracketed my face again and I turned up my face to receive the kiss. His lips grazed mine again before moving lower to the same spot along my neck he'd tasted in the car. This time he flicked his tongue against the vein in my neck that began pulsing and the sensation moved down my spine, igniting my whole body on fire.

I needed to get out of my clothes. Jacob sensed this. His hands moved down the sides of my body. He was pulling my shirt over my head in no time, discarding it. He took a step back, his eyes sparkling as he admired me standing there with no shirt on. I forced myself to hold his gaze, but when his hands went for the straps of my bra I stopped him.

He pulled back, questioning.

"Bra on."

He eyed me wordlessly for a half a breath before nodding. His hands moved down to the waist of my jeans and I sighed in relief. From there, no words were exchanged between the two of us as we undressed one another.

I grimaced at the purple and yellow bruising that was still visible on Jacob's chest. Moving in, I kissed his bruise and peered up at his face, making sure I wasn't causing him any pain.

He merely looked down on me, approving.

I kissed it again and again, feeling that somehow my lips could heal him. And I didn't mean just the physical bruises either. Jacob had dark secrets. They were hidden in the depths of his eyes, in the way he talked without revealing too much of himself, in the composed manner in which he held himself together even in the operating room.

"I want you on all fours, first," he demanded while taking my hand and leading us over to my high-sitting, queen-sized bed.

"No," he insisted when I went to pull back the light lavender and purple blanket that covered my sheets of my bed. "On top."

Crawling on top, I tried to move toward the center of my bed.

"Ohh, shit!" I cursed when before I could fully position myself, Jacob's large hands grabbed me by my cheeks, parting them to trace the lips of my pussy with his tongue. I'd never experienced a physical sensation like it in my life. My body instinctively arched, granting him better access to my hotspot. And Jacob took full advantage.

His hold tightened around the mounds of my ass and it felt as if he tried to bury his entire face in my nether region.

A purring sound began pouring from my lips as Jacob feasted on me. It felt too good. I wanted to beg him to stop and plead with him to never turn me loose. Fisting the blanket in my hands, I arched my back higher. That must've pleased him because a satisfied groan came from his mouth. His hands moved lower, cupping the backs of my thighs, spreading my legs farther apart to completely expose myself to him. I complied easily, feeling more turned on and wanted than ever before.

"J-Jacob, p-please don't stop!" I pleaded, my eyes squeezed shut, and at that moment I was glad he was behind me and couldn't see my face because I knew it was twisted up in the ugliest grimace imaginable. But I couldn't help it. Every time I tried to take a breath or regulate my heart rate it was like he sensed it and would double his efforts. Eating pussy should've been his specialty. Forget surgery, this was where he shone. And just to prove it, my thighs began shaking from the effort of trying to contain my orgasm.

I was falling over; it seemed much too quickly, but it was inevitable.

I inhaled deeply and let out a deep mewling sound as the orgasm flowed through my body. All ten of my toes squeezed tightly and I lowered my head to the pillows in front of me, attempting to crawl away from Jacob's still prodding mouth. The man was trying to end me, I could feel it.

"How was that?" his deep baritone had the damn nerve to question at the same time he flipped my entire body over, moving to hover over me.

I narrowed my gaze on those grey eyes that dared me to lie but didn't say anything. Instead, I lifted my hand and moved it down his chest, lightly caressing the bruises at his side and sliding lower, reaching for his—

"Don't," he ordered firmly just before I could grab his dick.

I blinked at the authority in his voice.

Lifting both of my hands to either side of my face, he ordered, "Leave them here."

I remained in that position as he lifted himself from the bed and sauntered over to where his jeans rested on my carpeted floor. I took the time to let my eyes carefully scan his muscular frame. He was a work of art. There wasn't an underdeveloped muscle to be found on his body. He looked as if he'd been playing sports the entirety of his life instead of studying hard in the library to earn his educational credentials. Briefly, I wondered if he played sports as a child. I bet he excelled at them if he had. He was the type to excel at everything he touched.

But it was when he turned around and headed in my direction with the foil-wrapped condom in his hand that my eyes drifted lower. My mouth watered and thighs instinctively parted even farther at the sight of the thick erection pointing directly at me. Nope. He wasn't small there either.

I wanted to offer to undo and put the condom on him, but something told me that wasn't a wise idea. Jacob seemed to need to be in control of this moment. And, contrary to my very nature, it wasn't even a question of whether or not I would allow him this control.

"You're so fucking perfect."

I smiled at him, feeling the compliment all the way to the tips of my toes. I ignored the voice inside of my head that tried to remind me that I actually wasn't perfect. I was scarred, but that didn't matter right then as I watched Jacob sheath himself and then turn his lust-filled gaze on me. At that instant, I had no idea how I'd lived this long on the Earth without being looked at like this.

I lifted up on my elbows as he moved in between my legs, angling my head up. Complying, he lowered his head, allowing our lips to touch … but the kiss was too short, not nearly enough of what I wanted. Jacob was teasing me as he let our lips brush across one another's but never fully connect.

A frustrated sound emanated from the back of my throat.

Jacob chuckled and I swear I wanted to throttle him. "You want a kiss, baby?"

I nodded because the use of a pet name had melted my annoyance just enough to calm down any sarcastic retort I had in mind.

"Say please."

I leaned back to look into his eyes. He was completely serious.

"Please," fell from my mouth before I could contemplate his demand too much. And thank God it did, because in an instant Jacob was devouring my lips again, and I his.

His hands went to both of mine, intertwining our fingers and placing them back to either side of my head. He adjusted himself in between my legs and I moaned almost painfully when his cock grazed against the lips of my core.

Jacob pulled back with his gaze still locked on mine, as he began to slide inside of my body. I was instantly reminded that it'd been a while since I was in this position with a man, but instead of asking him to stop or slow down I wanted to beg him to hurry up. My body grew hungrier and hungrier for him with each passing half an inch.

"You feel so good, baby," he panted, and I swear I could feel myself growing wetter just from his words.

"You're so deep." He felt like he was going to enter my stomach at any moment.

"You can take it," he demanded.

Licking my lips, I nodded because damn straight I could. I wanted to feel every last inch of him inside of me. Thankfully, my body agreed, and the tightness subsided. Once it did, I found myself laying on my side, face-to-face with Jacob. He'd turned our bodies to face one another, my leg hiked high around his waist—the new position allowed him to slide even deeper inside of my core.

My mouth opened and closed as I tried to pant his name but only gasps of air came out. His long arm draped over my waist, his hand moving to squeeze and knead the globe of my ass.

"Shit!" he cursed angrily. "How the fuck do you feel this good?"

His words sent me even higher than his pulsating cock.

I covered his cheek with my hand and moved in, taking his lips because words just weren't enough, even if I could manage to form any.

So damn good, was all I could manage to think as he retreated and entered over and over again. I arched my back, pressing the entirety of the top half of my body into him. For the briefest heartbeat I wished I could've been totally unclothed with him. To drop my bra and have one hundred percent skin to skin contact.

"Stay with me, baby."

His words again pulled me back from my wandering thoughts. I returned my gaze to his and found his eyes staring deep into mine. The regular storminess that was always there had dropped, replaced by a different kind of storm, one that had my body producing even more lubrication for him to glide in and out of.

His hand reached lower and his thumb grazed across my clitoris. The movement wasn't much, but I didn't need too much contact. It was just enough to give my body exactly what it wanted. Release.

I squeezed my eyes shut as all the muscles in my body tightened with the rush of my orgasm. For his part, Jacob gave me no favor when he moved his forearm under my leg, pulling it up even higher on his body and pushing in just a quarter of an inch deeper.

"Oh! Oh! Oh!" I groaned over and over, my head thrashing against my pillow.

I felt Jacob's body tense up as well in my arms; his throaty groans telling me that he was going over as well. His lips moved to the crook of my neck, kissing and licking there until we both returned to ourselves. Only when our breathing returned to normal did he pull back. I immediately wanted to follow because the separation felt like too much to bear.

We laid there facing one another, silently staring into each other's eyes, both conveying that what we just experienced exceeded either of our expectations. I knew sex with Jacob would be good. I didn't expect it to be otherworldly.

When Jacob finally pulled out of me, I felt bereft and as if something I thought I'd known for a very long time had just been completely turned on its head.

I silently stared as he flipped himself onto his back and removed the condom, licking my lips the whole time. He stood, and I watched his tight ass flex as he strode to the door, passing to the bathroom across the hall. A few second later, my toilet flushed and he was back in the room.

Turning on my back, I waited for him to climb back into bed with me. I began to fold down the light blanket and sheet, to get underneath them, when I noticed he'd put his boxer briefs back on and was searching for what I presumed to be his pants. I sat up.

"You're leaving?"

His head popped up and he paused but didn't say anything.

"Don't," fell from my lips. "Stay." I hoped I didn't sound as desperate and pleading as I thought I did. But I didn't want to be alone.

He dropped his jeans back to the floor and moved closer to the bed. Leaning back, I held out my hand to him.

His gaze moved from my hand to the bed coverings. "I don't like sleeping under blankets … or sheets."

My eyes dipped to where he stared and then back up to his. He was warring with something and whatever it was could cause him to bolt at any moment. But he didn't want to. I could feel that just as deeply as I'd felt him imbedded in my body only a few minutes earlier.

"Stay. We don't have to use the blanket or sheets."

His jaw went rigid as he clenched his teeth together, but finally, he nodded. I pushed out the breath I was holding. He moved across the room, turning off the light before coming back to the bed. He hesitated for a half a breath before climbing back onto the bed and laying on his back.

Turning on my side, I saw him staring at the ceiling. I wanted to ask what he was thinking about, what had him scared, but that may have led to him asking me the same thing and I wasn't ready to go there just yet.

"Can I put my hand on your stomach?"

He looked over at me and nodded.

I stretched out my hand and gently laid it on his rock-hard abdomen. How a man found time to be a high level plastic surgeon and be as fit as he was, I had no idea, but Jacob seemed to be able to make up time where no one else could. If he wanted something he got it done. No excuses.

His large hands covered mine, holding it tightly to his body.

Easing my head down to the pillow, I let our breathing patterns fall in line with one another's until we both drifted off into a confused, yet blissfully sex-induced sleep.

CHAPTER 12

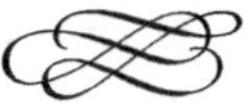

*J*acob

I'm not in my bed.

That was my first coherent thought of the morning. My eyes popped open in alarm, and sure enough I wasn't in my condo. The warm bed linens beneath my body was my first clue. As I circled the room with my gaze, the second indication that I wasn't at home became apparent. The third was the scent I inhaled as I turned my head. The pillows. They smelled of sweetness. And it was that smell which aided in calming the raging anxiety sleeping away from home often brought.

When I turned, expecting to see Grace lying next to me, I was surprised to see the other half of the bed was empty and made up. That was when the coldness set in. The usual cold, lonely feeling I'd learned to live with over the past twenty plus years of my life.

Sitting up, I rubbed my eyes and stood to find my clothing. As I searched out the room, I noted the lavender and purple decor. I padded my way across the room on the purple carpet to the white, low sitting chair in the corner where my clothing had been neatly folded and placed. However, on top of my clothing was a towel and other toiletries along with a note in her feminine handwriting. Yes, I'd memorized her handwriting from the charts at work.

You were sleeping so peacefully, I didn't want to wake you.
Bathroom's across the hall.
Take your time.
I'll be in the kitchen preparing breakfast.
~Grace~

Who leaves notes to inform someone they're in the kitchen making breakfast? More importantly, who saves those notes because the damn paper reminds him of the scent of the woman who wrote it? Me. That's who.

I folded the note and stuck it inside the pocket of my jeans before grabbing the toiletries and heading across the hall to the bathroom. I hadn't paid much attention the night before to the room that Grace had furnished in earth tones. The different oranges and browns gave the bathroom a warm feel, and I paused, examining the shower curtain that was designed with the image of the Serengeti desert at sunrise. At the forefront a curvy, dark-browned skin woman carrying a basket on top of her head stood facing front with a gorgeous smile on her face.

I showered quickly, noting the specialty shop soaps, face washes, and lotions Grace had neatly tucked in the shower's caddy around the sink. Most of the toiletries were handmade or made from basic ingredients such as coconut oil, cocoa, or shea butter.

About twenty minutes later, I sauntered up the hall, being pulled by the scent of freshly brewed coffee, and that siren voice of Grace's, as she sung another song I wasn't familiar with but wanted to hear more of.

Rounding the corner, I stopped short. Grace's back was to me as she continued to sing. She stood at the stove in just a sleeveless black T-shirt and a pair of yellow boy shorts that hugged her ass nicely. When she started swaying her hips with whatever she was singing, my dick stood up, asking for some attention. An image of me bending her over the counter she stood at, my hand burying into her hair as I pulled her head back, ordering her to say my name, flashed before my eyes.

That was when I cleared my throat and moved forward.

She abruptly stopped singing and smiled as she moved around the kitchen island with a cup of coffee in her hand. "Morning."

She held the mug out for me to take as she moved closer, but the damn coffee was the last thing I needed. I dropped my head, before taking the coffee, beckoning her lips. Complying, she lifted her head to allow our lips to touch. Not until I pulled back did I retrieve the cup from her hand.

"Morning. Have you been up long?"

She shook her head and took my free hand in hers, guiding us to the stools at the kitchen's island. "Not too long. I would've woken you but ..." She trailed off and shrugged. "Did you sleep well?"

"Yes," I answered, clearing my throat because that was the truth. I don't ever sleep well, much less in a foreign bed. However, last night I had.

I watched as she slid a veggie omelet onto a plate and then another. That was the first time I actually looked at the kitchen island. There were two bowls of salsa, one of cheese and another with avocado slices in it. A glass pitcher of fresh-squeezed orange juice. I knew it was fresh squeezed because I saw the recently used citrus fruit juicer parts in the sink. And something told me the salsa wasn't from a jar. She'd prepared a whole spread. She had to be up for the past hour, at least.

That was when my eyes went to the time on the electric stove. It read just after nine o'clock. That was sleeping in late for me, even on a weekend.

Lifting the coffee to my lips, I took a sip, my eyes closing at the strong taste; I was thankful for the fact she knew I took my coffee black.

"Thank you," I said when she placed my plate in front of me.

She turned to retrieve her plate, but my arm moved around her body, trapping her to me, instead. Forking off a piece of the omelet, I held it up to her lips even though my own stomach began growling at the smell of the food.

"Jacob, that's yours. I have my own omelet."

My eyes dipped to her lips and a smile touched my own. She was such a caretaker. At work and at home. It came to her naturally. Caring and doing for others.

"We're sharing. You've been awake for some time preparing all of this food. The least I can do before I bend you over your own kitchen counter is let you have the first bite."

Her eyelids fluttered and slowly her lips parted as she received the omelet I fed her. Pulling the fork free from her lips, I buried my face into the crook of her neck and licked before sucking the spot where her vein protruded, telling me her thoughts without words. My hand slid underneath the T-shirt she wore, but when I attempted to move it higher, her hand stopped mine.

Leaning back, I looked down on her. There was uncertainty and a touch of fear in her eyes. I hated it; she didn't deserve it. I brushed my lips across hers and then hopped off the stool, doing what my cock and brain had been begging me to do ever since I rounded that fucking corner.

I spun Grace around, and before the gasp could fully escape her lips, I had those teasing boy shorts down, around her ankles. I removed the condom from my back pocket because foresight had told me I'd end up in this position before I left Grace's home.

Sheathing myself faster than I ever had before, I was sliding into Grace's wet core without so much as a second thought.

"Arch your back for me, baby."

Grace did as instructed, and I was able to slide inside of her deeper, exactly where the fuck I belonged. I reached up and yanked the band she used to keep her hair clasped in a bun loose. Her wild curls spilled out, and just as I had in my fantasy, I buried my hand in those curls, pulling her head backwards as I rode her deep from behind.

"You're driving me fucking crazy," I snarled in her ear.

"Me too," she scoffed. "I-I don't appreciate it."

I chuckled at the way she could barely get the words out as she bounced on my cock. Watching as my rod retreated and entered her body repeatedly, I squeezed her ass with my free hand and noticed how every muscle in my body went tight. My body filled with a sense of pleasure unlike any other as she called out my name repeatedly. She was mine for the taking, and I let my cock pleasure her in the ways I couldn't let come from my mouth.

"Shiiit!" she yelled as the orgasm rocked her body.

She trembled and her hands tightened on the edges of the kitchen island.

Seeing the ways her body responded to me had my dick filling with come. I felt myself preparing to release, and though I felt like I wanted to spend eternity inside of her wet, warm snatch, I let go. The orgasm was rushed, quick and everything I needed to keep me going for the day.

"I wasn't expecting that." Her breathless voice was full of awe.

I kissed the back of her neck before sliding out of her. I despised that feeling. Of retreating from her body. I hated it the night before, too, but I forced myself to remember that it was impossible to go through life attached to another person permanently. I had to pull out at some point.

"I'll be right back," I grunted before exiting the kitchen and heading to the bathroom to discard the used condom. A minute later I strolled back up the hall to the kitchen to find Grace sitting at the opposite side of the island. Her hair was still wild, her lips formed a teasing smile I was sure she wasn't even aware of, and the flushed skin all told of how thoroughly fucked she'd just been.

The dimples as she smiled, though, those were what caused my damn knees to nearly topple me. I made my way back to my original seat—thankfully, without falling—and took my position on the stool.

We ate in silence for a little while, stealing quiet glances across the island that spoke more than either one of us were ready to allow to pass through our lips.

"Breakfast was delicious," I finally stated after finishing my omelet with the home-made sweet potato hash browns she served along with it. And just as I suspected, the salsa in the bowls had been freshly made as well. The thought of the effort she put in made me want to pull her over the island and have my way with her again, but I refrained. I needed to keep my own sanity in check, and I doubted that having her for a third time in less than twelve hours would allow for that.

"Thank you."

"What are you—" My question was cut off by the opening of the front door.

"Grace, I– Oh, you have company," Grace's sister Journey interrupted when her eyes moved to me.

I frowned, hating the interruption, and loathing even more that I had completely forgotten that her sister was staying with her. If I'd been in my right mind, I would've thought twice about taking her in her own kitchen.

"Journey." Grace stood from her stool, sounding surprised. "Your text said you wouldn't be home until this afternoon."

Journey shrugged. "I changed my mind."

For the first time, I was able to take a good look at Grace's younger sister. She was about two inches taller and her skin was more of a tawny brown than her sister's caramel coloring. Her hair was done in long braids that went almost to her waist. A few of them were multi-colored. She stood there dressed in a pair of high-waist jeans and a white crop top, her eyes bouncing between me and her sister.

"Journey, this is Jacob. We, uh, work together."

My head snapped to Grace as she moved beside me.

"Work?" Journey and I said at the same time.

No fucking way just a work colleague was going to be in her home at nine in the morning on her day off, eating breakfast in her kitchen after having just provided her with a mind-blowing orgasm.

"Well, obviously, we more than work together," Grace corrected, giving me a sideways look before she turned toward her sister, who was now staring at me.

"You a doctor?"

"I am."

"You were here the other night."

I nodded.

Journey's eyes lowered to the floor. Shame. I knew it well.

"Thanks."

"No thanks needed."

"Hey, I'm going to head to my room for a little nap." Journey tossed us both a chin nod and headed down the hall.

"That's my cue." I got the feeling Journey had more to say to her sister.

"You're leaving?" Grace questioned as she followed me down the hall to her bedroom.

"Yeah," I answered, searching for my wallet once I realized I forgot to place it in my pocket. I quickly grabbed it from the desk, but my movement was too fast and it slipped from my hands, causing it to fall to the floor.

My license slipped free and landed near Grace's feet. She bent to pick it up, scanning it before handing it back to me.

I placed the license back and stuffed my wallet inside of my back pocket. Moving closer to Grace, I placed a kiss to her forehead.

"Thanks for breakfast."

She lifted on her tiptoes, her hand curling around my wrist, and pressed a kiss to my lips. "Thanks for being truthful with me last night."

All memory of the night before, prior to us arriving at her home, was forgotten until that moment. I remembered taking her to the Underground and revealing one of my many secrets. Lowering, I brushed my lips across hers, feeling closer to her than to anyone.

"I'll walk you out."

I released a breath, grateful that she didn't need me to say anything else or explain myself further.

"Call me when you get home? So I know you made it in okay."

My lips spread. "Sure thing, Nurse Young," I teased.

She punched me in the shoulder.

"Hey, did you forget about my injury? What type of nurse are you?"

"The kind that remembers your injured ribs are on your left side, not your right. And the type who isn't falling for that *'I'm hurt'* crap when you were just making me scream your name like there was no tomorrow in my kitchen."

I tossed my head back, and for the first time in probably a decade I laughed. It was more than a chuckle; it was a sound that came from my toes. It surprised even me, but I couldn't help it.

When I lowered my head, Grace's gaze read surprised. She bit her bottom lip, as if turned on by my reaction.

I gave her one last kiss, then dropping my arm from her waist and stepping back, taking her in one final time before turning and heading to my car. She waited for me to get inside and start the car before closing her door with a final wave.

As I pulled out of her driveway, I began to regret every morning of my adult life that I'd woken up without this. Without her.

* * *

GRACE

It took me a while to gather myself after Jacob left. As I made breakfast that morning, visions of us spending the day curled up in one another's arms, watching trashy TV, interspersed by periods of making wild, passionate love had danced in around in my head. And I wasn't a woman who daydreamed about that kind of thing. More like, on my days off, in between cleaning, volunteering at a local health clinic that cared for underserved patients, and cooking or getting in a workout at the gym or pool, I would take the occasional nap, or thumb through songs to practice for my next set at Rocket.

And if that wasn't enough, I would sometimes find myself at the hospital, making sure that I'd given the correct instructions for a patient's care. But rarely, and by rarely, I mean never, did my thoughts center around spending my free time wrapped up in a man's arms.

I sighed as I got out of the shower, realizing that had been exactly how I wanted to spend my day. And while I loved and deeply cared for my little sister, a small part of me wished she hadn't come home.

I immediately lowered my head at that thought, feeling ashamed. I knew she was going through a tough time. And she knew it, as well. I was the one she ran to when she needed to help. She might've lived with our dad and stepmom—she had since she was eleven years old—but she still came to me when things got overwhelming.

I avoided looking at my own reflection in the mirror as I dressed in a matching pair of black panties and bra, and slid a simple summer dress over my head. Exiting the bedroom, I turned down the hall to the guest room where Journey was staying.

"Journey, sweetie," I cooed as I knocked on the door, opening it. I was grateful the door wasn't locked; another indication that my sister had been waiting for me to come to her.

"Oh, sweetie, what's wrong?" I questioned, rushing to the bed when she rolled over and I could see the tears streaming down her face.

"I'm s-sorry," she sobbed. "I didn't mean to interrupt your d-date." Her shoulders jerked in the way they do when one struggles to cry, breathe, and talk at the same time.

"Don't worry about it, Journey." Another pang of guilt fluttered through my body as I remembered I'd just wished she hadn't been there.

"What's wrong?"

"Everything, Grace. Everything's wrong." Curling up, she placed her head in my lap and cried even harder, wrapping her arms around me.

"Journey—"

"I know I'm just like Mama." She sniffled. "I don't wanna be, Grace. I don't wanna be sick like her."

I blinked away the tears forming, not wanting to delve into my own sadness and fear over my sister's condition. She needed me to be there for her right then.

"Journey, look at me," I prodded while pulling her arms free of my waist so she could position herself to sit up. "What makes you think you're like Mama?" I asked once she calmed down.

I hadn't wanted to force my opinion on her, knowing that it would make her even more reluctant to come to me for help. We both grew up with our mama, living in fear each day of what we would walk into because her moods were so all over the place. That only got worse once my father abandoned us.

"I know it, Grace. I didn't tell you this because I didn't want you to be mad, but a few months ago, I-I quit my job and then maxed out all my credit cards, buying a new wardrobe and taking my friends out on shopping sprees. Then I met a guy and that's when I followed him to Chicago."

"And then you came here?"

She nodded. "I felt myself getting sadder and sadder each day. I wanted to be closer to you, so I used meeting him here as an excuse. Then I just …"

"Couldn't outrun it anymore."

She shook her head. "I was so tired."

Remembering how much she slept after I found her nearly passed out at my front door, I nodded. She slept for almost two days straight, aside from being prodded to wake up to eat.

"I remember. I was young, Grace, and you tried to hide as much as you could from me, but I remember coming home to Mama dancing on the table while she repainted our ceiling. And then how she cursed at you when you tried to get her down. She yelled at you to get her another beer from the fridge. And then the time she couldn't get out of bed, crying for hours and days at a time. And how she made you …"

"Sing," I sighed.

Journey nodded. "I remember that glossy look in her eyes when she got like that because I know that feeling."

Journey's red-rimmed eyes filled with tears again and her bottom lip quivered.

"Have you gone to a doctor, Journey?"

She looked away from me before shaking her head. "Will you go with me? I think I can go if you're there."

Inhaling deeply, I wrapped my arms around my sister, rocking her back and forth as her body began to tremble again from the crying. "Of course, I'll go with you, Journey."

This wasn't all bad news. My mother never wanted to seek treatment. Not like we could've afforded it after my father left, anyway. While he'd been there, he would tell me things like, "There's nothing wrong with your mama. She's just worn out from raising you kids," or, "She's a little extravagant. Most kids would be thrilled to have a mama that's not so boring all the time."

I shook my head, remembering that even then, at seven years old, I knew something wasn't right with my family.

CHAPTER 13

*G*race

"Hi, Grace, this is Dr. Mitchell's office, calling to remind you that it's time for your annual tests. Please give us a call back so we can get that set up as soon as possible. The number is ..." Pulling the phone from my ear, I pressed the button to save the message, as a jolt of nervousness ran through my belly. I swallowed and inhaled deeply, trying to remind myself that it was only some testing I was making the appointment for. I needed to be as strong for myself as I was for my sister this morning.

"Hey."

I turned and my worry was replaced by joy when I was met with Jacob's hard gaze on me. My smile widened at the cup of coffee he held out to me. I could already smell the vanilla flavoring coming from the steam that rose through the little mouth opening of the lid.

"I forgot to have this this morning," I said, plucking the cup from his hand and holding it up to him before taking my first sip. "Thank you." Closing my eyes, I sighed, feeling warmed already.

"When I got your text, I figured you would've."

After speaking with the charge nurse, I sent him a text that morning telling him I'd be in late for my shift because I was going with Journey to her doctor's appointment. Thankfully, the doctor's office was at Memorial, just on the other side of the hospital. She took an Uber back home once the appointment ended.

"You know me so well, huh?"

I was teasing but his face turned serious. "I'm learning."

That piqued my interest. I suddenly wanted to know how Jacob saw me. And as if on cue, he began telling me.

"You've been a caretaker your whole life. No wonder nursing comes so naturally to you."

And if I ever had any doubt as to whether or not Jacob had problems with discernment, they would've been eviscerated in that instant.

"I'm that obvious?" I lifted an eyebrow, taking another sip of my coffee. I grinned when his eyes followed the movement of my mouth as I licked the corner of my lips.

"To anyone who watches as closely as I do." His voice had dropped.

"You know me so well … what am I planning to do now?"

"Visit Johnny Westbrook."

I giggled, because of course that's what I was on my way to do.

"How's he doing?" I asked.

Jacob shrugged. "I presume he's doing well. I haven't seen him yet this morning. Wanted to wait on you."

Somehow, that seemed sweet to me. As if it was *our thing* to check in on the patient we worked on together in the ER and through his first two surgeries.

"He has another one scheduled for later in the week."

I nodded, not letting my face show any emotion as we approached Johnny's hospital room.

"Good morning." I beamed as we entered the room.

Johnny's father was right by his son's bedside, looking tired and uncomfortable. The man still had a leg and an arm in a cast, had just had his wife's funeral the week before, and was trying desperately to comfort his son who was in an immense amount of pain. Thankfully, Johnny hadn't woken up for the day.

"I like to let him sleep as long as possible before the first round comes in," his father whispered, apologetically.

"Absolutely." I waved him off. "We don't need him awake. Just checking in to see how he's doing."

His father frowned. "He hates the daily bandage changes."

My heart dropped. Yeah, those were painful.

"If I could take his place, I would. In a heartbeat." His face was so full of sincerity and heartache. A part of me wanted to reach out and comfort him somehow, but then I heard Jacob clear his throat behind me.

"It's better you're here for him. His vitals look good. We'll let him rest." His voice sounded surprisingly distant. His gaze was shuttered as he looked at the boy's father. I got the sense this was more than a doctor working to keep his professional distance.

"We'll perform another skin graft later this week."

"Do you have to operate again? So soon?"

Jacob nodded. "It's what's the best for his healing. I'll check on him later." He turned and headed out of the room.

"We'll take good care of him in surgery, Mr. Westbrook."

He nodded, eyes full of grief, and I headed out behind Jacob.

I wanted to ask him what that was all about. Why he couldn't show even a small fraction of emotion for a man who was obviously in as much emotional pain as his son was physically. But Jacob's face stopped me. The voice in my head told me there was more to his story. I wanted to ask him … no, beg him to let me in, to help him with whatever was going on, but this wasn't the time or place.

"Hey, did you hear? The hospital execs are bringing in some healthcare consulting firm to oversee the hospital's operations."

He frowned as we began moving down the hallway. He grunted. "I heard. Bunch of asshole suits who breathe down our necks and tell the staff what we're doing wrong."

"You seem cheery about it," I teased, nudging him with my elbow.

He grunted again.

"I get it. None of us are really looking forward to it, but maybe it'll help in some way. And if it doesn't, whatever." I shrugged. I was all for improving hospital operations if it meant improving the quality of care patients received. But often it just meant even more administrative work for staff, namely, nurses, to have to get through.

"How did this morning go?"

I blinked remembering Journey's appointment. "I'm not sure. She was tight-lipped once she left the psychiatrist's office."

"Can't blame her. Who the hell wants some head doc poking around up there? They're not even real doctors as far as I'm concerned."

I giggled. "Not everyone can be a surgeon. The *gods* of the hospital," I bemoaned, jokingly.

"Shame for them." Pausing, he looked down at me in the way he does when his mind was working. He slid his hands into his pockets. "There's a final summer concert down at Williamsport Park this weekend. Want to go?"

I was well aware of the concert. It was the ending of the park's Summer in the Park series. There'd been live bands and artists throughout the summer.

My eyebrows dipped. "A park with a bunch of people? Not something I thought *you'd* be a fan of."

He shook his head, a half smile emerging. "Hell, me either. I don't like crowds or people too much. But I figured you would enjoy it."

I had the biggest urge to throw my arms around him and press my lips to his, but we were at work. I cleared my throat. "Yes. I would love that."

He moved his hand from his pockets, giving me one final look and squeeze before heading back to his office for an appointment with a patient.

Standing there, I sighed as he walked away. Jacob had me forgetting all about my sister and her worries, and the message I'd gotten from my doctor's office.

* * *

Jacob

What the hell was I thinking? I fucking *hate* crowds.

"I don't like people," I grunted as I scowled at another couple who rushed past us to get a closer view of the stage. We were in the middle of Williamsport Park for their end of summer concert. It was the last official day of the summer season, which meant it was slightly chilly out. But there were throngs of people about us, many of whom had spread themselves out onto picnic blankets or beach chairs with coolers of food around them.

I hadn't thought of any of that, but of course, Grace had. When I arrived to pick her up, she had a wicker picnic basket full of Greek salad, sandwiches, fruit, crackers, and a bottle of red wine. And the blanket to match, of course. Luckily, I did have a blanket in the back of my own car, which was there in the case of emergencies, but I'd forgotten all about it.

Since these blankets were for sitting, I didn't mind using them in the park.

Grace giggled as we held either ends of the blankets, unfolding them. "You're a doctor."

"So?"

"So? That means your very job, by definition, is to heal people for a living."

I shrugged. "I'm a plastic surgeon, most don't see that as healing." They were wrong but I didn't waste my time defending my profession to people who didn't matter.

"You and I both know plastics is more than just nose and ass jobs to rich people who want to look good on their yacht. Besides, most of those types of plastic surgeons own their own practice. You, on the other hand …" she slipped off the gold sandals she wore and padded across the blanket, reaching me. Lifting her hand to my chest, she turned her head upward. "… work for a hospital providing care to little boys in the burn unit. Tell me again how much you don't like people."

"Kids are different."

She giggled and didn't bother reminding me that most of my patients were adults.

"Kiss."

That was all I said before she raised on tiptoes, her lips touching mine. That was the reminder I needed of why I brought her to this concert, amongst hundreds of people, when crowds weren't usually my thing.

"Are you hungry?" she questioned, our lips still touching.

"Not for food."

She pulled back, laughing when I threw my arm around her waist. "That's all I'm offering in this park, Doctor."

Shit.

Never, and I swear I mean *never* had I ever had a fantasy of a woman dressed in a nurse's dress while calling me doctor. I'd never been turned on by that, but goddammit if Grace didn't just make that happen.

"I hope you have an extra pair of scrubs."

"What?" She frowned.

"Nothing."

"Sit," she insisted as she pulled open the huge, heavy picnic basket. I knew how heavy it was because I was the one to haul that thing from the car to where we were, which had been about a half a mile walk due to all the cars and filled parking.

My stomach instantly growled when she took out paper plates and loaded them with turkey and Swiss cheese sandwiches on whole grain bread with salad and fruit. I'd eaten at restaurants that cost an arm and a leg, whose food didn't have half the attention and detail put into the way she plated it.

When she handed me my plate, it was all I could do to keep from bringing her with me. As soon as she opened her door, I told her that she hadn't needed to prepare all of this. That we could've picked up something on the way or gotten food from one of the many vendors down here at the park.

"Ah," she'd waved dismissively, "who knows what's in that food. I like quality and flavor."

She also liked serving others. She didn't say it, but it didn't need to be said, either.

I watched her while she ate, happily. Her ears perked up as the music by a local jazz band began to play.

"These guys play at Rocket sometimes." She faced me with a wide grin on her face as she bounced in time with the instrumentals.

She seemed so carefree and in her zone that, yet again, my own discomfort of the crowds around us fell away. Pulling Grace into me, I adjusted our bodies so that her back was to my chest as we finished eating.

I set my plate aside and let my hands rest on her sleeve-covered arms, rubbing them up and down. Grace pushed up farther to my chest, resting her head on my shoulder. We listened to the music as one by one a number of local and some well-known artists around the country entered and exited the stage, gracing the audience with two to three songs a piece and wishing farewell to the summer.

"You belong up there."

Grace turned her head to stare up at me. "I don't."

"You're better than anyone who's touched the stage tonight." I could've been my biased, but her vocal talent was in-line with what I heard coming from the microphone on stage.

"I don't want to be famous or well-known. I don't sing for that reason."

I moved my arms around her body, coming to rest on her abdomen. "Why do you sing?"

There was a heartbeat before she said, "For me. I stopped singing after my mother died. Thought I hated it. Then … I got on stage one day and remembered I enjoyed the feeling of letting music flow through my vocal cords."

"That's why you sing at Rocket."

She nodded.

Leaning lower, I nibbled on her earlobe. Her gasp shot right to my cock.

"Put the blanket over you," I ordered in her ear.

"Jaco—"

"Unless you want these people to watch us like we're the entertainment, you should do it. And be quick about it." My voice was determined, and my hands were already moving to unclasp the button of her dark denim jeans.

Grace didn't give any more challenge than that. Grabbing the excess portion of the top blanket, she covered her lap and bottom half of her stomach with it. As soon as my hand slipped inside of her panties, I knew why she gave little pushback. She was just as ready as I was. I briefly lamented over the fact that I wasn't in a position to sink my rapidly hardening cock into her from this position, but hearing her sing out her orgasm my hand was about to bring her to would have to do for now.

"That feels sooo good," she hummed, lifting her face to mine as my two fingers worked over her clit. When our lips locked, I moved my hand lower, sinking into her wet folds. She moaned into my mouth and I swore I was going to fucking lose it.

I wanted to reach up and cup her breast with my free hand, but I knew her hand would be there, stopping me. It always did when I got too close to her breasts. And I wasn't in the mood to be stopped right then. I needed to feel Grace shudder and climax for me.

"Come for me, baby. Sing for me," I insisted.

She complied.

Her lips tightly sealed, she let out a moan only I could hear.

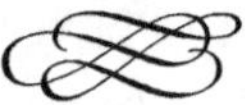

race

"What were you like as a kid?"

I felt his entire body stiffen behind me. The question had clearly thrown him off and instantly I wanted to know more.

"You don't have to go into too much detail if you don't want. Just a hint of what you were like."

"I didn't have a personality as a kid."

I wanted to turn and look up at him. To see his eyes as he said those words. However, I knew he would clam up even more if I stared directly into his gaze. We were still at Williamsport Park. The main event had just appeared on the stage, and all the people around us were enthralled with the music. Some stood and danced while others sat cuddled up with their partners, just as Jacob and I were. A few others ran after wandering toddlers, laughing as they tried to get away. I still couldn't believe that in the midst of all of this I'd let Jacob bring me to orgasm with his hand. I hadn't done anything that crazy since … ever.

"You had to have some sort of personality." My hands moved to cover his which rested on my belly.

He didn't say anything for a full minute but I waited him out, just as I did with patients who didn't want a procedure done that they knew had to be completed. I waited with the patience I learned very early on.

"I wasn't allowed to have a personality, or wants, or desires as a kid. The only thing that mattered in my household was that we all looked good from the outside … not good, perfect. I had to have the perfect grades, be the star athlete on whatever team I played on, outshine everyone in any science competition I joined. If I didn't there was hell to pay. Not much room for personal development when you're forced to achieve someone else's standards."

The bitterness in his voice made my heart ache. Jacob always seemed to have an intensity about everything he did, from the operating room to fighting, and even the way we began. To know that that kind of fierce concentration had been drilled into him as a child hurt even more. But it explained, at least in part, the storms that were constantly brewing in his eyes. It explained why he was often closed off around patients.

"My mother's illness left little room for personal growth also."

"My mother wasn't ill … she was pure evil."

I swallowed and sat up, turning to face Jacob. His eyes had a far-off look as he avoided my gaze. I don't know why, but I'd assumed the parent he was referring to was his father. Not his mother. Mine, I could reconcile as sick as to why she did the things she did. Jacob didn't have that.

"You really think there's a such thing as pure evil?"

"I don't have to think. I was born in it. We looked cookie cutter from the outside, but …" He trailed off, shaking his head. "I left home at sixteen and never returned." His gaze lowered and I saw shame, apparent as ever, in his facial expression.

"You did what you needed to do to save yourself. Don't be ashamed of that."

He lifted my fingers to his lips, kissing them, but not saying anything. When I realized he wasn't going to continue talking, I turned around and laid back his chest again, hoping that he believed what I said, at least on some level. There was something that he was holding himself on the hook for and had been for a very long time.

* * *

Jacob

I patted my hand against the pocket of my jeans and felt nothing. I checked the other side, knowing my wallet wouldn't be there. I never stuck it in my left side pocket.

"Shit," I grunt as I pull up to a stop light.

"What's wrong?" Grace questioned, glancing over at me from the passenger seat. We were heading out to dinner at one of her favorite Italian restaurants in the downtown area of the city. I just picked her up.

"I forgot my wallet." I frowned, hating that I would have to add another fifteen minutes onto our drive to head back to my place.

"No worries, I can pick up the tab tonight."

My frown deepened and I looked over at Grace.

She giggled. "What? Too macho to let the woman pick up the bill for the night?"

I nodded. "Damn straight," I responded just as I made a U-turn, heading in the direction of my condo.

"Jacob, are you seriously going back to your place for your wallet? I really don't mind picking up the bill."

"My license is also in there. I need I.D. on me."

"You don't keep yours in the car?"

My eyebrows dipped as I looked at her as if she were crazy. Another round of laughter and the muscle at the left-center of my chest responded by beating faster. "Why the hell would I? Is that what you do?"

"Yeah. After forgetting my wallet one too many times, or changing from one purse to another, only to leave my license at home, I just decided to leave it in my car." She shrugged. "Worked well for me so far. I just remember to retrieve it when going out, like tonight."

I shook my head. "I'm not doing that. This'll only take a few minutes."

I had the urge to step on the gas to reach our destination sooner, but I wasn't in the mood to risk getting pulled over without my license on me. Eight minutes later, we were pulling up to the front of the high-rise building housing my condo. I chose to park out front in the ten-minute parking lane, instead of in my spot in the garage.

"I'll only be a minute."

"Can I come up?"

I stopped, my body halfway outside of my car, with the other half still inside. Lifting my eyebrows, I stared at Grace.

The expression on her face was hopeful.

Again, my heart lurched. "You want to see my place."

It wasn't a question but she nodded.

I swallowed because this would be the first time I'd ever let a woman who wasn't my cleaning lady, or the person who dropped my groceries or dry cleaning off, into my home.

"Yes," I finally answered, getting out of my car and then going around to Grace's side to hold the door open for her.

I held firmly to her hand as I punched in the code to grant us access to the front entranceway of my building.

"Fancy," Grace stated, smirking over at me as we entered the elevator. I knew her comment was more to break up the silence of the moment than anything else.

We got off on the tenth floor and she followed me down the hallway where only three condos resided. Mine was at the far end, on the right side. I slid the keycard into the door and the lock clicked as it disengaged. Inhaling, I pushed the door open and stepped aside to make room for Grace to enter. As soon as she did the automatic lights I had installed came on, illuminating the living room space and foyer of my home.

Her heels sounded against my hardwood flooring, which brought my attention to her legs. She was dressed in a forest green, asymmetric shoulder, jumpsuit that covered those well-sculpted legs of hers, but I'd committed them to memory.

"Are you going to show me around?"

I blinked out of the trance staring at her put me in and held out my hand. She took it and I began the tour, showing her the open-floor plan living room, with the low sitting, black leather couch and loveseat, which faced the flat screen just above the mock fireplace. We then entered the kitchen where I watched her eyes widen, admiring the shiny countertops and large stove top that rarely ever got turned on. I remembered how much Grace enjoyed cooking, and for an instant I could envision her in my kitchen, cooking in just a T-shirt and panties as she'd done at her place.

"This is the guest room," I stated, pushing open the door of the room that was only partially decorated. Pictures that I purchased to go on the wall were still sitting on the floor, and the half put together bed remained bare.

Grace giggled. "Please tell me no one has actually ever slept in here."

I shook my head. Just the way I liked it. Why the hell I even chose to call it a guest room was beyond me. My decorator had thought it would be better as a guest room than an office. And at the time, I was so preoccupied with work that I let him do what he thought was best.

"I'm thinking of turning it into a home office instead."

After shutting the light off, I took Grace by the hand, showing her the room down the hall, which was the bathroom, but then I hesitated on the next room. My bedroom wasn't unlike most single male bedrooms but there was one aspect I knew that stood out above all others.

I swallowed and went for it, something telling me that this was the right move. I pressed the door of my bedroom open and flicked on the light switch.

"This is huge," she admired, looking around.

But I caught the moment she spotted it. She paused, and from her profile I could see her eyes widen when she took in the sight of my huge bed, with a completely empty mattress, smack dead in the center of the room.

"You really don't like bed linens." Her voice was low as she continued to stare at my bed.

I grunted in response, that uneasy, queasy feeling in my stomach rising at the thought of bed linens.

"No."

She turned to me and her lips parted as she started to say something, but whatever it was, she kept to herself. Instead, she moved closer, placing her hand on my chest and rising to kiss my cheek.

"Thank you for showing me your home."

The way she said it told me that she knew this wasn't something I regularly did. I didn't open myself or my home up to just anyone. She'd been the first. And the fact that she didn't question me about the bed issue told me I made the right call in letting her be the first.

Moving toward the nightstand where I spotted my wallet, I remembered that I'd forgotten to set up the recording for the fight that night.

"One sec, I need to record something." I picked up the remote and turned the television on.

Grace moved closer. "What're you recording?"

"The NFA fight."

"NFA?"

"National Fighting Association."

"Oh, I've heard of it." She silently stood by as I pressed the necessary buttons to ensure the fight would be available whenever I arrived back home to watch it.

"We can stay in and—"

"No." I shook my head. "You didn't get dressed up to spend the night at my place watching a fight. We're going out." Grabbing her hand, I led her back out of the room, down the hall, and out the door.

The drive to the restaurant from my condo was only about ten minutes, which we filled with conversation about work, our latest patients, and our plans for the weekend. Grace told me how her sister was doing. She was still wrestling with her possible diagnosis.

"Her doctor believes she has Bipolar II disorder. I tried to explain to her that that's possibly good news since the symptoms aren't as severe as Bipolar I, but all she heard was that she's defective. At least, that's what she heard at first, but she's coming around. She went back home to our father's for a few weeks to talk with him and our stepmom about it and see what types of treatment she should get on."

"Does she have doctors at home?"

Grace nodded. "They're good about communicating with her psychiatrist here in Williamsport since he was the one who originally diagnosed her."

We pulled up to the restaurant and I chose to have the valet park the car. After giving him my keys, I placed my hand at Grace's lower back and escorted her inside, for the first time feeling honored to have a woman on my arm.

* * *

GRACE

"No!" I stated adamantly again, shaking my head. "It's not my night to sing."

"What the hell does that matter?" Jacob insisted, his brows furrowed.

He looked so damn hot when his face turned serious.

"I'm not singing."

We had come to Rocket after our dinner at the Italian restaurant, even though I wasn't on the schedule to sing that night. Apparently, there was a cancellation in tonight's lineup, and now Jacob was insisting that I was the only person who could take that person's spot.

"We didn't come here for me to sing. I'm certain there's someone else who can—"

"I don't want to hear anyone else," he demanded. "No one has a better voice than you."

I rolled my eyes to keep the grin from covering my face at the way the compliment easily flowed from his lips.

"Fine. *One* song."

That grin of his immediately flashed in triumph, but it didn't even matter because it made me happy to please him.

"One song," I reiterated, trying to convince myself to keep that vow to myself, but the way Jacob's eyes sparked with achievement, I feared my willingness to go back on my own word and perform as many songs as he'd ask.

I followed Jacob to the stage by the hand as if he knew the way better than I did.

"Hey, guys. Heard you're in need of a singer."

Jackson's head popped up from the saxophone. "We sure do," he said, standing and making his way toward the staircase to hold out his hand to help me up.

Before I could even lift my hand to take his, Jacob's voice interjected. "I've got it," he snapped, shooting bullets, forget daggers, at Jackson with his glare.

"Thank you." I pressed a kiss to his cheek and stepped onto the stage on my own, heading to the microphone. "Good evening, everyone. I'm not the regular lineup for tonight, but since Shelly couldn't make it, I thought I'd take a chance to sing a song or two for you. Everyone cool with that?" I questioned, and giggled when a round of applause went through the night club.

I took a step from the microphone, looking over my shoulder to the band to tell them the song I planned on singing. I turned to the audience and my eyes lowered to the front stage, dead center where I knew he'd be standing. Even in a dark room of about two hundred people, I could feel his presence. His energy drew my eyes to him. And those grey eyes held me captive as the chords for Snoh Aalegra's "I Want You Around" began playing.

Staring directly at Jacob, my lips parted and I began singing the words of the song. This was another added component to singing I hadn't ever anticipated. It expressed the words and sentiment that I was either in denial about or just wasn't ready to say on my own.

Jacob's gaze never wavered from mine. He was as caught up in the lyrics of the song as I was.

The song ended all too soon, and I knew I wouldn't be singing another one … not from the stage, anyway. Because as soon as I placed the microphone back into its holder, Jacob leapt onto the stage with such grace, ease, and fluidity that it stole my breath.

"It's time to go now," he growled in my ear.

I nodded because I felt the same. I didn't need to ask where we were going. The gleam in his eyes told me where. Away from the prying eyes of those who were surrounding us at the present moment.

Less than five minutes later, Jacob was holding the passenger side door of his car open for me, waiting for me to climb in. Once he got in, we were pulling off in the direction of my home.

CHAPTER 15

*J*acob

As soon as we entered her front door, my hands were reaching for the end of the bow that held the belt of Grace's jumpsuit together. She managed to turn on a light inside of the foyer of her home so I could fully see what I was doing, but I soon frowned upon seeing the gold zipper that also held her jumpsuit in place.

"Mmm," she hummed as I licked the side of her neck, while also guiding her body down the hall to her bedroom.

My hands lowered over her front, pushing her jumpsuit down, but just when I reached the top of her breasts, per usual, Grace's hands stopped me. I could feel her holding the strapless bra she wore in place with one hand, while maneuvering the rest of her clothing down her waist.

I pulled back, growing impatient and agitated because I wanted to see *all* of her. She still hadn't granted me that pleasure yet. Turning, she peered over her shoulder at me, uncertainty filled her eyes, and I had a decision to make. The uncomfortable way my cock rubbed against the zipper of my jeans made the choice for me.

Wordlessly, I pushed the rest of her clothing down, until she remained there in a bra and panty set that nearly perfectly matched the coloring of her own skin.

Grace's hands moved to my shirt and I raised my arms high, allowing her to remove it. She tossed it onto the chair that sat at the corner of the room before her hands moved to the belt buckle. She quickly undid the belt and zipper of my jeans but that was as far as I would allow her to go. I wasn't ready for a woman to fully undress me.

"I want to taste you," she whispered.

My body froze.

"Will you let me?" Her voice was bordering on begging and my heart lurched against my ribcage.

This was an aspect of our sexual relationship I hadn't let her cross. I looked deep into her eyes and the sincerity, want, and small amount of fear I saw there actually calmed me down, enough that I nodded.

"No hands," I added. I still couldn't let another woman's hands touch my cock.

"Okay."

I let out a breath, watching as she lowered to her knees and waited for me to step out of the rest of my clothing. Leaning forward, her lips parted, and her tongue connected with the tip of my cock. I inhaled sharply and held my breath, waiting for the wave of nausea to pass through me, telling me that I couldn't go through with this.

It never came.

Mostly because as I stared down and watched Grace take my cock into her mouth, I was able to just watch *her*. To be present for this experience and this one alone. Memories of the past didn't come flooding back to mind as they usually did. This was Grace with her mouth around my shaft, no one else.

My hips picked up on Grace's rhythm and I began moving in and out of her mouth with ease. She kept her hands at her sides, allowing me to control the pace. I reached around and buried my hands into her thick hair—which she'd worn down that night—and began pumping into her mouth more rapidly. She moaned, and I felt myself grow even harder from the sound and the vibrations it sent down my shaft.

"I'm going to come in your mouth," I gritted out through my teeth, feeling my orgasm welling up in my body.

Grace's watery eyes rose to mine and she nodded.

That was all the inspiration I needed to let loose into the channel of her mouth. I spilled into her as she swallowed. I watched as some of my semen managed to spill out of the corners of her mouth, but Grace didn't quit. She continued to suck me off until the last drop came from me.

But even when it did, I didn't feel satisfied. Watching Grace swallow my cock had been a life altering experience but I still wanted more. Less than a minute after my orgasm, I found myself positioning my body on Grace's bed and bringing her to straddle me, once I covered my length with a condom. I held onto either side of her hips as she slowly lowered onto my rod, both of us letting out loud moans as I filled her. She was way beyond ready for me.

Not for the first time, I regretted the use of the latex material that separated our skin to skin contact. I wanted to know what it felt like to have her muscles stroking my cock without anything between us.

"You feel so g-good," she panted, her eyes tightly closed, lips parted as her hips rode me.

"Open your eyes, Grace." I needed to see her, to see the pleasure she derived from this moment. It was the only way I could stay here, with her, and keep the memories at bay.

Slowly her eyes opened, and she peered down at me, her gaze hungry for more. To honor her silent request, I let my hips surge upward, my hands still holding her, as I began riding her from the bottom.

One of her hands went to the bra she still had on, holding it in place, while the other hand went to my abdomen, holding her steady. We stared and watched one another, our moans and the sounds from the bed being the only noises coming from the room. When Grace's face tightened, I knew she was close.

"Sing for me, baby," I demanded, wanting to hear the high notes she was about to deliver. And did she.

She tossed her head back, stopped biting her bottom lip, and let out a note only a satisfying orgasm could bring on.

The tightening and milking of her pussy muscles around my cock was enough to deliver my own climax. I tightened my hold on her hips and surged into her one final time before every muscle in my body squeezed and I let out a shout as I came.

I heaved hard as my body tried to regulate its breathing, holding Grace to me until she raised her body and slid off me. I still couldn't get over how cold I felt every time our bodies separated. Any other time, I couldn't wait to get away from a woman post coitus, but not so much with Grace.

Reluctantly, I sat up and pushed myself off the bed to head to the bathroom to remove the condom and relieve myself before going back to the room. Grace was waiting for my return, lying on her side, facing me.

I headed to the bed, pushing the blanket and top sheet away from me. Her hand moved to my stomach and I covered it with mine. This was our usual way of sleeping after we'd made love. Silence filled the room.

"Sing to me," I said as I stared up at the ceiling.

"I already sang once for you tonight."

A half smile was pulled from me as I turned my head in her direction. "You've sung more than once for me tonight, baby."

Giggling, she tucked her head.

My hands tightened around hers.

As soon as she lifted her head, she began humming. It was preparation for whatever song she was about to begin singing. When she opened her mouth, from the very first word, I felt like she chose this song with me and only me in mind.

I listened carefully to the words of the song, and only flinched inwardly when I heard words like "Lord" and "bless my soul." I ignored those phrases and chose to focus on the fact that Grace's voice was filling the room, along with that space at the center of my chest that'd felt empty for so long.

I turned on my side to face her completely as the crescendo of the song built. She cupped my cheek, her thumb going to the indent in my chin, stroking as she sang, looking me directly in the eyes. Only when she sang the final words of the song did I recognize that goosebumps had sprung up all over my arms and chest.

"What's the name of that song?"

She cleared her throat. "It's called 'Jacob's Song' by Briana Babinueax or Bri for short." Her eyes dipped.

"It's a religious song."

She nodded. "I know you're an atheist, but it reminds me of you a little bit."

I lifted her hand to my lips. "For the first time, I don't mind it." I rolled back over to my back, keeping her hand to my abdomen.

"Were you always an atheist?"

I shrugged. "We went to church every weekend. Sat in the front pew every damn Sunday. And then returning to our house felt like entering hell. I couldn't reconcile a supposedly loving God that allowed my home to be filled with such pain. And I couldn't stand supposedly religious and devout people who overlooked things they knew were happening. Not just to me or my home life, but …" I shook my head.

"I get it."

I faced her. "Do you?"

She nodded. "I'm not an atheist, but the things we see sometimes … Even in our line of work. It makes you wonder."

I turned my gaze to the ceiling, nodding.

No more was said after that as we laid there silently, enjoying the closeness of one another until we fell asleep.

* * *

WHEN MY EYES SPRANG OPEN, the nervous feeling I had the first time wasn't there. No, I wasn't in my own bedroom but this one had come to feel more and more familiar. *Almost as if it's home.* I quickly shook that thought free. Grace and I had only been together about a month and a half, it was way too soon for me to get to thinking of her place as my home.

But even as I tried to force myself to think rationally, her lingering scent in the linens warmed something deep in my belly. It wasn't unusual for her to wake up before me. She often left me sleeping while she got up to shower and fix breakfast for the both of us. As I stood up to stretch the kinks from the night out, I heard the shower running and instantly, my legs headed in that direction. All I could think of was the night before and other nights we'd spent in her bed, but Grace had never fully bared herself to me. I wanted to see her, all of her.

I slid into the steamy bathroom without making much noise, and in two steps I was yanking the shower curtain back.

"Wha—" Grace yelled, jumping as she turned to face me, her arms instantly going to cover her breasts. "Get out!" she yelled.

Her tone screamed angry and surprised, but her eyes—those brown pools—read afraid.

I stared into her eyes, my expression unflinching as I raised my leg to step fully into the shower. Her eyes glanced all over my body, her lower lip sucked in between her teeth when she caught sight of my half erect cock pointing toward her.

"Jacob, I'm not done showering." Her eyes went to the shower curtain as I pulled it closed, caging us in.

"Move your hands, Grace."

She shook her head.

Lowering my face to hers, I kissed her lips. My hands went to her wrists. "Move your hands, baby." It wasn't a question, but the order had come out patiently. Fear already glittered in those eyes of hers and that cut me deeper than anything. I didn't want to alarm her any more than she already was. But I needed to see all of her.

The muscles in her arms relaxed slightly, and slowly—half inch by half inch—she allowed me to pull her arms away from her breasts. I stared into her eyes at first. They grew watery.

Gradually, I moved my gaze lower from her eyes, to the rest of her face, her neck, the top of her chest, and then to her left breast. My cock twitched at the sight of the perfectly formed, caramel brown globe with the darker brown areola and pert nipple. I let my gaze shift to her right breast and it wasn't the same perfection as the left. In place of where her nipple should've been, was a long, healed-over scar. It was a scar I'd seen many times on women who came to me for reconstructive surgery after surviving breast cancer.

I looked back up to Grace. "How long ago?"

"Five years," she whispered.

I did the quick math. "You were twenty-six." My eyes went back to her scars.

"Twenty-five at the age of diagnosis and the mastectomy. Followed by a year of chemo and radiation."

I swallowed, knowing the regiment well.

She gasped when my right hand rose to touch her scar. I ran my thumb over the semi-raised skin. Her body stiffened but she didn't push me away.

"Why didn't you tell me? I'm a plastic surgeon, Grace. You've stood next to me as I operated on women with scars just like—"

"I didn't want you to see me like one of them! Not like I was a patient or just another body on your table to be fixed. I didn't want you to see me as broken. I still don't." Her voice trembled with the tears she held back.

Lowering my lips to her scar, I kissed it once, twice, three times, before standing back up to look her in the eye when I said, "Baby, out of the two of us, you're not the one who's broken." My lips crashed down over hers, my hand still holding onto what was left of her right breast, as I kissed her furiously.

I pivoted her body so that her back was pressed against the tiled wall of the shower. Leaving my hand where it was, and keeping my thumb grazing across her scar, I sank to my knees, and with my free arm lifted her left leg to place over my shoulder.

"Jacob!" Grace's voice pleaded.

I buried my face into her center, spreading her labia to give my tongue better access to her clit. With my mouth, but without words, I expressed how perfect I believed she was. Because the word perfection didn't even begin to describe what she was to me.

She moaned above me as her hand came down to cover mine, which still rested over her scar. Her hips began to buck against my face, and I felt as if I couldn't get enough of her. I squeezed her left thigh as it rested against my shoulder, adoring the feel of her body against mine. I swallowed every bit of moisture her body produced for me. Ignoring the pelting water that had begun to turn cold, I lapped at Grace's pussy with a vigor even I didn't know I possessed. And when her body began trembling, and her cries became hoarse, and her flower opened and clenched from her coming, I still couldn't get enough.

I licked and suckled until her throat muscles gave in and she couldn't scream any longer, wringing a second orgasm free from her. When all was said and done, Grace was forced to push me away from her, lest I continue feasting off her pussy and bringing her to climax a third time, giving my own self lockjaw. But I would've been willing to make that sacrifice.

And as I stood, holding Grace up on her shaking legs, I kissed her scar again before connecting with her lips.

Absolute perfection.

* * *

GRACE

"How come you never went in for reconstructive surgery?"

I nearly choked on my freshly squeezed grape juice. Jacob and I sat around my kitchen island, eating our breakfast even though it was sometime after noon. We hadn't come up for air after the shower for a while.

"You don't know how to be subtle, do you?"

He shrugged a shoulder, his elbows planted on countertop, fork dangling from one hand as he peered over at me.

I licked my lips at the sight of his flexed muscles because he was shirtless.

"Subtlety isn't my specialty."

"I've noticed."

I took another sip of juice before placing the glass down. "I was tired of being a patient." I looked to him. "After surgery and almost a full year of treatment, I couldn't bear the thought of going in for another surgery and the healing time it would take. I wanted to put cancer in my rearview mirror. So, I figured I would live with the scars, or maybe get surgery sometime in the future."

"Five years later and you still haven't."

If any other man had said those words, I would've taken it as an accusation. But Jacob didn't mean it that way. He was just curious.

"Same reason. I enjoy taking care of others but am not so good at letting others do the same for me."

"They say doctors make the worst patients, but the truth is, *no one* is worse than nurses."

I giggled because I suspected there was some truth to that. Everyone knew nurses were the heartbeat of any hospital. Sure, doctors gave out prescriptions and diagnoses and treatment regimens, but nurses were necessary for the follow through. Most doctors couldn't do half of what nurses did on a daily basis, but it was a secret we kept to ourselves. And with that much knowledge and responsibility, yes, it was difficult as hell to let go and allow yourself to be taken care of.

"Come here."

His deep voice pulled my attention to his perfect lips. I admired the little bit of dark stubble growing around his mouth thanks to the fact that he hadn't shaved that morning.

I did as requested and stood from my seat, circling the island, to perch my body on the edge of Jacob's stool. He adjusted, giving me a little more space to fit comfortably while his left hand circled my waist, holding me in place.

He kissed me behind my ear before taking another bite of the blueberry pancakes I made us for breakfast. His hand moved underneath the black, sleeveless T-shirt I wore, up to the space that had been my right breast. I stiffened when his fingers traced the scar at the same time he brought a forkful of pancakes to my lips.

I opened my mouth, allowing him to feed me, but my body was still tense. It'd been a long time since I allowed anyone accept my doctor to touch me there. Apparently, he was making sure I got used to it.

"Does this make you uncomfortable?"

I nodded as I swallowed the pancakes.

"Do you want me to stop?"

Sighing, I laid my head back against his shoulder. "No."

"Good."

I grinned and placed a kiss to his jawline.

"You like the grape juice, huh?" I asked as he refilled his glass for the second time.

"I do especially since you kept the pulp in it. Same when you make orange juice."

"Pulp is the only way."

He kissed my cheek in agreement before taking a sip of the tart juice.

I closed my eyes, sighing and feeling grateful that I got to spend the day just like this.

CHAPTER 16

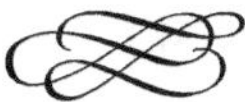

*G*race

Looking down at my cell phone at the text message I just received, I frowned. It was only a confirmation text for my appointment the following week, but that damn fear which always came up regarding this particular appointment rose.

"What's that all about?"

I lifted my gaze to see Jacob coming toward me, a frown on his own face, as if my displeasure somehow caused his.

I took the cup of coffee he offered. "Thank you." Shrugging, I took a sip. "Just not looking forward to the staff meeting this morning."

Jacob lifted an eyebrow, watching me carefully.

"You know about the consulting firm, right?" I asked because his gaze was becoming too unraveling to my nerves.

"I heard about it."

He said it as if it were no big deal to him. *Typical.*

"I mean, you don't have much to worry about anyway," I continued as we proceeded down the hall toward the large staff room where much of the surgical staff was to be introduced to the new consultants. "You have one of the best rated outcomes for your surgeries.

Probably because you barely let any of your residents touch anything in the OR," I giggled, nudging his side with my elbow.

He glared down at me, but a tiny smile played at his lips.

"Thank you," I said, passing through the door he held open for me.

"Oh, thank you, Dr. Reynolds," another feminine voice purred behind me.

I immediately rolled my eyes at the sound of Suzanne's voice. I wasn't a jealous woman, I swear I wasn't. Even with boyfriends of mine in the past, I didn't think much of other women trying to flirt with them because if they were easily able to fall into that trap, then the guy wasn't meant for me. But that logic did not seem to apply when I glared at Suzanne as she smiled, staring up into Jacob's face, standing closer than I deemed appropriate.

I had to remind myself that we were at work and yanking her away from him by her hair wouldn't be looked upon as a good thing.

Jacob merely nodded in Suzanne's direction and stepped past her, placing his hand at the small of my back to guide us in the direction of two empty seats in the auditorium-style room.

It didn't bother me one bit that Jacob's and my relationship was becoming more and more apparent to our co-workers. We were never in anyone's face about it, and of course, kept it professional while at work. I'd even convinced Jacob that he couldn't schedule me for every single one of his surgeries. Though, I assisted with many of his surgeries, I still worked with other surgeons, and he other nurses.

"We need to get this over with. I have a consult later this morning and a surgery this afternoon."

"Nose job, right?"

He nodded. "You can ditch Jeffries' hip replacement and assist me instead."

Giggling, I shook my head. "We've talked about this. Dr. Jeffries is already expecting me."

He frowned but didn't protest any further.

A minute later, the heads of the hospital walked in along with the chief of surgery and an older man who didn't look familiar. I was surmising this must be the new consultant when Jacob's abrupt movement to my left had me looking over at him instead.

His back was ramrod straight as he stared ahead, glaring at the man. Tension filled his body just that quickly and the guy hadn't even said anything.

"Thank you all for coming in on time," the hospital's president began. "As you know, Memorial Hospital has decided to hire a consultant to help us determine how we can improve operations and better serve our patients. We have decided the most critical departments to start with are the emergency department and the surgical unit, which is why we've asked you all to join us. I would like to take this time to introduce you to Daniel Reynolds from Healthcare Solutions. Mr. Reynolds comes to us all the way from the West Coast, and is delighted to be joining our team for a while to help Memorial be the best hospital it can be. Mr. Reynolds, please introduce yourself."

The president stepped aside, holding out his hand to Mr. Reynolds who then took his place at the center of the lecture stage.

Reynolds.

I turned again to Jacob who was sitting still as a statue. His face appeared as if it was made out of granite. The scowl that he'd always worn when I first met him was back, and though I couldn't see them from this angle, I imagined the dark storm clouds that were often in his eyes were in full force.

Jacob is from the West Coast, my brain reminded me.

He had grown up in Washington, the Seattle area. I turned to look down at the man who was now speaking about his record as a consultant with various hospitals around the country, and his career in the healthcare industry prior to starting his own company. Squinting, I tried to ascertain whether or not I could glean any resemblance between the man down front and the man sitting next to me.

But I didn't need to. Once Mr. Reynold's eyes circled the room as if searching for something while he continued to talk, they paused ... or rather, hesitated, when he peered up and his gaze landed on Jacob. The movement of his feet halted and he stumbled slightly, but he quickly recovered. It was obvious then that this man was related to

Jacob. And I would venture to guess, by the way Jacob glared at him, this Daniel Reynolds was his father.

* * *

Jacob

"What the hell are you doing here?" I growled at the man who dared to enter my office.

My father's lips pinched, and a crease appeared in his forehead.

"Jacob, you left the room before I could get a chance to speak with you. You didn't even bother to come say hello."

"Did you honestly expect me to?" I shoved my hands into the pocket of my scrubs.

The displeased expression on his face deepened, causing me to scoff even more.

"Jacob, we haven't seen you or your brother in years. It is not fair—"

"Fair?" I paused to gather myself, and lowered my voice, stepping closer to my father. "You want to talk about fucking fair?"

"Listen, son, I know I wasn't around a lot when you were younger, and your mother … well, she had unconventional ways of raising you two boys, but we wanted the best for you—"

"*Unconventional?* Are you out of your—" Inhaling again, I pulled my gaze away from my father. I centered my gaze on the familiar sight of my office, my name placard on my desk, and the stack of patient files directly behind it. All of this reminding me that I was no longer a child, living in his home, at the mercy of his absenteeism and my mother's destructive and soul-crushing rearing.

Slowly, I exhaled, peering back up at my father.

"Jacob, today is not a day you should be spending without family. It's your—"

"Do you know what I told that bitch the last time I laid eyes on her?"

My father's eyes ballooned. "Do not refer to your mo—"

"Do you know what I said to her?" I growled while I stepped

closer, getting directly in his face since we both stood at six-feet-two inches. "I told her that if she *ever* tried to contact me again, I'd tell you and anyone else *exactly* who she was."

My father's head jerked backwards, a stunned expression mirroring his face. "I-I know who my wife is."

"Are you sure about that? That horrified look in your eyes tells me you don't. Or perhaps you do. Maybe you do know, or at the very least, suspected all of the ugly things that cunt you married and fathered two children with is capable of."

He sputtered for a few moments, his hazel eyes circling the room, as he tried to find words to fill the moment.

"She's dying, Jacob. She didn't want me to tell you, but she has an inoperable brain tumor. It's already caused her to have one major stroke. Doctors give her only about six more months to live."

Pinching my lips, I cocked my head to the side. "Is she in any pain?"

"Yes."

"Good," I responded, staring him directly in his eyes. "Now get the hell out of my office," I seethed, hands fisting in my pockets, searching for something to hit.

I guessed my father finally recognized that I wasn't going to bend. He took a couple of steps backwards before turning and exiting without another word. I was left there still bristling with anger. So much so, that sitting down to read a couple of research studies I'd planned on reading wasn't about to happen.

I started to get that jumpy feeling I got when I need to be in the ring and hit something or someone. But since it was the middle of the day, that wasn't going to happen. I had surgery in another hour, which would serve to calm me down. I decided to head to the nurses' station to check on the board to see who was scheduled to operate with me, since Grace would be with another surgeon.

While walking down the hall from my office to the board, I mentally went over the procedure I was going to be completing to help me remember everything, and calm my nerves. Thankfully, my father was nowhere to be found in the hallways, but the memory of his appearance lingered in my mind.

"Dr. Reynolds."

Immediately, my eyes rolled at the sound of her voice. I paused and glanced over my shoulder by way of answering.

Suzanne's smile widened. "Looks like we'll be in the OR together today." She moved closer.

I lifted an eyebrow.

"I'll be the surgical nurse assisting you for the batwing surgery." She giggled.

I narrowed my gaze. "The arm lift," I corrected.

"Yeah, that one. I was thinking maybe we could go over the surgery beforehand. You know, maybe—"

"Unless you're the one cutting into the patient, that won't be necessary." I turned and walked away, still feeling her eyes on my back.

"Hey," another feminine voice rang out as soon as I rounded the corner, but this I welcomed. "Where'd you disappear to after the meeting?"

"I had to print out some articles in my office before surgery," I explained, unfamiliar with explaining myself to anyone, let alone a woman, since I left home as a teenager.

"Are you all right?" Grace questioned, her hickory eyes searching mine.

I blinked, shuttering all the emotion that was still coursing through me. "Perfect. Still pissed you won't be in surgery with me."

Those dimples that appeared as she grinned helped to extinguish just a portion of the fire that'd begun to burn in my chest ever since I first laid eyes on my father in that auditorium.

"Sorry about that." She sounded decidedly non-apologetic. "But maybe this'll make up for it." She pulled two tickets from the front pocket of her scrub shirt, holding them out to me.

I took the two tickets from her hand and read them. My gaze lifted to hers.

"NFA tickets." It wasn't a question. It's obvious what these were.

She nodded. "I saw all the recordings you had of those NFA fights, especially of that Luke McClennan or McDonald—"

"McConnell," I corrected.

"That's it. Luke McConnell. He's fighting here in Williamsport this weekend. It's supposed to be a big deal. Anyway, we're going."

"You bought us tickets." I don't know why this stunned me so much. "Why?"

"Because it's your birthday."

I frowned, trying to remember when I told her about my birthday. It's not a day that I ever celebrated, so the chances of me actually going out of my way to tell her the date were zero.

"I saw it on your license. When you dropped it in my bedroom, after our first night together, and I picked it up and handed it to you."

I nodded, remembering every moment we spent together.

"We'll go out to dinner before the fight. Sorry, I can't celebrate with you tonight, on your actual birthday, but I'm working a twelve-hour shift and am usually exhausted after those."

Was she honestly apologizing?

"I gotta go." Moving in, she lifted on her tiptoes, checking around to make sure it was just the two of us in the hallway, before pressing a quick kiss to my lips. Instinctively, my desire took over and I pulled her to me, deepening the kiss.

Grace pulled back, giggling and slapping my shoulder. "We're at work. Bye." She waved and headed in the opposite direction, presumably to prepare for her next surgery.

It was also what I should've been doing but I just stood there, staring at the two tickets in my hand, and the name of the two fighters. I'd never been to a live NFA fight for reasons I wasn't ready to share with Grace. But she'd gone out of her way to not only remember my birthday but to make it special. Saying no wasn't an option.

CHAPTER 17

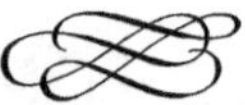

Jacob

"You're awfully quiet tonight. I mean, even more than usual," Grace joked as we exited the Indian restaurant we decided to have dinner at before heading over to the fight.

"I'm enjoying listening to you and hearing about your day more than I like talking." That was a more than half truth. The sound of her voice whether, she was talking or singing, was my favorite sound. I enjoyed it more than my own voice.

"You sure it has nothing to do with the fact that we're about to go watch one of your favorite athletes live?"

"Possibly." I shrugged while pulling out my key to unlock my car doors.

The drive to the sporting complex where the fight was held was only about fifteen minutes from the restaurant, but it took a while to find parking.

"Ugh, I should've sprung for the reserved parking," Grace lamented. "It's going to be a mess getting out of here."

"It's fine."

"At least we're early and our seats are already reserved. Oh, and I have a surprise for you after the fight."

After finally finding a space, I turned off the car and raised an eyebrow in her direction. "I don't like—"

"Surprises," she repeated at the same time I did. "I know, I know, but you'll like this one."

I sighed and pushed out of the car, going to her side to hold the door open for her. We made our way to the arena and spent twenty-five minutes getting through the security line. By the time we made it inside, we only had ten minutes until the fight began, which was fine with me since I hated sitting and waiting for things.

"I had no idea cage fighting was so popular," Grace stated, looking around at the hundreds of ticket buyers who passed us, anxiously heading toward the concession stand or their seats. "Did you know it's still not legal in some states?"

"It's a brutal sport, some say."

She nodded.

"You want popcorn or anything?"

She shook her head. "Our seats are upfront."

For the first time I actually looked down at the seat number on the ticket. I was in seat B12 and Grace was B13. We were in the second row, right at the center. I hadn't even looked at the seat numbers because I'd still been working through my tension of actually going to one of these things.

It'll be fine. The voice in my head worked to calm me down as I stepped aside, letting Grace pass me once we got to our row. Not until she sat in her seat, did I take the time to look around the room. There had to be over two thousand people in this audience. And at the center of the room stood a huge, octagonal-shaped cage that spread thirty feet in diameter. The cage sat atop a platform, allowing the fighters, once inside, to be more visible for the entire audience.

I watched as the lights around the auditorium dimmed and the walkways in which the fighters came out were illumined.

"Here they come," Grace cheered.

"Ladies and gentlemen …" the announcer began over the loud-speaker, introducing the first fighter. His name was something Ramirez or whatever; I barely paid attention. He wasn't who I came to see. When the second fighter was introduced, I sat up straighter in my chair.

I watched as Luke McConnell strolled out of the dark entranceway into the light that shone on the walkway down to the cage. His face was set in stone, as it always was, and he didn't look around or wave like his opponent had. His entrance wasn't extravagant but the audience cheered nonetheless.

"I don't know why they're cheering. I hear he's washed up."

I turned and gave the kid behind me who'd said that a hard glare before turning back around.

I pushed out any outside noise as the commentators again introduced the fighters by their stats. Next, the bell went off and the two fighters went at it.

"Oh!" Grace cheered when Luke landed a punch to his opponent's ribs, almost sending him to his knees.

I remained silent as I took in the skill of each fighter. Luke had a lightness about the way he fought. It brought back memories and I lowered my gaze briefly. Only when I heard Grace beside me, did I lift my head again, seeing Luke against the cage, after having received a brutal punch to his left cheek. I grew pissed at the way the announcers kept replaying the hit over and over again, as the referee got in between the fighters, saying something that only they could hear.

The fight commenced, and I found myself feeling proud when Luke delivered a knee strike that sent Ramirez down. Luke landed on top of him and wailed on him, eventually getting him into an arm lock position that if pushed too far could've easily snapped Ramirez's arm. That should've been the end of the fight. There shouldn't have been a reason the fight kept going. But for some reason, Luke raised his head, looking around the audience.

His eyes scanned the front rows and that's when they landed directly on me. He squinted as if trying to discern whether or not he was seeing a ghost. I felt it the moment he realized it wasn't a ghost. His eyebrows shot up and the fight that should've been taking all of his attention was pushed to the background of thought. Unfortunately, his grip on Ramirez must've slackened considerably because a second later, Luke found himself flat on his back, as Ramirez worked, trying to put him into a chokehold with his legs.

"Oh no!" Grace screamed next to me, bringing me out of my trance. "What happened? He was about to win!"

"Five … four …. Three …"

Just as the audience began to count down along with the referee, Luke broke Ramirez' hold, preventing his loss. But he never fully recovered the vigor he began the fight with. In the end, the fight went in Luke's favor but it wasn't one of his better matches. And he knew it.

A pissed off Luke snatched his arm from the ref's hold as soon as he was declared the winner and stormed out of the cage, down the same walkway he entered on.

"Why is he so upset? He won, right?" Confused, Grace looked to me.

"He did but it wasn't one of his better fights," I tried to explain.

"Maybe he's a perfectionist, like someone else I know." Laughing, she nudged me with her elbow.

You have no idea.

"Well, I hope that doesn't spill over into the surprise I have for you."

I glanced behind me, her hand in mine as I led us out of the row toward the staircase. "How would it impact your surprise?"

She shook her head, and I sighed because she still wasn't divulging her secret. I truly did not like surprises but the excitement on her face kept me from demanding she tell me.

"No, we're not leaving yet," she finally said when I started heading for the main exit.

I turned.

"We're going this way. I got us VIP tickets to meet Luke McConnell backstage." Her smile was brighter than the lights of the arena. I don't think she even registered the dismay on my face as she grabbed my hand and led me toward the side door marked "VIP Access ONLY."

"Hi," she greeted the huge security guard who stood outside of the door.

Only his dark eyes moved as he looked down at us.

She handed him our tickets and he let us pass.

"Are you excited? You get to meet your favorite boxer."

"He's not a boxer."

"Fighter, whatever. You know what I mean."

Her enthusiasm was what kept me from turning around and walking right out of this arena like this night never happened. I told myself that Luke would likely be in a decent mood since he did win the fight, after all. Plus, we probably weren't the only ones with VIP tickets to see him. He'd likely not even notice we were there.

"Who the hell is this?" I heard his voice bellow, and my stomach turned upside down. It'd been so long since I heard him speak in person and not from behind a television camera.

"These are the VIP ticket holders you agreed to meet, Luke," a male voice, which I didn't recognize, said.

"Fucking A," he huffed. "Fine. I'll be out in a minute."

The man whose voice I didn't recognized stepped from behind the door with a pasted smile on his face. "I'm sorry, Mr. McConnell will be out in one moment."

"Oh, please, tell him to take his time. We're not in a rush, right, Jacob?" Grace turned to me, smiling.

I grunted because the truth was I was actually in a rush. I looked around, and to my dismay didn't see anyone else lined up behind us outside of the door for this meeting.

"Where's everyone else?" I questioned.

The skinny guy appeared to be confused.

"For the signing or whatever this is?" I reiterated.

"Oh." His eyebrows rose and he shook his head. "Mr. McConnell said he would only take a few VIP guests. He's usually very tired after a fight." The way his eyes dipped and he avoided my direct stare told me he was lying.

"All right, where're they a—" Luke McConnell's deep voice demanded as he pushed the door open with so much force, Grace actually jumped back.

I stepped halfway in front of her to keep her from getting bowled over by him.

"You fucking shitting me right now?" His voice read incredulity as he glared at me.

"Luke—" I started.

"Don't *Luke* me! I thought that was you in the audience. I should've forgotten all about Ramirez and fucking jumped you!" He charged, grabbing for my shirt.

"What the—" I heard Grace exclaim behind me, shocked and obviously confused by his reaction.

I didn't have time to tell her what was going on. I only had a second to push her farther out of the way of the speeding train that was Luke McConnell's anger before he took his first swing at my face.

Seeing it coming, I ducked, narrowly missing his massive fist.

"Oh my God! Security!" Grace screamed. "Get off of him!" She was yelling at Luke who continued to charge me. "Someone call the police!" she demanded just as two security staff got in between Luke and I.

"No! Don't call the police," I demanded, my chest heaving the same way Luke's was as he shot bullets in my direction with this glare.

"Why not? He attacked you!"

"Because he's my kid brother." My stare was transfixed on Luke McConnell, who'd grown up as Luke Reynolds. He changed his name once he began his professional fighting career.

"What?" she cried incredulously.

I didn't have time to answer Grace's question before Luke said, "So you fucking remember you have a brother?"

His angry hazel eyes quickly moved from me to the woman behind me. "You thought bringing your bitch here tonight would get you—"

I don't know what the hell he'd been about to say because it was halted when I lunged out of the grip of the security guard and my fist connected with his jaw. All I saw was fucking red and hearing him call Grace a bitch over and over in my head as I kept swinging.

"Break it up!" someone yelled frantically.

I felt a stabbing pain in my side when one of Luke's hit made contact but I kept going.

"Don't ever call her out of her name again!"

"Don't ever call yourself my brother, you fucking shithead! You weren't there for me before don't bother showing up now!"

"You have no idea what I protected you from!" I roared with more anger than I'd felt in a long time.

I was heaving as security again separated Luke and I.

Stopping in his tracks, my brother stared at me as if what I said hit him right between the eyes. Just as I intended it to. But I wasn't about to explain anything to him or anyone else. I hadn't set up this meeting. Had no intention on ever disturbing Luke in his life as it was.

"I think we should go." Grace voice finally broke through our stare off.

Luke's angry gaze fell to her but nothing came from his mouth.

I unballed my fists and snatched away from the security guard who still held me. Taking Grace's hand in mine, I turned and started for the exit, without another word.

* * *

Grace

Well that didn't go as planned. I sighed to myself as I looked across the console to the driver seat to see Jacob's stone-faced profile. He hadn't uttered a word since we left the arena. Nothing.

Part of me wanted to be angry that he hadn't told me before that Luke McConnell was his brother. And that obviously, their relationship wasn't on good terms. But the bigger part of me felt guilty for screwing up his birthday. I wanted to make it special for him, and instead, it turned into a total disaster.

I glanced out the passenger side window to see familiar sights and streets passing us by. Jacob was headed in the direction of my home. Ten minutes later, he pulled into my driveway and cut off the ignition before sitting back in his seating, running his hand down the side of his face.

I reached over, placing my hand on his shoulder. He flinched a little but didn't push me away. That had to be a good sign.

"Well, we both seem to have interesting younger siblings," I tried to joke.

Jacob turned to me with those storm clouds in his eyes. My heart ached. He looked like he had the weight of the world on his shoulders.

Sighing, he shook his head. "Journey had you, at least. Luke …" He broke off, shaking his head again. "I wasn't the brother he needed."

I scrunched my face, frowning. "How could you've been given—"

"He wasn't wrong. What he said. I wasn't there for him. I left that house when I was sixteen years old, and for all he knows I barely looked back."

My hand went to the nape of his neck, running my fingers through the hair there. "Jacob, you were a kid. What were you—"

"You should go inside." His voice was firm as he stared straight ahead.

"Are you coming in with me?"

"No."

I inwardly jolted at the lack of emotion in his voice, and the feeling of rejection it produced in me. He was pushing me away.

"Where're you going?" I knew the answer to the question, but I wanted to hear him say it.

He remained silent.

"To fight," I sighed.

"Go inside, Grace." He lowered his hand to mine, squeezing it, but he didn't look at me.

I waited for a few more seconds, hoping that he'd change his mind, but it was fruitless. Opening the passenger door, I fished my keys out of my bag and walked to the front door, unlocking it. Not until I fully entered and turned on the lights inside did I hear Jacob's Range Rover start up and begin backing out of my driveway. I knew he was headed to get into a fight of his own that night. I just hoped he would be okay.

CHAPTER 18

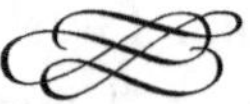

*J*acob

My entire body tingled with the need to get into the ring as I pushed through the doors of the changing room. I was dressed in my typical fighting shorts, and my hands were tightly wrapped thanks to Buddy who'd taken one look at me when I showed up at the Underground and bumped another guy so I could be in the next fight.

"Take it easy on Brick tonight, 'kay, champ?" Buddy teased, smacking me on the shoulder.

I grunted and swatted his hand away from me before entering the ring.

Fighting Brick was exactly what I needed. Unlike some of the other regulars, he didn't hold back when it came to fighting me.

"All right, boys, you know the rules. Avoid the face but everything else is on the line. Hope you wore your cups. Brick, I wouldn't get on this guy's bad side if I were you. He looks pissed," Buddy warned.

Scowling, Brick snorted. There was no love lost between either one of us.

"Okay, gentlemen. To the victor goes the spoils!" Buddy dropped his arm and moved out of the way much quicker than anyone would've believed a man in his sixties could move.

The cheers and yells from the surrounding audience began. It was a much smaller crowd than had been at the arena earlier that evening, but hearing them took me back to that place. Back to the moment when Luke's gaze landed on me and the hatred he felt emerged. It was so raw and uncut that I felt it all the way down to my toes.

That was when Brick took his first swing at me, hitting me in the left side of my ribs. I pivoted quickly enough that the hit was more of a graze than a direct hit, but it was the same spot that Luke had made contact with earlier and I grimaced. Both from the physical pain and the memory of his face earlier that night and years prior.

I sent a left hook to Brick's stomach, causing him to stumble just long enough that I could get my bearings back. But a memory of the past came barreling down on me, throwing me off so much that Brick was able to land an elbow and then a side sweep, taking me off my legs. I found myself pinned on my back, struggling to breathe and shake off the memory of the past to focus on the here and now.

But Brick hadn't earned his name purely from the look of him. The motherfucker was almost impossible to shake once he had you pinned. I struggled and fought to break free from his arm, which was the damn size of a tree trunk. Somehow I managed to maneuver my leg in a way that I was able to send a kick to his throat, causing him to let me go as he began gasping for air. But he wasn't done.

I had just enough time to stagger to my feet before another one of Brick's fists came my way. This time I blocked it with my elbow and sent a jab to the soft part of his belly.

He grunted in pain and stumbled back a couple of times.

Again and again, Brick and I went blow for blow. Exhaustion began to engulf my limbs the same way the pain of seeing my kid brother again in person had. Brick's movements were slowing down as well, telling of his fatigue. But we kept going.

I became absorbed in the fight, knowing that when this fight ended and I stepped out of the ring, all I had left was to deal with all the shit that had begun bubbling to the surface. That was the last thing

I wanted. Seeing my father earlier in the week, learning the witch of a woman who birthed me was dying, and then seeing Luke. It all had sent me to the ring. Where I could, for a time, exchange the physical pain, for the emotional. In the ring I could focus my anger and aggression on my opponent, as opposed to fighting ghosts of the past.

"That's enough boys!" Buddy finally declared, pulling Brick and I out of our arm and arm head lock. "We've got other fighters who want to get in the ring tonight."

I finally dropped my hands and stood up straight, looking across the ring at Brick. The slant of his eyes and his heavy breathing, which mirrored my own, told the story. We were both done for the night.

"Touch gloves," Buddy insisted.

Instead of reminding him that we weren't actually wearing any gloves, I held out my right fist. Brick tapped his knuckles to mine and I ambled my way over to the ropes, climbing down and out of the ring.

I didn't bother with showering or changing back into the clothes I arrived in. I simply unwrapped my now swollen hands, threw a dark T-shirt over my head, grabbed my keys, and headed for the exit. The brisk night air of late fall sent a shiver through my body, jolting me out of my exhausted stupor just long enough that I felt refreshed enough for the drive back home.

It was semi-dark when I pulled into the garage that connected to my building, but I didn't miss the woman who got out of the car, as I parked in my usual parking spot on the second floor of the garage. I climbed out of the car and circled around to the passenger side to come face-to-face with Grace.

She didn't say anything at first. Instead, her eyes lingered on my body, slowly scanning me. She frowned when her eyes caught sight of my hands. She lifted her gaze.

"You ready to talk now?"

* * *

GRACE

No, he wasn't ready to talk. But sometimes if you wait for someone to be ready for something, they'll never do it. At least, that'd been my experience. Jacob knew it also, because instead of answering me directly, he took me by the hand and led me to the elevator that took us up to the tenth floor where he resided.

He was silent as we headed down the hall, and he paused to unlock his door, stepping aside to let me pass before he entered.

Turning, I watched him dump the gym bag he carried his fight clothes in by the door and turned toward his hallway. I stepped out of the sneakers I wore and kicked them next to the door before following him. He removed his shirt, and I covered my mouth to prevent the gasp from escaping at the sight of the bruises covering his torso.

Squeezing my eyes shut, I turned and headed out of the room, making my way back up to the kitchen. I grabbed the kitchen towel that hung, neatly folded over the stove's handle, and then moved to the freezer, opening it for some ice. Better than the ice, I found a couple of ice packs. I searched for a second towel, and finding it, I wrapped the two ice packs in the towels before heading back down to Jacob's bedroom.

He laid across the empty mattress with one arm covering his face, in only a pair of boxer briefs. Even with the bruises, his body was truly a work of art.

"I don't need ice."

"Shut up," I demanded, taking his hands into mine for him to sit up.

He did so, and I placed the ice packs over both of his hands to cover his swelling knuckles.

"You have surgery on Johnny Westbrook in two days. That little boy needs you to be at optimum level. You're icing these knuckles tonight."

He grunted but didn't give anymore pushback, leaving his hands in his lap with the cold compresses covering them and doing their job.

I checked the time on the clock to make a mental note to remove the packs after twenty-minutes.

"I hope you won, at least."

He frowned. "It was a draw."

"Who'd you fight?"

"Brick."

I frowned. "Considering he was your second fight of the night, I'd consider that a win."

He grunted but I suspected it was supposed to be a laugh.

I couldn't help it when my eyes trickled down his body again to stare at the bruising. The question that'd been on my mind for days finally came out of my mouth.

"Daniel Reynolds from Health Solutions. He's your father."

Jacob's eyes spoke before he did. "Yes."

"Luke McConnell, he's your brother, but—"

"He uses our paternal grandmother's maiden name."

I nodded.

"He seems to be a fan of yours."

He didn't say anything.

"Interesting you both have found the same method to release your aggression." I'd been thinking about it ever since Jacob dropped me off.

Luke ended up becoming a professional fighter, and a pretty good one by most people's standards, and Jacob, it wasn't his profession, but it obviously was a hobby of his.

"We learned at a young age." Jacob finally looked at me. "I was five and Luke was three the first time my mother made us fight. Luke had soiled himself while we were at the babysitter's and that she-devil thought an appropriate punishment would be to push aside the furniture in the living room and make me fight Luke, to teach him a lesson."

"The first time?"

He nodded. "It only got worse as we got older. Whenever one of us brought home anything less than an A from school, she'd force the other to hit and beat on them for not doing our best, as she called it. If we didn't want to, she would do the job herself, smacking, kicking and clawing at us until we fought one another."

I shook my head in disbelief because I couldn't fathom what he was saying.

"And what about your father? He allowed this to go on?"

Jacob shrugged. "He was hardly around. In my family, you either achieved or you didn't exist, period. The Reynolds are prominent in Washington. My grandfather was a U.S. senator, and his brother was on the short list to become a U.S. Supreme Court justice. One of my uncles is a world-renowned cardiologist, while the other sits on the state's highest court. If you were born a Reynolds, you were going to be either a lawyer or a doctor, and not just an average, run of the mill doctor or lawyer, either. My father decided to become both. He got his medical degree, and after residency in internal medicine, went to get his JD/MBA. His first job at a law firm is where he met my mother. She was a legal secretary. They married, and she became the stay-at-home Stepford wife that everyone believed was perfect. But while he was out building his empire and adding to the family name, she was at home terrorizing us."

I shook my head again because the pain in his eyes ripped at my insides.

"I think I hate him more than I hate her. A father is supposed to protect his family."

I nodded, agreeing and feeling the same way. "Some of them didn't get the memo."

Jacob's eye rose to meet mine again, a curious look crossing his face.

"My father wasn't good at protecting us either. He ignored or tried to downplay my mother's illness until one day he finally couldn't take it and left when I was nine years old and Journey was just three. He left the two of us to fend for ourselves in a home with a very sick woman."

"Do you hate him?"

I shook my head. "I thought I did. Even when he took Journey in when she was eleven, after our mother died. She'd parked her car on the train tracks of an oncoming train during one of her depressive episodes. I was seventeen and refused to move in with my father."

"How could you not hate him for making you live through that alone?"

I removed the ice packs from Jacob's hands and massaged his knuckles with my fingers to warm them back up. "When I was diagnosed with cancer, he and his wife, Elaine, were there for me. I'd bought my home by then, and they practically moved in to help take me back and forth to my treatments, clean, grocery shop, handle the bills. Everything. I don't know what I would've done without them. He'd apologized for leaving before but his actions spoke louder than words. But I still get angry sometimes."

"Over Journey."

I nodded. "He ignored her symptoms for a while. Same as with my mother, but he's coming around to accepting the reality of her diagnosis."

"You were there for your little sister. I wasn't there for Luke. Not the way he needed me to be. I graduated high school at sixteen and went to college, leaving him behind. I wouldn't have survived another moment in that fucking house." The guilt written all over his face was crushing.

"Jacob." I leaned forward, gripping his hands tighter. "What were you supposed to do? You were a child. A scared child of a very sick and demented woman."

He grunted and looked over my shoulder.

There was more to this story. More to his guilt than he wasn't letting on. However, I wouldn't push it.

"You look tired." I ran my hand down the side of his face. His eyelids hung heavy. "Lay down."

I would've gone to cover him with a blanket or sheet, but none were present, just like the last time I was at his home.

Their absence didn't seem to bother Jacob, as he curled an arm around one of his pillows and laid on his side.

"I'll head out."

My departure was stopped by his arm gripping my wrist. "Stay."

"Are you sure?"

He didn't answer with words. Instead, his strong arm tugged me back down to the bed.

He pulled me into his side and wrapped his arm around me, eliminating any space between our bodies. Even if there were a blanket, I doubted I'd need it considering the warmth of Jacob's body so close to mine, warming me to the core. I listened carefully as his breathing eventually slowed into a rhythm alerting me that he'd fallen asleep. I closed my eyes and gave over to sleep soon after.

CHAPTER 19

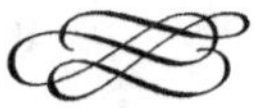

race

"That was beautiful stitch work you did on the procedure the other day, Dr. Reynolds."

I stopped myself from grimacing at the sound of Suzanne's voice as I rounded the corner. Unfortunately, I wasn't skilled at schooling my face when displeased. The grimace returned full force. Suzanne was standing less than a foot away from Jacob, staring up into his face, in the middle of the hallway.

"I was thinking I could assist you sometime soon on your next ca—"

"That won't be necessary."

She jumped when Jacob and I both spoke at once. I watched her dark brown eyes narrow, but then the crease in her forehead smoothed out as she forced a smile. "Grace, I didn't know you were there."

"I bet you didn't. Anyway, I think Beth's trying to find you," I said, referencing the charge nurse who'd just taken over for our shift.

"Guess I should go see what she wants."

"Probably." I stared at her until she passed me and strolled down the hallway.

174

I turned back to Jacob who was watching me with a twinkle in his eyes.

"She was standing too close."

He didn't respond; instead, he glanced over my head as if spying to see if anyone was around. I went to ask what he was looking for when suddenly his arm wrapped around my waist and he pulled me through the door we stood next to. The movement was so quick and unexpected, that it took me a couple of breaths to realize that he'd pulled me into one of the empty patient rooms.

His lips collapsed into mine and I hummed against his mouth, sighing at the kiss.

"I didn't get a chance to do that this morning," his deep voice said once he pulled back from the kiss.

"I had to come in early," I explained why I had to leave his place before he even woke up that morning.

"Next time, wake me up," he growled before covering my lips once more.

Unfortunately, again the kiss ended too abruptly when my cell phone buzzed. I jumped and quickly pulled it out to see yet another alert from my doctor's office reminding me of my appointment.

"I have to go do rounds," I stated.

Jacob's eyes lifted and he nodded. "Same. Dinner, tonight?"

I nodded and headed out as he held the door open. It'd been a full week since the night of the fight, and while he and I had grown closer, I got the sense that there was so much more bubbling beneath the surface. Seeing his father and brother within the span of a few days couldn't have been easy. No matter how much he tried to say that it didn't matter to him, I knew that it bothered him. He wasn't over whatever happened to him in those dark days of his childhood and adolescence. It was evident but he wasn't ready to open up about it either.

"Grace, you still have to leave at one-thirty, right?" Beth questioned, interrupting my thoughts as I moved behind the nurses' station.

I nodded. "Yeah, why? Do you need me to stay?"

"No." Beth shook her head. "Suzanne will cover the surgery with Dr. Ross, and I think we're all clear this afternoon. You'll be back by three?"

"I should be." My stomach turned as nervousness seized me. Hopefully, I would be back that afternoon after my appointment with nothing else on my mind. Lifting my head from the computer screen I'd been staring at, I found Suzanne's eyes locked on me.

She quickly averted her gaze, but the feeling in the pit of my stomach sent off alarm bells, telling me she was trouble. I didn't have time to give it too much thought when she stood up and made an announcement about going to prep her patient for surgery. Ignoring her, I finished inputting some information into the computer, before checking on a couple of patients and then heading out for my appointment.

* * *

My palms were sweaty, and I ran them up and down my thighs, using the material of the scrubs I still wore to dry them off. I glanced up at the clock on the wall to see the minute hand had only moved from one black line to the next, telling me only a minute had passed since the last time I stared at it.

Ugh! my brain shouted internally. I stood up and began pacing the waiting office. There were about five other people waiting as well, one whose face was pale as a ghost. She had no eyebrows and wore a yellow bandana around her head; she looked frail. I tried hard to avoid her, but my eyes kept going to her and the man who sat behind her. My gaze drifted lower, to spot the wedding ring on his left ring finger. Hers was bare, but upon closer examination, I could see her rings hung from a chain around her neck. Her fingers probably had become so thin they no longer fit properly.

I glanced down at my own hands, remembering how thin they had gotten while I underwent chemo. My heart squeezed as I painfully remembered back to that time. These annual checkups always brought out this fear again. But as I went to squeeze my hand into a tight fist, another masculine hand stopped mine.

Gasping, I lifted my head, and my gaze crashed into those grey eyes. An immediate calm filled my body even as my eyebrows wrinkled in confusion.

"What're you doing here?"

"You came into work early this morning, you had a two o'clock meeting, and I spotted the reminder text message confirming your appointment with Dr. Mitchell, one of the top oncologists in the city."

I narrowed my eyes on him and let out a small smirk. "You were spying on my messages."

He shrugged. "You spied on my birthday. Turnabout is fair play."

The lump in my throat prevented me from responding verbally. I was left with squeezing his hand in mine to display my gratitude that he took the time to show up even when I hadn't asked.

"Is this for your yearly checkup, or do you suspect …" He wouldn't or couldn't finish the question but I knew where he was going.

"Yearly checkup."

Releasing a breath, his shoulders relaxed a little. "You should've told me." His voice deepened and gaze was intent.

I frowned. "I'm used to doing this alone."

He shook his head. "That's not the way this works anymore." His hand tightened around mine.

I still wasn't used to letting others take care of me.

"Thank you," I whispered past the lump in my throat.

"Grace Young."

I turned and nodded at the receptionist who waited at the door to show me down the hall to Dr. Mitchell's office.

I looked back to Jacob.

"I'll be right here when you get out."

"But you have a me—"

"I'll be here when you get out," he stated again, more firmly. "Oh," he began while cupping my chin in his hand, "and don't think we're not going to discuss why you chose not to clue me in on this appointment in the first place."

I ducked my head to hide my grin and pushed up on my tiptoes to press a kiss to his cheek, before pivoting on my heels to follow the receptionist down the hall. As I walked down the hall with my chin lifted, I realized that the fear had lessened. It was still there, but even more palpable was the knowledge that I had gone and thoroughly fallen head over heels in love with the man who'd shown up for me, just to wait and hold my hand when I hadn't even asked him to.

"I do think that's the first time I've seen you walk into my office smiling," Dr. Mitchell mentioned as I entered her office.

Dipping my head, I tried to cover the smile I wasn't even aware of as I moved to sit in the armchair across from her shiny wooden desk. "I'm sure the day you officially gave me the news I was in remission, I wore a smile."

Dr. Mitchell nodded, the long dreadlocks she wore in a high ponytail shifting as she did so. "You had a smile *leaving* my office, not upon entering. And that one was more of a tentative grin, rather than the full-on, happy to be alive glow you've got going on. If I didn't know any better, I would suspect that you're in love."

My eyebrows rose and eyes enlarged. "Dr. Mitchell, I thought you were an oncologist not a psychiatrist," I teased.

She giggled. "You know I did consider psychiatry as a specialty early on in medical school, but ultimately chose oncology."

I shook my head. "Maybe that's evidence that you *needed* a shrink instead of becoming one."

She let out a laugh that was so infectious I began giggling myself. One of the things I appreciated about her was her sense of humor. She was undoubtedly one of the best in her field, but she had a way of making her patients feel at ease. At least, that's how I always felt around her, and I'd heard many others say the same. And considering the work she did day in and day out, that was no easy task. I wondered how she kept her spirits high when faced with so much disease and pain. But I didn't ask that, I was in too good a mood.

"So, Dr. Mitchell, I hope you have some good news for me," I said once she ceased laughing.

Dr. Mitchell nodded and opened the folder that was in front of her. Her dark brown eyes shifted downward, and she read over the results of the examination and blood work I'd taken as soon as I arrived in the office, about thirty minutes prior.

When she lifted her head with a smile on her face the remaining tension I'd been feeling dissipated.

"Looks good."

Dr. Mitchell kept talking but I didn't hear anything after those two words. I didn't need to. All I knew was that I remained cancer free and the man I loved continued to wait for me in the lobby of Dr. Mitchell's office as I left.

Stepping over the threshold of the door that separated the lobby from the back office and exam rooms of Dr. Mitchell's office, my eyes immediately scanned for Jacob. He didn't waste any time when he lifted his head from his cell phone and saw me standing there. He rose and met me at the door, his lips landing on mine.

"Looks good." I was barely able to choke out the words.

His lips parted. "Celebration dinner tonight."

I nodded and let him lead the way out of the doctor's office.

CHAPTER 20

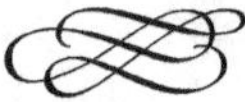

*J*acob

I'm not particularly prone to fear. My profession is to cut people open for a living, fix whatever is ailing them, sew them back together again, and to let their bodies take over the rest of the healing process. I was good … fuck that, *great* at my job and only getting better with time, age, and experience.

I grew up in a manner in which fear was just a part of my daily life. You either let it overwhelm you and take you out, or you made the daily choice to live through it, survive anyway you could until you were able to get out.

I could go up against an opponent twice my size in a cage-style fighting ring without an ounce of fear over what will happen to me, or even the potential harm it could bring to my professional goals.

I say all of this because it truly astounded me the fear that rose up in my gut when I spotted the text from Dr. Mitchell's office on Grace's phone. I knew Dr. Mitchell to be a top-notch oncologist in Williamsport. I'd even operated on a few of her patients who had mastectomies and other procedures as part of their cancer battles. What frightened me even more was the fact that Grace hadn't brought her appointment up.

Sure, I was well aware of the fact that even patients in remission had to have annual appointments with their oncologists as a precaution. However, logic and even my extensive medical knowledge didn't suffice in the face of my fear, that perhaps Grace's cancer had returned. That fear had threatened to strip all of my common sense and ability to think straight, which was already growing questionable in the face of recent events.

I still wasn't over my father being so fucking close to me, or seeing Luke a few weeks ago. And though my father remained out of my hair for the most part, as his team did whatever the hell they were doing, I still knew he was around. I could still feel his eyes watching me whenever I passed him in the hallway. The dumb fuck was waiting it out, hoping that I'd come to my senses and want to be a part of his life. To ask him how his wife was doing and go see her. It'd be a cold day in hell before that happened.

"What are you thinking about?"

I was yanked from my thoughts by Grace's question. I peered across the table, the pungent scent of the Indian food spread out in front of us rising to my nose but not detracting from the gut punch that struck me every time I looked at Grace's smile. Those dimples were deep enough for me to fall into. And, who the hell had I become?

"I'm thinking we should've taken this food to go because you're wearing too many clothes right now." I didn't even blink as I told her the truth, my hand moving across the table, covering hers.

Her head dipped and I remembered how when I first laid eyes on her and that lifted chin as she stared me down, without the slightest bit of intimidation, I would've never guessed she could appear this demure. And, unlike what I found with some other women, it wasn't a put on.

"We're celebrating."

"Goddamn right we are, and I'm even more anxious to get home and celebrate with my di—"

"Dr. Reynolds and Grace, how nice it is to see you here."

My frown was instantaneous as the annoying and familiar voice of Suzanne interrupted me telling Grace all the ways I was looking forward to stripping her naked and celebrating the good news of her test scans, all night long.

I turned my head to the right, glaring at the woman smiling down on us expectantly. Her eyes were cast in my direction. I barely paid her a glance and let my gaze shift to her left. There was a man standing next to her.

"Suzanne," Grace responded. "How great to run into you tonight." She sounded about as grateful as I was at that moment.

"Isn't it? This is my brother, Glen," she introduced as if either one of us gave a fuck.

Again, I gave no reaction.

"He's only a few months shy of completing his RN degree. He wants to be a surgical nurse just like his older sister." She smiled at the man who had yet to speak. "Anyway, I told him about the opening at Memorial and that if he worked there, he would get the opportunity to work with world class surgeons such as yourself, Dr. Reynolds."

The conversation would've been annoying enough if Suzanne had left it at that. But at the very least, I would've easily dismissed and forgotten ever seeing her if she just walked off. But she didn't do that. No. The woman—and I'm using that term extremely loosely—had the audacity to lower her hand and run her fingertips along my bare fore-arm. I immediately pulled back my arm, anger rising in my stomach.

"Maybe you should keep your hands to yourself." Those tight words came from Grace, who responded before I got the chance to.

Suzanne seemed startled for a second as she looked between Grace and me. But it was a put on, the woman was pretending.

"My apologies, Jacob, I tend to be the affectionate type with every-one. Right, Glen?"

And for the first time, the man beside her spoke. "Yep. She's always been like that." Then he let out the most awkward laugh I'd ever heard.

"Enjoy your dinner. And it's Dr. Reynolds," I retorted, dismissing the both of them before turning my attention back to Grace, who appeared to be as annoyed as I felt.

Out of the corner of my eye, I watched as Suzanne hesitated but then tapped her brother with her elbow and made a jerking motion with her head. The two headed off in a different direction, where I didn't give a shit. As long as they were away from us.

"I think you were right."

I lifted an eyebrow.

"We definitely should've taken this to go. My mood to be alone with you has grown two-fold."

"It's not too late," I began at the same time I raised my arm to call our waiter over. "We'll be taking this to go."

Our young waiter nodded and left to retrieve the containers that we'd carry most of our uneaten meal in.

I pulled out my wallet and placed a few bills on the table before standing. "I'm going to run to the bathroom."

Grace nodded.

I wound my way through the dining area and down the hall to the bathrooms. I quickly handled my business and exited, only to meet up with Suzanne yet again, in the rather small hallway. And I knew this meeting hadn't been a chance encounter, either. I didn't say anything and started to move around her to get back to the only woman who mattered, but she wasn't taking a hint.

"Jacob, I didn't mean to interrupt your meeting with Grace. I'm sure you two have some important work to discuss or whatever," she said, moving closer than necessary, "... seeing as how she's maneuvered her way into so many of your surgeries, but—"

"Let me stop you right there, Nurse Greene, because you seem to not be getting the picture. Grace, is the *only* woman from work who gets to call me by my first name. And I assure you, that what she and I have to *discuss* goes far beyond anything that may or may not happen in the OR." I stepped closer because I wanted to make myself crystal clear. "Let's get one thing straight from here on out. Anything that happens between Grace and I is none of your goddamned business. And just in case you had any sneaking suspicion, the answer is no, *hell no,* I wouldn't touch you with a ten-foot pole."

I moved past Suzanne, ensuring that no part of my body touched hers because the thought alone caused a sickening feeling to overcome me. She reminded me too much of another woman. One who was dying back in the state I'd left for good.

I did my best to tamp down on those feelings as I moved back to the table where Grace sat. Only when she turned and smiled up at me, placing her hand in mine, for us to leave, did the feeling begin to subside.

* * *

"Fuck!" I tilted my head back and cursed from the depths of my soul, as Grace continued to work me over with her mouth.

This woman was beyond amazing. She was unbelievable. Tonight's celebration was supposed to be about her. It was her victory that we were celebrating. Another year of being cancer free. But once we got back to her place, I couldn't keep my hands to myself. I forgot all about our uneaten dinner and tried to make her my dinner instead. And yet, she turned the tables on me.

She'd gotten on her knees in front of me and begged me to allow her the privilege of sucking me off. And with those brown eyes filled with need staring up at me, I wasn't strong enough to say no. I just wasn't. When she placed her hands behind her back, clasping them because she knew I still didn't like for anyone's hands to be near my dick, my knees almost gave out.

Now, I was standing in the middle of her bedroom, head pointed toward the ceiling gasping for air as I fed her my cock, and she took it all, more ravenously than any meal I'd watched her consume.

Grace was a caretaker through and through. Even when something was supposed to be for and about her, she found a way to take care of me. Case in point, the way she was sucking my soul through my cock. And I gladly gave it to her.

I looked down and placed both hands in the mass of curls she always wore down when we went out because she knew I liked it. My hips pressed in and out of her mouth in timing with the jerking motions of her head. My hold on her hair tightened when she moaned around my cock. My toes curled into the plush carpeting, the muscles of my backside tightened up, and before I could yell out a warning, I was gushing into her mouth, feeding her.

And my woman took it all.

"Aargh!" I roared as my come seeped into her mouth, spilling from me. That orgasm alone should've been enough, but it was far from it.

When I abruptly picked Grace up and placed her on her back on the bed, she yelped in surprise.

"You're going to injure yourself if you—"

Her protests were cut off by my mouth covering hers. Within seconds she gave up hopes of trying to reason with me into being careful and fell into the kiss. I broke away from her mouth and lowered myself, kissing down her neck, chest, and then what'd become my favorite spot on her body.

Her scars.

I kissed the mound of breast tissue her surgeon had left behind, along with the scar of where her nipple had once been. I felt the tension in her body ease with each kiss. She still wasn't a hundred percent comfortable with me touching this part of her, but she didn't stop me, and she grew more relaxed each time I did it.

I reveled in that spot on her body because it was the physical evidence of her being a survivor. But she was more than a survivor, she was a warrior. And as I slid inside of her body, unsheathed for the first time, ever, I delighted in the feeling of being fully skin to skin with her. Of how tight her muscles clamped down around me, and most of all of the way she reached for me, pulling me to her as she called my name.

"You feel so good," she crooned, her eyes reduced to slits, heavy with the weight of the passion and feeling of our lovemaking.

My own, were the two words that continued to run through my mind as I pistoned my hips, pulling out and then thrusting back into her body.

Two words I never imagined calling any woman. But here she was.

And while she writhed beneath me as the force of her orgasm rocketed through her body, I wondered just how long I could keep her before I fucked it all up.

CHAPTER 21

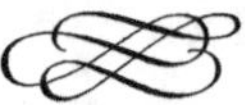

Jacob

"Come in," I called, not looking up from my computer screen which sat on the desk in my office.

"Did you hear Johnny Westbrook is being discharged today?" The smile was evident in Grace's voice.

I lifted my head. "You don't have to knock before you enter my office."

She frowned. "What if you were in with a patient?"

I shrugged. "They'd get over it."

Giggling, she shook her head.

A pang of regret hit me in the stomach because I missed the way her curls dance around her shoulders whenever she moved her head. But since we were at work, those curls were confined to a tight bun at the nape of her neck.

"I'm not going to just barge into your office. Anyway, did you hear what I said?"

I nodded and stood. "I was just finishing up some work so I could go and check on him before he left." I knew she'd be aware of the fact that Johnny was being released from the hospital today.

"His grafts are looking good. He's still in a lot of pain, though," she sighed.

"He will be for some time to come." *Probably years.*

I held the door open for her to pass through before exiting and closing the door behind me. We strolled down the hall together talking about a few other patients and a couple of surgeries I had coming up in the next few days.

"Dr. Jeffries has already pulled me for his hip surgery this afternoon."

"Goddamned carpenters," I grunted.

Grace giggled. "You know those carpenters aren't all that fond of plastics. They joke about you all doing butt lifts and whatever."

I rolled my eyes. "That's because those punks don't want to admit they don't have the finesse to create a butterfly stitch so perfect you wouldn't even know a scar was there, after it heals, or couldn't do a skin graft with so much grace that even the body swears it regrew the skin on it's own."

"So humble. But I'm guessing ortho would remind you that plastic surgeons such as yourself have never replaced a hip or a knee joint."

I frowned as we neared Johnny Westbrook's closed door. "I could've learned if I wanted to."

Grace's smile grew as she spun around to face me, placing her back against the door and her hand on the knob. "You absolutely could have. You could've done anything you set your mind to."

My nostrils flared and my hands tightened in the pockets of my lab coat because I'd be damned if I didn't want to mount this woman right there and then. Lucky for her, she turned and pushed the door open as she used her free hand to knock.

"Hi," she greeted Johnny, his father, and one of the boy's uncles. "Today's a big day," she sing-songed.

The boy in the bed let out a small smile. "I'm going home."

His father frowned. "Not quite home, just yet. First the rehab center."

And he would likely have to come back to the hospital for a few more surgeries before he could go home, but I didn't feel the need to add that bit of news to his happy mood.

"I know, Dad, but you said rehab is one step closer to going home, right?"

"He has a point," I interjected.

"See?" he said, looking between me and his father.

Most of the adults in the room let out a laugh at the boy one-upping his father. My lips even cracked a bit before I went about going through the release procedures with the family and answering any questions they might have.

"Dr. McCall will be in shortly to give you more information on what Johnny can expect at the rehab facility."

"Thank you, Dr. Reynolds." Johnny's father stood and made his way over, extending his free hand for me to shake. In the three months since the family's accident, Mr. Westbrook's leg had healed, so he was out of the cast, though his right arm was still in a sling.

"My pleasure," I told him, shaking his free hand.

"I think he's going to be all right," Grace sighed as we exited the room.

I didn't say anything because while Johnny's spirits were high now, he was only nine years old. I didn't want to imagine what the teenage years would be like for him as an adolescent with scars and burn marks over fifty percent of his body.

"You like kids?" I suddenly questioned as we both walked back down the hall to my office.

She seemed startled by the question as she pulled her lips in, forming a line. "Yeah, of course. They're pretty cool. More durable than adults, that's for sure. Someone twenty years older than Johnny in his same position would be having a much more difficult time with what he's coping with. Their healing process would've been slower, too. You know all the studies that say kids are just more resilient."

She stopped short, only a few feet from my office, checking her buzzing cell phone.

"Gotta go check on a patient and then I have to prep for surgery. See ya later." She scanned the hallway, making sure it was just the two of us before lifting on her tiptoes and kissing my lips.

I would've told her it didn't matter if the whole damn hospital was around, as long as I felt her lips on mine before she walked away, but I didn't get the chance because my own pager went off.

I checked the message that had been redirected to my cell phone and found that the patient I was consulting on another doctor with was on her way up, with Dr. Lyons in tow.

I placed by pager back on my hip and my cell on my desk and was just preparing to wait for both the patient and doctor when my door suddenly opened. Assuming it was Grace since she'd just left, and the person hadn't knocked, I turned with a half grin on my face.

"You're getting used to entering without kno—" I cut myself off when I saw when it wasn't Grace but a different nurse. "What the hell?"

"Hi," Suzanne purred, looking over her shoulder as she slid the door to my office closed.

"Nurse Greene, what do you want?"

"Oh come on, Jacob. Grace isn't around. You can drop the Nurse Greene crap." She moved closer and the gleam in her eyes told me she was serious and had no intention of stopping.

Her eyes were filled with lust and a primal drive to get what she wanted. If it had been coming from Grace, I would've welcomed it with open arms, but coming from Suzanne both angered and sickened me. It threw me back to a long time ago.

Before I could part my lips to tell her to get the hell out in a much less polite manner her hand was reaching for my cock.

"Oh my God, you're bigger than I thought."

I don't know if it was her hand on a part of my body that I hadn't even let Grace touch, the tone of her voice that was lined with both awe and a hint of laughter, or if it was the look of winning in her eyes that did it. Possibly all of these things combined.

But without a clear thought in my head, my mind snapped, every muscle in my body coiling with anger. My left hand darted out and clasped tightly around Suzanne's throat, squeezing it as I pinned her against my file cabinet.

I registered the moment her eyes turned from lust to sheer panic and fear. That turn made me squeeze tighter. I wanted to remove the life from her very body.

"Take your fucking hands off of me," I growled in a voice that was utterly foreign to me.

By that time Suzanne's hand had long ago dropped from my cock. She was now clawing at my wrist and hand, trying to get me to free her from my grasp.

"Dr. Reynolds, oh my God!" someone yelled behind me.

That snapped me back to reality and my grip fell from Suzanne who bent over, as she gasped for air.

"Oh my God!"

I turned to see two women, one of them Dr. Lyons, the colleague who paged me earlier, and the other woman her patient, I hastily assumed.

"What is happening?" Dr. Lyons, demanded.

"H-he tried to kill m-me. Help!" Suzanne replied, still gasping for air. "Call security."

"Dr. Reynolds?" Dr. Lyons questioned, looking to me, obviously for answers but I didn't have any to give.

"Get her the hell out of my office!" I yelled.

"I'm calling security," the woman with Dr. Lyons said. "If this is how he treats staff at this hospital there's no way he'll be operating on me."

I would've told the woman to go fuck herself, but words eluded me at the moment. I had nothing to say to anyone.

Even as Suzanne fled my office, tears streaming down her face and telling anyone who would listen that I'd attacked her, I said nothing. I even tried to replay the events over and over in my head but failed at that small task. I couldn't remember what happened. One minute I was standing there and the next I had my hand around her throat ready to kill her. I might've done it if Dr. Lyons and her patient hadn't entered the room.

"Dr. Reynolds, we're going to have to put you on immediate suspension until we can sort this thing out. We're going to have to ascertain whether or not the police should be brought into this matter to file criminal charges."

I barely heard the words of the hospital's top lawyer.

"Nurse Greene is very adamant that we fire you but I told her that cannot be done until a full investigation is made. With that said, this is not looking good for you, Dr. Reynolds. Considering there were two witnesses and you haven't said anything."

I glanced around the room, in which there were three other members of the hospital's legal team. We all sat around a huge, shiny conference table on the eighth floor of the hospital. From the window I could see down into the parking lot. I just needed to get outside of this damn hospital.

"Dr. Reynolds, where are you going? Do you have anything to say?"

I didn't answer as I strolled out of the door and down the hallway to the elevator. I punched the down button repeatedly until the damn thing arrived.

Stepping on, I was grateful that I had the presence of mind to grab my keys and my wallet from my office before heading up to the hospital's executive office suites.

I didn't say a word as I stepped off the elevator and passed through the double doors, exiting the hospital. I got in my car and started it up, not sure of where the hell I was going, but knowing I needed to get as far from this hospital as I could.

* * *

Grace

"You were great in there, Nurse Young," Dr. Jeffries stated as we exited the OR.

I smiled as I peeled the scrub cap from my head. "Thank you, Doctor."

The hip replacement surgery had gone on longer than expected due to some complications. Thankfully, Dr. Jeffries was able to stop the excess bleeding that had occurred, and we were able to get the patient stabilized enough to finish the surgery. Though, he would likely have a much longer recovery time than anticipated. I didn't envy Dr. Jeffries whose job it now was to go in and tell his patient what happened.

I watched as he strolled down the hall, the resident who aided in the surgery next to him. I had to admire surgeons for what they did. It took a hell of a lot of guts to literally pry another human being open with the confidence that you could fix whatever it was that ailed them.

I shook my head at the thought, rounding the corner to approach the nurses' station. Out of the corner of my eye I saw three nurses huddled together in a corner, but didn't think much of it. Gossiping at the nurses' station wasn't an uncommon occurrence. I took a seat at the desk to input some information into one of the computers.

"Did you hear what he did?" Lucy, another OR nurse, questioned, sounding outraged almost.

"He tried to kill her. I mean, we were only half joking when we called him Dr. Jackass but he has gone too far. He needs to be fired."

My ears perked up because I knew that was the name many of the nurses referred to Jacob as, although most hadn't called him that around me lately.

I turned in my chair because it'd become obvious they *wanted* me to overhear their gossiping.

"Who are you all talking about?" I tried to be polite about asking but there was some hostility apparent in my voice.

"You were in surgery when it happened."

I blinked at Lucy. "When what happened?" I hated when people tried to be cryptic for dramatic effect. "Just spit it out."

"Your boyfriend attacked Suzanne. He tried to strangle her."

"Lucky for her, Dr. Lyons and a patient walked in on him."

Rising, I began shaking my head in denial. "Someone's lying."

"It's the truth. There were witnesses, just like Angela said," Lucy interjected.

"What? Why would Jacob do something like that?"

"The same reason he's always so pissy to the rest of the staff and even patients."

"No, Jacob has never been abrasive toward a patient." A little or a lot standoffish, sure, but never abrasive or harmful.

"Not that we know of," Lucy scoffed, and I wanted to slap the shit out of her and that look off her damn face.

"Look, Grace, we know you like him or have been seeing him or whatever."

"That's none of your concern."

Angela blinked, shocked, but she shook it off. "Yeah, well, he attacked Suzanne and he's already been suspended for it. He'll likely lose his job and he'll be lucky if he stays out of jail."

"You're lying. Jacob wouldn't attack—"

"Oh yeah?"

I turned to see an angry and scowling Suzanne standing on the other side of the nurses' station.

"That monster attacked me in his office for no reason."

I shook my head as my body began trembling with anger.

"You don't believe me. Just look at my neck!" she yelled, snatching the silk scarf she tied around her neck off.

Gasping, I covered my mouth in horror when the red marks around her neck became obvious. The world stopped spinning for a few heartbeats, and all was silent as my mind tried to reconcile what it was seeing.

"Dr. Lyons walked in on him, and if she hadn't, he would've killed me. I was terrified for my life." Suzanne began sobbing.

Two of the nurses behind me brushed past me to move to comfort Suzanne, hugging her.

"He's a m-monster," she heaved at me through trembling lips. "You don't want to believe it because he's your boyfriend but he's danger-ous, Grace."

"I'm sorry, Grace." Lucy came up behind me, placing her hand on my shoulder.

I shook my shoulder free, turning to face her. "We don't know what happened in that room."

Lucy's eyes narrowed on me; obviously she couldn't believe that in the face of such mounting evidence I would even consider still defending Jacob.

"We do know that Suzanne has some obvious injuries, and that Dr. Lyons and a patient of hers all back up her claims. We know Dr. Reynolds is not the friendliest staff member on this floor. Look, I'm sorry but the facts don't lie. And his case isn't helped by him not saying anything."

I tilted my head. "What do you mean he hasn't said anything?"

"According to my friend who works as one of the administrative assistants in the legal department, Dr. Reynolds never even spoke when asked what happened. Never said what precipitated him attacking Suzanne. But he never denied it either. He just walked out of the office."

I wrinkled my forehead in utter confusion. "He left?"

Lucy nodded. "Without a word."

Turning, I gave Suzanne one final look as she proceeded down the hall, her shoulders shaking as she cried, being comforted by the two other nurses. I narrowed my gaze on her back. Something just didn't feel right. I'd never trusted Suzanne, and she was talking about the man that I'd fallen in love with. I would've automatically dismissed her claims as lies, but the red marks around her neck and eyewitnesses were two things I couldn't get passed.

"I'm sorry, Grace," Lucy said before passing me and heading down the hallway.

I stood there alone and trying to comprehend this situation. When I couldn't, I pulled out my cell phone and tried to call Jacob. His phone went straight to voicemail. I sent him a text asking where he was.

Glancing at the clock on the wall, I sighed realizing I still had an hour before my shift was over and a ton of more work to do that would likely take me well past that hour. I sent him another text telling him that I would get out of work past my scheduled time but that I'd head directly over to his place afterwards.

I didn't receive any message back, not that I expected to. Jacob was clearly in the wind.

CHAPTER 22

*J*acob

I stuffed my cell phone back into my pocket, barely letting the two text messages I received from Grace sink in. She'd be at my place once she got off work.

I won't be there, was the only coherent thought that came to mind. I couldn't face her. Out of everyone, she was the one person who I couldn't or just didn't want to look in the eye at this moment. That dirty feeling I'd had ever since Suzanne fucking touched me wouldn't let up throughout the day, even as I left the hospital and found myself drinking well into the early evening. I lost count of how many drinks I had.

And when the alcohol and the three showers I'd taken, scrubbing my body over and over until my skin was raw, didn't work, I found myself at the only place that I hoped could alleviate this feeling.

"Looking rough tonight, Doc," the guard noted as I passed through the doors of the Underground.

"Argh," I grunted and kept walking. I wasn't in the mood for talking. I was only here to hit or be hit. I didn't mind either one at this point.

"Buddy," I called, having to pause to get steady on my feet. It'd been a very long time since I drank as much alcohol as I'd consumed that day.

He turned to me and immediately frowned as he approached. Though it was dark in there, he glared at me as if he could see me clearly. "You're drunk."

I scowled. "I'm sober." Not the truth but not a total lie either. "I don't need an addictions' counselor either," I growled. "I just need a fight."

I peered over his shoulder to scout the rest of the room. There were two guys in the ring with some guy I didn't know taking Buddy's usual place as referee. I could feel Buddy's gaze still studying me but I didn't say anything. Wasn't about to give a further explanation beyond what it was I needed.

"You'll be up next. There's a new guy in town. Maybe you can show him around the block."

I quickly nodded at Buddy, acknowledging his words, and then move passed him to the door leading to the changing room. I changed out of the sweatpants and T-shirt and put on the shorts I typically fought in, and proceeded to wrap my hands, only to spot a pair of large hands reaching for mine.

"Don't touch me!" I snatched my hands free and looked up to see a scowling Connor peering down at me.

"You need your fucking hands wrapped," he insisted.

Reluctantly, I let him continue wrapping my hands tightly in my own wraps.

His face was contorted as if he wrestling with what to say.

"Just don't fucking kill anyone tonight."

How he knew I was in the mood to kill, I had no idea, but I didn't say anything. I heard the door open and glanced over Connor's shoulder to see Buddy standing at the door.

"You ready?"

I nodded and flexed my hands, feeling out the wrap job Connor had done. I didn't say anything to him but I could feel his glare on my back as I passed through the door. As soon as I entered the ring, the palpable energy that'd been coursing through me since I left the hospital earlier, increased. It was as if the room shrank in size, down to nothing besides that sixteen by sixteen foot square.

The cheers and applause of the guys standing around watching, anticipating, melted away. I looked past Buddy to the corner of the room and found a guy who I didn't know peering back at me.

"Doc, this is Chuck. Chuck, Doc," Buddy introduced, getting in the middle of us.

Chuck. The hell kind of name is that?

I grunted by way of introduction and *Chuck* did the same.

"All right, you both know the rules." Buddy lifted his arm and lowered it, a little bell went off, and Buddy jumped out of the way, as Chuck and I began circling one another.

"You sure your delicate surgeon hands can handle this?" he snarled.

I rolled my eyes. *This guy's a fucking talker.* I hated talkers. All the new guys started out as talkers, until they got popped in the face. Yeah, hitting in the face wasn't *supposed* to be allowed, but every now and then the situation required it.

"Ow, shit!" Chuck cursed right after I chin checked him with a left jab. "No hitting in the fucking face."

"Go cry about it, you little bitch!" I lunged at him but missed as he jumped back, avoiding the right hook aimed at his ribs.

"Haha! The only bitch around is the one who gave birth to you!"

As soon as his words registered it was as if my entire body went numb. I didn't hear, feel, or see anything but red and his face. My memory flashed to earlier that day of Suzanne grabbing me in my office, and then just to fuck me over some more, it happened. My brain flashed back to another pair of hands reaching under the sheets of my bed when I was just thirteen years old.

"This is just our little secret ..." the owner of those hands repeated.

I blinked and I was thrown back to that time, more than twenty years ago, but this time I fought. I punched and kicked and yelled as I rained blow after blow, desperately seeking to get those fucking hands off of me. But they wouldn't budge. The harder I fought the tighter and tighter her hold became over me.

"Doc! Doc!"

"Get off of him, man!"

The hands felt tighter and tighter around my body, which forced me to continue to fight more aggressively to free myself.

"Let him go. Shit!"

"Jacob, stop!"

It was the last voice that finally pulled me out of my trance.

Grace.

I looked up and blinked, my eyes colliding with her brown orbs. My chest immediately panged with guilt, shame, and worry because her eyes were filled with such fear. She was standing only about a foot away from me. I went to reach for her and that's when I saw a pair of hands pulling her away.

"Grace, you shouldn't be in here," a vaguely familiar voice called to her.

"Don't touch her!" I growled and began lunging toward whoever it was that thought they could take her away from me. Could put their fucking hands on her. I tried to lunge but was held back by someone.

"Doc, calm—"

"Fuck you." Turning, I swung on whoever the hell was trying to hold me back. And then I continued swinging, not seeing anything or anyone. My fists made frequent contact, but it wasn't until a sharp pain radiated through my hand that I slowed down. Strong arms enveloped me from behind.

"Doc, calm the fuck down!" Connor growled.

The pain had made me coherent enough that I could discern whose voice was speaking. I blinked and scanned the room with my gaze. There were at least ten pairs of eyes on me, staring, befuddled. I pushed out of Connor's hold, stumbling and looking back, realizing that somehow I made my way out of the ring and was halfway through the audience. I swallowed and stared down at my throbbing hand. It took some time for me to realize that my right hand pinky was sitting in a very awkward manner.

"He's hurt."

Grace.

I lifted my head from my hand to find Grace coming to kneel down in front of me, since I'd somehow sunken to the floor.

She took my injured hand into hers. "This is bad, Jacob. We have to get you to the hospital."

"Wh-What are you doing here?"

She looked up. "I came looking for you."

I sealed my lips shut because I didn't know how to respond to that. Why would she come looking for me?

Nothing was making any sense, and the constant buzzing sound in my head was growing louder and louder.

"He needs a doctor." I heard Grace say.

"He *is* a doctor."

"He needs an ortho doctor. I'm pretty sure his finger is broken."

"Is he catatonic?"

Is that Joshua?

"I've never seen him get that fucking crazy before." *That has to be Damon.* I was pretty sure it was, but the damn buzzing just continued getting louder and louder.

I squeezed my eyes shut and hit my forehead with the palm of my left hand, trying to make it stop, but it wouldn't. Even worse, were those fucking hands kept coming back, grabbing at me. Moving underneath the sheets and touching at me.

"We'll take him to Memorial."

"No! He works there. He won't want to go there. I'll take him to Central. I used to work there. I know them."

Someone or something began lifting me up. I tried to push it away but felt too weak and too heavy to do much good.

"Jacob, we're taking you to get your hand checked out."

Grace.

Her voice was the perfect embodiment of her name. It made the buzzing sound dull just enough that could feel like I wasn't completely losing my damned mind. When she talked the hands went away, too.

"Keep talking," I heard a far off voice say but the words had come from my mouth.

"What do you want me to say?"

"Anything. Just keep talking, please." I loathed the sound of my own voice. It sounded so fucking weak and tired.

"Um, I hope you're happy that I missed my swim workout for you. I stopped by your condo first and didn't find your car. I was going to go up but I knew you wouldn't be there …" She kept talking as the cool, night air grazed against my sweaty body.

We were outside.

Someone was leading me, holding me up, as we moved farther and farther away from wherever we'd been. But I couldn't figure out where we were going. All I knew was that I needed to continue following the sound of her voice. It was like a siren call. As long as it kept going, I would follow.

"We're going to the hospital, Jacob. I'll take you to Central. I know the staff there, okay?"

Was it a question?

It might've been a question but I had no answer to give.

* * *

"How bad is it, Mark?"

I blinked and looked around the room. I was in an exam room. Peering down, I saw that I was dressed in a hospital gown. I was the patient and not the doctor.

That was when I did a double take. The room had all the markers of a typical exam room in an emergency department, but this wasn't Memorial. We weren't at the hospital I worked at.

"Grace, you know I can't tell you."

"I know the rules, Mark, but please, just this once."

"Look, I'll go in there and ask him if it's okay that you see his records."

"But he's—" Grace and whoever this Mark character was she was talking to, startled when I abruptly pulled back the curtain of the exam room, staring at the both of them.

"Jacob."

I turned to Grace and saw the fear and hesitancy in her eyes.

"Why am I in a hospital gown? And why—" I went to hold up my right hand and that's when pain radiated up my arm and down the whole right side of my body.

"Jacob," Grace called as she moved to my side, helping me back to the gurney I'd hopped off of in the first place.

"What the hell am I doing here?"

Grace looked at me with a pained expression, before glancing over at the guy she called Mark. I recognized the green scrubs and lab coat, marking him a doctor.

"You don't remember anything?" Grace's voice was soft. Too soft. The kind of genteel she used with patients in anguish or young children who were frightened in the hospital. It wasn't the type of voice she used with me.

"Why are you talking to me like that?" I insisted. "Were we in an accident?"

Blinking, she shook her head. "Jacob, your pinky is pretty badly broken."

I glanced down at my right hand, seeing my finger in a splint. I squinted because for the fucking life of me I couldn't remember how it happened. And that's when I started to feel the physical pain even more. It was as if my body took that exact moment to remind me that whatever I went through it'd been hell.

Using my uninjured hand, I pulled free from the hospital robe I wore. I glared, stunned at the red and purple bruises that'd begun forming.

"Did I go to the Underground?" I questioned, not even peering up.

"Yes."

I moved my gaze from my body to Grace but I couldn't look at her for too long. Something in the solemn way she was staring at me, almost as if she felt sorry for me, pissed me off.

My gaze moved past her to the doctor. The one she called by his first name. "How bad is my finger, *Mark?*" I snarled because I hated how close he was standing to Grace.

He blinked and looked to her and then to me.

"Am I your patient or is she?" I growled, feeling angry because I couldn't remember how the hell I'd gotten here, and because I loathed the feeling of being treated like a damn child. I didn't need caution. Just tell it to me straight.

"Jacob—"

I lifted an eyebrow. "Dr. Reynolds," I corrected.

He frowned and cleared his throat, his dark brown eyes darting to Grace again. Thankfully, she didn't say anything.

"Dr. Reynolds, we don't know the extent of your injuries just yet because we haven't been able to conduct an X-ray. You were, uh, pretty agitated when you arrived here at the hospital."

I looked him up and down, first sizing him up, it was an instinctive reaction. And secondly, I wanted to see if he had any injuries that maybe I caused. I didn't notice anything.

"I suspect you have a fracture of the metacarpal bone of the fifth finger."

"A boxer's fracture."

He nodded.

I looked down at my swollen hand and had essentially the same diagnosis. In other words, I fractured my pinky knuckle, commonly referred to as boxer's fracture because it was often the result of punching an immovable object such as a wall or a person's jaw.

Blinking, I tried to force my mind to remember what the hell had happened. I squinted as I remembered climbing into the ring with some new guy and Buddy giving the directions as usual before the fight, then everything goes dark. Except, that nauseous feeling welled up in the pit of my stomach and I felt hands touching me.

"Don't touch me!" I snarled and yanked my body away, causing the table with the medical supplies sitting on it to go flying through the air, making a loud banging sound as the bowl hit the ground.

I jumped down from the exam table, my legs feeling shaky ... so much so that I nearly toppled over.

"Jacob, it's okay. Mark just wanted to take you to get some X-rays so he can diagnose the extent of your injury."

Grace's voice had a soothing affect on my nerves.

I turned to her and our eyes collide. All I saw was worry and fear in the depths of those brown pools.

Again, I had to turn away from her to the only other person in the room.

"Fine," I grunted. "Let's get the X-rays."

He swallowed and nodded before leaving the room without another word.

There was silence for a long while before Grace spoke up. "Jacob …" She didn't finish because too soon *Mark* was back with an X-ray tech and the huge machine I'm very familiar with.

"Dr. Reynolds, we're going to need you to—"

"I know how this works," I cut him off, feeling impatient because they were treating me with kid gloves.

"Grace, I need you to step outside of the room."

Grace's eyes moved to me for reassurance and I nodded. She gave me a final look before turning and exiting the room.

I watched as Mark and the technician went through the motions of setting up the X-ray equipment, and I positioned myself on the gurney so that my hand would rest on the square for the correct image. It hurt like hell just laying my hand in the flat position. As the pictures were taken, Mark talked about some bullshit that I already knew but I didn't bother stopping him. All I kept thinking about was the possibility of bone fragments having broken off and needing to be repaired surgically. That would put me out of the OR for months likely, and then there was a chance that the bone would never heal properly, possibly ending my career as I knew it.

I knew you were a screw up!

Squeezing my eyes tightly, I shook my head as the sounds of my mother's voice echoed in my head.

"Dr. Reynolds, are you all right?"

"Are you fucking done yet?" I snapped.

"Y-Yeah, we're done. We should have the images for you soon," the frightened X-ray tech answered before looking to the other guy, and then quickly setting up the machine to push back out of the room.

"I'm not having surgery here," I stated, hopping off the gurney and searching for my clothes. There were better orthopedic surgeons at Memorial. If I was going to let anyone operate on me, it would be one of them.

"Dr. Reynolds, where are you going? We haven't confirmed your injury yet."

That was when Grace stepped back inside the curtain, her eyes growing wide as she watched me struggle to pull the T-shirt I must've worn here over my head.

"Jacob, what are you doing?"

"Leaving," I grunted out, due to a combination of the pain in my body and anger.

"You can't go, you haven't even gotten the results of your X-rays back yet."

"I don't need– Shit!" I cursed from having stubbed my damn toe on the side of the bed. I hadn't even realized I was barefoot.

"Jacob, calm down, please."

"I'm not letting them operate on me. My chances will be better at Memorial," I demanded, searching out my shoes.

"We don't even know if you need surgery. Let's just take this one step at a time."

"And stop using that fucking tone with me!" I snarled at Grace, causing her to stiffen in shock. "I'm not your patient. I'm your—" Pausing, I looked around the room before my eyes fell back on Grace. "I'm not your patient."

Her watery eyes blinked and she shook her head. "No, you're not my patient. I'm sorry."

Her apology calmed the raging bull that'd been awakened inside of me, even for just a little bit. Unfortunately, I was starting to discern that whatever had been awakened inside of me that day, wouldn't be put to sleep so easily. My brain still wasn't letting me remember the entirety of that day. Just pieces and glimpses. Deep down, I knew something had gone terribly wrong, however. I had a strong sense of my world being off its axis, and I couldn't shake it. That coupled with the possibility of a career-ending injury and I felt like I was about to explode.

"Dr. Reynolds, your X-rays should be back any moment. Let's wait until we know what's going on with your hand before we make any decisions."

I frowned, wanting to tell this guy to fuck off. I hated his voice, the fact that Grace was on a first name basis with him, *and* that she'd brought me to him in the first place. It showed that she trusted him. I hated him for that. But I ignored him. I placed my attention on Grace, and even though she remained silent, her eyes pleaded with me to do as he requested.

"Fine."

CHAPTER 23

Jacob

She flinched.

Grace flinched when I raised my left hand to run my knuckles across her cheek. She blanched at movement from me, and seeing that was a pain I'd never felt before. We were sitting inside of my car, in my parking space in the garage attached to my building. Grace had driven us from the hospital.

I lowered my hand to my leg. "Are you afraid of me now?"

Grace turned her head to face me but didn't say anything.

Reaching over, I pulled my keys from the ignition, and pushed open the passenger side door, climbing out while also forcing myself to ignore the pain the movement caused in my hand and the rest of my body. My fourth and fifth fingers were in a cast that extended all the way down past my wrist, holding the broken fragments of my bone in place to heal.

I don't believe you'll need surgery ...

The words of the orthopedic surgeon that'd been called down to the emergency department, to give me his analysis on my injury, rang out in my head, as I headed in the direction of the elevator. My long strides got me to the elevator in less than a minute, but I could hear

Grace's frantic footsteps behind me. She was jogging to keep up with me.

I wanted to tell her to go away. All I kept seeing was the image of her flinching away from me in my car.

But just as I slipped inside of the elevator, to carry me up to my condo where I could shut out the rest of the world, she jumped in right behind me.

"What are you doing?" I questioned at the same time I pounded the button for the tenth floor with my new cast.

"Jacob, you're going to make your injury worse doing that."

"Stop babying me." My voice was low, but it bubbled over with rage. I wasn't angry at Grace but she was there, and she always had a way of bringing up emotions that I either never knew existed in me or I tried to suppress.

"I'm not babying you. I'm just concerned."

"I don't need your concern."

The elevator dinged and I didn't wait for her to catch up as I exited and headed down the hall to my condo. But again, Grace was right on my heels and her insistence on following me kept the war inside of me going. Part of me wanted to pull her to me and never let her go, while the other kept replaying her flinching away from me, and wanted to push her away.

"What're you doing here, Grace?" I questioned, spinning on her as she shut and locked my door behind her.

"What do you mean, what am I doing here?" Folding her arms across her chest, she huffed, a wrinkle forming between her eyebrows. She was growing pissed, impatient with my attitude.

Good. Maybe that meant she'd leave on her own so I wouldn't have to push her away.

"I know what you're doing," she said, moving closer.

"And what would that be?" I cocked my head to the side. I would've folded my own arms across my chest but the throbbing in my hand and wrist stopped me from doing that.

"You're trying to push me away. Goading me so you think I'll leave. You might be nothing more than an ass to people who don't know you and who you can intimidate, but I'm not them." The final four words of her declarations were punctuated with a poke to my chest from her forefinger.

Truthfully, it would've been funny and sexy as hell, her anger, if I wasn't pissed off in my own right.

My nostrils flared and I remembered back to that fear in her eyes at the hospital. I shook my head. No. She needed to go. She didn't need to be around me. She didn't deserve to be around all of the fucked up shit going on in my head that was only bound to spill out one way or another.

"You need to leave."

"I'm not going anywhere?"

"Why?" I yelled and growled, slamming my left fist into my countertop.

Grace jumped, and that was the moment I thought would do it, but I should've known better. Grace was a hell of a lot braver than I was. She didn't run.

"I'm not leaving, Jacob."

"I want to be alone."

"Too damn bad."

Stubborn woman. It'd piss me off even more if it didn't actually turn me the hell on. It was incredibly ridiculous that as fucked up in the head as I felt in that moment, that the set look on Grace's face and the fact that she hadn't run screaming from my craziness, made my cock come alive.

But I continued to push. "You already admitted to being afraid of me." I took a step closer, and then another, forcing her to retreat backwards.

"I never said I was afraid of you."

"You flinched, in the car. And you didn't answer me when I asked."

"I'm not afraid of you," she said though her lips trembled.

I placed my hands up on the wall behind her, bracketing her body between it and my own. "Then what are you?"

"I'm afraid *for* you, you crazy son of a bitch!"

I frowned, and the tightening in my stomach muscles increased.

My cock began to feel heavy as it strained to get closer to her entrance. I lowered my gaze and realized she still wore her electric blue scrubs. She must've come looking for me right after her shift ended.

Lowering my left hand to her left breast, I pinched her nipple through the material of her scrubs and bra. She let out a strained whimper.

"Y-You're in trouble at w-work …"

I barely heard what she said. The time for talking was over. My mouth seized hers. I roughly bumped my hips against her body, letting her feel my hardness, how much I fucking wanted her right then. I pinched her nipple again, harder this time, and the painful, guttural, wanting moan she let out into my mouth made me rock hard in an instant.

Again, my mind went fuzzy, but this time instead of seeing red and anger, all I felt was need, a desperate need to remove the clothing separating us.

The pain in my hand and body subsided as I fought to pull Grace free from the scrubs that contained everything I wanted to see. I roughly yanked and tugged at the black bra she wore underneath her scrubs, freeing her body from its shackles. Before her bra could even hit the floor, I was undoing the drawstring of her pants and frantically pulling them down over her hips.

"J-Jacob!" she gasped when my free hand went to squeeze the globe of her ass.

"I can smell you," I growled into her neck. She was just as turned on as I was.

Sinking to my knees, I pressed my face against the curly hairs of her mound, and inhaled deeply. She smelled like heaven. A forbidden oasis that somehow, someway I'd been invited into. I wasn't about to turn down the opportunity.

I still couldn't remember everything that happened that day, but I knew it wasn't good. Grace's face, her cautionary words, and the feeling in the pit of my stomach told me the shit wasn't good. But as I spread Grace's thighs apart, lifting one of them over my left shoulder, and using the thumb and forefinger of my right hand to spread her pussy lips open to me, I didn't give a damn about whatever had happened that day. All I cared about was lapping at Grace's pussy.

The first swipe of my tongue had Grace's head lolling backwards against the wall and her hips pushing outward to meet my tongue again. I wouldn't let her down, as I went in for more. The taste and smell surrounding me encouraged my hunger, and it grew heavier and heavier. It was as if the more I consumed of her, the more my body craved her. There was no satiating me.

"Jacob!" she yelled after she came the first time.

But that was hardly a drop in the bucket for me. I needed more. I continued lapping at her pussy. Letting my tongue glide over and over her clitoris, seeking out more and more pleasure from her body. I ignored the ache in my cock that demanded I drive myself into her.

The mewls and screams coming from Grace's mouth were enough to keep my hunger building. When she began trembling again before clenching her thighs, I felt her second orgasm rain down on my tongue. I feasted on her body as if there were no tomorrow.

I couldn't even wait until the shivers from her second orgasm disappeared before I was lifting her by the knees, wrapping her legs around my hips and carrying her to my bedroom. I ignored the pain in my right hand that shot up my arm because my need for her was much stronger than the discomfort.

"Jacob, w-we should t-talk," she tried to stumble out.

"Less talking, more fucking," I grunted at the same time I dropped her on her back on my bed.

Grace hesitated, her right hand instinctively going to the right side of her chest, covering over her scars.

"Move your hand, Grace." My voice sounded so dark, I barely recognized it.

She was still hesitant about her scars. The same ones that I adored on her.

"Move. Your. Hand."

Slowly her hand fell away.

"Spread your legs," I demanded as I stood over my bare bed with an equally naked Grace laying on top of it.

Her knees fell apart and her beautiful, brown pussy was bared to me.

I fisted my cock in my hand, not even remembering when I'd removed my own clothing.

"Open her to me. I want to see her."

She bit her bottom lip and the sight was almost painful. Those brown pools of hers spoke of her hesitance, her internal war. She wanted to talk. Wanted to hash out whatever the hell was going on in my head. But she also wanted to fuck.

To make her decision easier, I leaned down and pinched her nipple again, and then bent lower, running my tongue along the scar on the right side of her chest.

She gasped and her back bowed, pushing up deeper into my mouth.

"Now show me," I growled, lifting myself to stand again, to get a better view of all of her.

She did as told and used the first and second fingers of her right hand to spread herself wide for me.

I rubbed the drop of precum that'd emerged over the tip of my cock, gritting my teeth at the sensations that coursed through my veins at the sight of Grace so open and ready for me. I went to my knees on the mattress, moving in between her legs. I inhaled sharply when my cock bumped up against her entrance. Grace's mouth formed an "O" and I had to lean down to kiss her mouth.

Her head lifted to meet mine, and as soon as our lips touched, I pushed myself deep inside of her. I wanted to feel every inch of her muscles brushing up against and hugging my cock. She moaned into my mouth, and a shiver ran through my body, so profoundly, the entire bed shook. With my left hand I took her fingers in mine, intertwining ours, and moved her hand to the side, pushing her arm over her head.

I lifted my head, parting our lips so that I could see her more clearly, and I began hammering my hips into her. Her eyes squeezed shut, until I grunted and she opened them, allowing me to see everything she was feeling.

The awestruck look in her eyes that took place every time our bodies became one, along with her parted, kiss swollen lips, and the feel of her thighs against my hips, bouncing every time I pushed into her and pulled out, was almost too much for even me. But it was her gaze that kept me locked in. It pushed away all the heavy shit I'd been feeling up until the moment our lips touched. Whatever had happened earlier in the day didn't matter, whatever was going to happen after this didn't matter either. Just as long as I could keep peering down into those eyes, it was all I needed. It was more life saving than the oxygen I pulled in through my flared nostrils.

Grace's lips trembled and parted but no words were spoken. Every time it seemed as if she went to say something, I pushed harder, pounded deeper, and pulled her legs up higher, causing her to lose whatever words were on the tip of her tongue.

I felt like I could go on like this forever, like I wanted to go on forever. But there must've been a miscommunication between my brain and my body because the latter began to give out. Once Grace's pussy quivered around my thrusting shaft as a result of her third orgasm, the tingling in my toes started. The sensation moved up my legs and collided with the vibrations shooting down my spine.

The breath from my body ceased to exist, and with one final thrust and curse from my lips, I was coming.

My come spilled out of my shaft and coated Grace's womb as if it knew that was its home. Even after my initial release, I couldn't stop my thrusting hips, and with each thrust came another spurt of my come.

I couldn't remember how long it took for my body to finish its release, but safe to say it was longer than I'd ever experienced before. But even as I pulled free from Grace's body, my cock was still semierect. Just that quickly, it had renewed energy.

Peering down into Grace's half-closed eyes, I knew I wasn't done. She gasped when I flipped her body over and brought her up onto all fours. And just as quickly, I was pushing into her again and again.

It was a long while before I was finished and had wrung out at least two more orgasms from Grace. It wasn't until she literally begged for me to let her rest, pushing me off of her with her hand, that I set her free.

I stood on wobbly legs and moved to my bathroom, retrieving a washcloth to clean her. But not even a few minutes later, once I returned to the room, did I find Grace, laying, asleep, light snores pouring from her mouth on my bed. I used the washcloth on both of us before tossing it somewhere over the bed and then gathering her still sleeping form in my arms. It didn't take five minutes before the exhaustion of whatever had happened that day, plus the sex marathon we just engaged in, took over and I fell asleep.

* * *

THAT WASN'T THE ANSWER.

That lone thought is what jostled me out of a restless sleep hours later. I scanned the darkened room as soon as my eyes popped open. It was quiet but I could make out tiny snores to my left side.

Turning my head, I saw Grace, still sleeping, curled up on her left side, naked as the day she was born. And despite my mood and the numerous rounds we engaged in before falling asleep, when I let my eyes fall down over the rest of her body, my stomach clenched and tingling shot through my shaft, wanting her. But I refrained.

Instead, I got up and padded my way through the darkened bedroom, out to the hallway closet. Opening it, I pulled out the comforter I bought when I first purchased this condo, over two years ago. The damn thing still sat in its original packaging. Yanking it free, I made my way back into the bedroom and took care to cover Grace with the blanket, making sure not to disturb her.

The blackout curtains in my bedroom made it difficult to discern what time of the day it was. It could be pitch black outside or middle of the day, bright and sunny and I wouldn't know. I kept this room dark for a reason.

But as I took a step back and watched Grace, in her sleep, getting comfortable and adjusting to the warmth of the blanket, another one of those damn memories shot to mind. I found myself quickly exiting the bedroom, but not before throwing on a pair of boxer briefs, to head up the hallway. The first place I went for was the cabinet over my kitchen sink. I reached for the bottle of scotch but cursed and slammed the cabinet shut when I found the bottle was empty.

Absentmindedly, I slammed my hand into the counter, but too bad for me, it was my right hand.

"Fuck!" I grunted, looking down and remembering that I had a goddamned broken knuckle. But the pain also served to bring back the memories of the previous day. I blinked and turned toward the microwave that sat a top of the stove. The clock read 11:53 a.m.

I shook my head, wondering how the hell I could've slept so long. I vaguely remembered the clock reading something like 2:33 a.m. when we arrived back at my place, but I couldn't be too sure.

Finding my way to one of the stools that sat around my kitchen island, I sat in it and put my forehead into the palm of my hands, my elbows pressing against the counter. It was an awkward placement due to the cast but I didn't give a shit. Squeezing my eyes shut, flashes of the day and night before came back to me. I remembered coming home briefly, reaching for the bottle of scotch, and then heading out to a bar to drink when I finished that.

My mood was dark. Darker than usual. It was the type of mood that pushed me to the Underground for a fight. I remembered getting into the ring and fighting some guy I'd never seen before. He was a shit talker.

"The only bitch around here is the one who birthed you."

My breathing stalled at the remembrance of his words.

"... the one who birthed you."

My mother.

Then there were hands grabbing me, reaching underneath covers, and all I had left to do was fight. I recalled swinging wildly at any and everything. My fists made contact with skin and flesh, muscle and something hard.

"Jacob, stop!"

That was Grace's voice. She appeared out of nowhere, slowing me down. Then there were hands grabbing her, keeping her from me, and I kept going—hitting, clawing, and kicking whatever or whomever tried to stand in between me and her.

But what the hell sent me over the edge in the first place?

From what I could gather, I was fuming for hours before I got to the Underground. Something had ticked me off.

I pounded my fists against my forehead, hoping that would force my goddamn memory to work.

"He tried to kill me!" a feminine voice shrieked.

"Dr. Reynolds, we have to put you on suspension ..."

The words drove the memory alive for me. It all came rushing back to me. Me walking down the hall with Grace before she got called away. She kissed me and then left. I turned and smiled at her back because she put me in that type of mood. Then I was moving into my office waiting for another doctor to come up with her patient for a consult.

I looked over some forms with my back to the door. It opened and I turned, grinning because I assumed it was Grace again. It wasn't.

That's when the heat of my anger began to rise. *Suzanne.* The bitch wouldn't take a hint.

However, the memory that sent me shooting up off the stool was her hand reaching and grabbing me. I hated that feeling and I lunged at her, wrapping my hand around her neck. I had every intention of squeezing the life out of her. But something had kept me from doing so. Something kept me from crossing over to the dark side my mind was leading me to. And just before I could fully release her, my door sprang open.

The doctor and patient I'd been waiting on, moved inside and began hurling accusations my way. Suzanne, of course, cried and called for security.

I shook my head as the memory of the day before mingled with past memories. Ones I did my damndest to forget as soon as I moved out of that house. But the door had been opened, the gates wouldn't hold back the flood any longer, and it all came back to me.

The nausea that always came was even worse this time, and I ran to my kitchen sink and upchucked whatever food had been left over in the contents of my stomach from the day before. When my stomach had no more to give, my body continued to be wracked with spells of dry heaves as my mind kept playing the reel of my childhood and adolescence over and over again.

Anger mixed with fear and pain. The fear of a boy who was caught between being a child and a man. I pounded against the counter, slamming my hand against the kitchen countertops before moving to the stools in the kitchen.

Pure fury ran through my veins as I picked up the first stool and brought it down hard against the kitchen island. The sound of the wood breaking exhilarated me. It wasn't quite the same sound as bones breaking but it was close enough. I didn't even notice or pay attention to the splintered wood that fell to the floor as I picked up the next stool and brought it down against the floor this time around. It also splintered but didn't fully break apart. That was, until I brought my bare foot down against the wood, rendering the object useless against my wrath. Picking up one of the legs of the stool with my good hand, I swung it wildly at the contents that resided on my kitchen island.

The fruit bowl, salt and pepper shakers, and a few granite coasters were sent hurling to the ground. Somewhere around me I heard glass shattering but didn't stop my rampage to identify what it was. All I knew was that I was in the mood to break shit. It didn't matter to me that I was destroying my home. That I was breaking all the things that I'd built and bought through the hard work of my bare hands. In fact, that reminder forced me to look at my right hand in the cast and that caused my ire to grow even more. The knowledge that my career had been taken from me sent me spiraling even more.

"Jacob! Jacooob!" Grace's wails pierced through the veil of my rage. The violence I was inflicting on my own home halted as I caught sight of her wide eyes. Her breathing was heavy as she stood, warily, at the entrance of the hallway and living room. She was dressed in the dark T-shirt I'd worn the night before.

I stood there, chest heaving and sweaty, with one of the legs of my bar stools lifted over my head.

"What're you doing?" she questioned through trembling lips. And not the same trembling they did when my cock was deep inside of her.

I blinked my gaze away because I couldn't keep staring at her. Shame began to corrode my senses as I looked around at my destroyed condo. There was glass and broken wood all over the floor. Somehow, I'd made it from the kitchen to the living room, shattering the glass coffee table that sat between the black leather couches. I turned and almost flinched at the sight of my cracked flat screen dangling haphazardly by its cords from the wall.

I took a step but froze in place when Grace yelled, "Don't move! There's glass all around you. You'll cut your feet."

I swallowed and peered up at her, as she turned and raced back down the hallway. She was back before I even got time to ask where she was going or what she was doing. She moved toward me with my pair of slippers from underneath my bed. The pair I rarely ever wore. I briefly wondered how she knew they were even under there.

"Put these on," she directed, placing the black slippers on the floor in front of me.

I slid my feet into the slippers. There was silence as I continued to look around the room, assessing the damage I'd done.

"Jacob, tell me what's wrong. Why did you do this?"

I swallowed and turned back to Grace, shame invading every pore of my body. "Go home, Grace." My voice was so heavy with the burdens that sat on my shoulders, I had to struggle just to get the words out. I took a step and then another, carrying myself around her. I couldn't bear facing her right then.

"What?" she spun around and questioned.

"You should go home." As painful as it was to say those words, it was the truth. I should be alone.

"I'm not going—" Her retort became non-existent when I picked up another porcelain vase, one that had escaped my wrath the first time around, and slammed it to the floor. She jumped.

"Get the hell out!" I yelled. "I'm not one of your fucking patients!"

"Why do you keep saying that?"

"Because it's true! I'm not a fucking invalid. I don't need to be coddled and babied."

Her shoulders sank and the guilt began to weigh on me more than the shame. Together they both damn near crippled me.

"What do you need?"

"To be alone."

She shook her head. "Bullshit."

I turned my head from her because she was right. I was full of shit. I knew it and she knew it. But I still didn't have the words to express what I was feeling. What was going on inside of my head.

When I turned to face her again, she was closer, moving my way. Her eyes were intent as she captured my attention and held it.

"I'm not babying you or treating you like a patient when I tell you, you're full of shit, Jacob. You need help." She looked down and around at the disaster of my home before her gaze came back to me. "You're not well."

I knew her words to be the truth. Anyone with eyes could see that. Regardless, I wanted to deny them. To tell her I was fine and didn't need shit from anyone because what I needed in the past hadn't been granted to me. I'd sought and gotten all of my needs on my own since I was sixteen. If anything was wrong, I figured it out and didn't bother to stop and ask for help because help wasn't coming. And good riddance.

But standing there with Grace's penetrating gaze on me, I knew what she said was true. For once, I'd come to a precipice that I didn't know how to face. This one was higher than any I'd faced before, and the darkness of the bottom that stared back up overwhelmed me.

"G-Go home, Grace," I managed to choke out one final time, before sliding to the floor, propping my elbows on my knees and lowering my head.

I heard her footsteps as she retreated. They grew softer and softer as she padded her way down the hall to my bedroom. The distance between my body and hers allowed me to push out a breath, my shoulder slumping even farther. The weight of the world was still there, hanging as heavy as ever, but maybe I wouldn't have to burden Grace with it either. She didn't deserve that.

I didn't even look up when I heard her approaching again. But I felt her warmth as she moved closer. I felt her shadow descend over my body as she lowered herself to the floor, in front of me. And I felt the tips of her fingers when she reached through the hole in my arms, and lifted my chin, forcing our gazes to meet. She was dressed in her blue scrubs again.

I saw her coming in for the kiss before she even moved. The look in her eyes told me what she was planning to do. But it came so sudden, I didn't have time to catch it before she was pulled away. The whisper of a kiss ordinarily wouldn't have been enough. But my body and my burdens were too heavy to bring our lips back together again.

"Jacob," she began, just above a whisper, "I love you. I love you more than I ever thought I could love a man, and you need help. More help than I'm capable of giving. Don't hate me for what I've done."

I narrowed my eyes because hating her would never even cross my mind. *How could she even think—*

The pounding on my front door stopped my questioning.

Grace gave me a final, worried look, and then stood, quickly moving to the door.

I didn't say anything as she pulled the door open because a sneaking suspicion began to consume me. She was expecting whoever was on the other side of that door.

"He's here." She glanced from the door to me, worrying her bottom lip. She only did that when she was extremely nervous. I'd seen that expression before on her face twice. Once when we were in the OR and things got really dicey and a patient almost bled out, the second time was when I pulled back the shower curtain, exposing her entirely nude body to my gaze for the first time.

The hairs on the back of my neck stood up.

She stepped away from the door and an older man entered behind her. I caught sight of his hazel eyes, which resided behind the lens of his glasses. His thin lips were formed into a grim line when he turned to stare down at me after glancing over the damage surrounding me.

I wanted to ask who the hell he was, standing in my damn home, but I was utterly drained. Too tired to even talk.

"Jacob," he began, kneeling in front of me, "I'm Dr. Kearns. Grace is a friend of mine." He paused to look up at Grace who was standing, hovering over us.

I turned my attention to Grace, but her eyes skittered away from mine. I lowered my gaze back to the man in front of me.

"What kind of doctor are you?" I knew the answer before it was asked.

"I'm a psychiatrist."

A muscle in my jaw ticked and I narrowed my gaze on Grace. "You called a fucking shrink?"

CHAPTER 24

race

Every morning for the last four mornings I woke up with two things: a piercing headache, and the strain of the guilt that just wouldn't go away, no matter how hard I tried to convince myself that what I did was for his own good.

To say Jacob was furious when he realized I'd called a psychiatrist for him would've been a total understatement. The way his eyes conveyed his ire still stung every night when I tried to go to sleep. So instead of sleeping, I found myself rethinking about him over and over. I tossed and turned every night, hence the reason for my headaches.

As I pushed the blanket from my body and sat up to get my day started, I made myself remember the words of Dr. Kearns'. He told me that I was doing this *for* Jacob and not *to* him.

"He's a danger to himself, and to you, Grace," he told me over the phone when I first called him, frantic that morning when I heard Jacob beginning to smash and break things in his kitchen.

That morning, I'd never been so thankful to have worked in the medical field in all my life. I knew to call Dr. Kearns instead of the police. I'd read too many news reports of people calling the police

221

when a family member of theirs was in a mental health crisis, only for the police to respond with bullets. Granted, sometimes the situation called for force, if the person was a threat to others, but a mental health professional who could calmly assess and assist in these situations was better.

I worked with Dr. Kearns at my old job, after a few of my former patients became his patients once they were discharged. He was always friendly to the nurses. I kept his card in my wallet, for what I didn't know, but I was glad to have had it that morning.

Jacob, on the other hand, probably still hated me for calling.

The way he tried to stand and tell both of us that he didn't need a damn shrink, still clawed at my insides. I stood there feeling so helpless after he stormed off down the hall, slamming his bedroom door shut. Dr. Kearns told me to leave. Of course, initially, I refused. I couldn't leave Jacob like that. But he'd convinced me, telling me that there likely was no way he could get through to Jacob if I was there.

"He needs to keep his pride right now, Grace," Dr. Kearns had said.

I wanted to tell them both to hell with his pride. He needed help. However, it wouldn't have done any good. So finally, I relinquished my position, grabbed my belongings, and headed out. I had to catch an Uber to the place where the Underground was held since my car had been left there overnight.

That was four days ago, and if I hadn't received a call from Dr. Kearns informing me that Jacob had agreed to his thirty day in-patient treatment center, I would have no idea what was going on with him. The man I loved.

My shoulders slumped as I proceeded across the hall to my bathroom to get showered and ready for the day. It'd been four days since I returned to work. I had two days off and called in sick the previous two days, hoping that time would give me the space and clarity I needed to be able to function properly. However, as I washed the soap off my body, my headache still pounding, I realized that'd only been a pipe dream. Ready or not, I needed to get back to work. The last thing I needed was to sit around my house for another day hoping for a call from Jacob or wondering what was going on with him.

So, an hour later, I found myself strolling off the elevator, an extra large cup of my usual vanilla-flavored coffee in my hand, which helped with my headache, and into the nurses' station. Per usual, there were a number of nurses hanging out at the desk, either completing some last minute task at the computer, telling the new nurses who were just coming on for our shift what patients to keep an eye out for, or gathering their belongings before heading out for the day. But my stomach dropped when, as soon as I approached the desk, it seemed as if all conversation stopped.

Sighing, I lifted my gaze, looking at my co-workers. Lisa, who sat at one of the computers darted her gaze away from me as if I were some sort of leper. There were two other women in the corner who were obvious about openly staring at me. I wasn't surprised to find one of those women to be Suzanne. A warning bell went off in my gut at the sight of her face. I never trusted her, though she never gave me a reason not to. She'd been good to all of her patients, for the most part, she did her job, and as far as I knew, she knew her stuff. But it was the way she always seemed to glam onto Jacob when he was around that I didn't like. Of course, most would just excuse that as petty jealousy on my part. And sure, that was likely part of the reason, but there was something else that didn't curl all the way over about her.

Now that she'd accused Jacob of attacking her, I really didn't trust her. Deep in my gut I knew there was more to the story than she was giving.

"Good morning, Grace. Glad to see you're back."

I smiled over at Charles, another surgical nurse on our floor. "Good morning, Charles. Thank you. How're you doing?"

He rolled his eyes skyward. "Ask me in about …" he paused to look at the watch on his wrist, "another four hours."

We both laughed.

Thankfully, Charles' little intervention seemed to break up the tension and the rest of the nursing staff went on about their business as usual.

"Grace, once you've gotten settled in, Marta from legal wants to speak with you in her office," Lisa stated before sliding a business card across the desk in my direction.

I leaned in and picked the card up, looking it over. Marta Ringwald, Esq. with the number of her office, which I recognized as being in the executive suites of the hospital. Again, it felt like the conversations around me halted and all eyes were cast in my direction.

I shoved the business card in the pocket of my scrubs.

"I'll get to Marta when I have time," I responded defiantly and lifted my chin. "Right now, I have patients to check on." I proceeded to the computer that was free, to Lisa's right, and logged in to look up the information on my patients for the day, before exiting the nurses' station to go check on the people in the hospital who really mattered.

"Let me help you with that."

I glanced over my shoulder to see Charles moving my way. I lifted an eyebrow and he made a face for me to just keep going as usual.

Once we rounded the corner and were out of earshot of the nurses' station, he leaned down and whispered, "I don't trust that one. You watch your back."

I frowned and wrinkled my forehead. "Which one?"

"Suzanne. Listen, I don't know what happened in that room with Dr. Reynolds, and yeah, the guy can be rude and off-putting at times, but he's one of the best surgeons I've worked with."

I nodded because that was the truth. Jacob's skills were second to none, and he was still young in his profession. I could only imagine where his career and abilities would take him. And why did I start thinking that? Because as soon as I did, my heart began to sink. I ached for the fact that he'd broken his knuckle, a fact that could be detrimental for a surgeon. Also, because I knew if he couldn't get past whatever it was he was going through, he would never be able to flourish in his career. And then there was this debacle with Suzanne, which could derail his career in so many ways.

"I don't trust her," Charles stated finally, drawing the same conclusion I'd come to months ago regarding Suzanne. "Just watch your back."

I nodded as Charles walked off to another patient's room, giving me one final warning look. Of all the nurses I worked with, I respected Charles' opinion the most. He was rarely the one to get involved in hospital gossip. He was efficient at his job and always willing to jump in and lend a hand when needed. If he was warning me about Suzanne, then I knew I was on the right track when my instincts were telling me not to believe a word she said.

* * *

Jacob

"What the hell am I doing here?" I asked to no one in particular as I glared at the ceiling above me. I laid in the bed of the single room I'd been assigned at the thirty day in-patient treatment center, Willow Springs Treatment Center.

"What the fuck kind of name is Willow Springs?" I asked Kearns as we drove into the circle driveway of the facility. He chuckled and said something about not being a fan of the name either, but he hadn't named it.

Now, I was here on my fourth day, in my empty, naked bed, the blanket and sheets bundled up in the corner of the floor, wondering how I got here. Yes, I agreed to come, but for the life of me I couldn't figure out how Kearns had gotten me to agree.

I finally got myself out of bed, sitting up and raising my arms overhead to stretch and work the kinks that'd formed during my sleep out of my back. Standing, I looked around the room, as I did every morning, appreciating the fact that I had a single occupancy room. I was not in the mood for a fucking roommate. Though not my style, the room that comfortably fit a queen-sized bed, a low sitting armchair in one corner, lamp, and a decent size desk, dresser, and closet wasn't exactly a shithole or a rubber room.

I snorted at the thought of being locked in one of those fucking rooms, with a straight jacket on to keep me from gauging my own eyes out. Shaking my head, I pulled open the top drawer of dresser and removed a T-shirt, bringing it to my nose and inhaling. The shirt wasn't mine. It was Grace's. She'd left it at my place, and while

225

packing to come here, I instinctively grabbed it, not knowing what for. But as I inhaled the shirt that smelled just like her, I knew why. It was my way of being close to her even when she wasn't physically present.

I used to think things like that were bullshit or for lames. Now, here I was, behaving like one of the men I despised who fell for a woman.

"I love you more than I ever thought I could love a man ..."

Those were some of the last words she said to me that morning. And to be honest, I think it was those very words that prompted me to take this step, to agree to be locked in this place for a month.

Fifteen minutes after awakening, I found myself rounding the corner of one of the trails on the Willow Springs property during my usual four mile run. After the first half mile, my lungs opened up and finally adjusted to the aerobic exercise. My brain switched off and my body took over, doing what it needed to do to make it to the next step, next mile marker, and the next phase of this workout. Running out here at Willow Springs came eerily close to what it felt like being in the operating room. All else seemed to fade away into oblivion, and all that mattered was the next step. I needed these morning runs to take the edge off in order to face what I had to face the rest of the day.

An hour later, I found myself sitting in Dr. Kearns office, on the comfortable loveseat couch I was pretty certain they make extra soft just to lull patients to open up.

"You're continuing to do your runs every morning, I see?" Dr. Kearns noted.

I nodded but didn't say anything since the answer was obvious. I was sitting there in a pair of track pants and T-shirt, after having just finished my breakfast after a run.

"Have you been able to come up with any other coping mechanisms that you can implement when things get too uncomfortable?"

"Fighting."

"Aside from fighting."

I grunted and stared across the room at the waterfall fountain that sat on his shelf. Water was supposed to bring tranquility—at least that was what I heard or read somewhere—but thinking of water reminded me of Grace. She loved swimming as her favorite activity. She could outswim me, which was no easy feat considering I was a pretty good swimmer. But it was her main form of exercise.

"Are you thinking about Grace?"

I turned sharply to Dr. Kearns, pissed that he could discern my thoughts so easily.

He must've picked up on my ire, because he soon added, "Your face gets more relaxed, calmer whenever you're thinking of her, or talking about her. I noticed it two days ago when she was mentioned."

I adjusted myself on the couch. "We're not discussing Grace."

He nodded. "You're right. We're not. We're discussing your list of coping mechanisms that I've been trying to pull out of you since our first session two days ago. We already have running on the list. And yes, fighting is your number one mechanism, aside from work and surgery, but considering your current state ..." his eyes lowered to the cast on my right hand, "it's imperative to come up with some other strategies."

Pushing out an impatient breath, I laid my head back against the wall behind me. "Getting drunk."

A chuckle came from across the room, but I didn't take my eyes off the ceiling. None of this opening up shit was easy, and we hadn't even gotten to the hard stuff yet.

"How about writing?"

I lifted my head and narrowed my gaze when I saw Dr. Kearns holding a black journal in his right hand. Leaning forward, he held it out to me.

I didn't take it.

"Why would I need one of those?"

He shrugged, still holding the book out to me. "You might want to write something in it. You were an English minor in college, after all."

I raised my gaze to him.

"You told me that during your initial in-patient interview."

I remembered that conversation. I had told him that.

"I suspect writing would be a good coping mechanism for you. You can either use this journal or write on your laptop."

"You guys don't allow laptops here."

He smiled. "No, we don't. But once you leave here, you can use it. For now, you'll have to stick to writing. Good thing you write with your left hand."

I snorted and glanced down at my fucked up right hand. Yeah, it was a good thing I was left-handed. Finally, I leaned over and took the journal from Dr. Kearns.

"What the hell am I supposed to write in here?" I flipped it over and over as if it were a foreign object.

"Whatever you want. No one's going to see it besides you."

I lifted an eyebrow. "You won't try to read it?"

He shook his head. "Only if you want me to."

"I won't," I insisted immediately, not even sure I was going to use the damn thing. I continued to flip it over in my hand, staring at it, and I flinched at a memory that came to mind.

"What just happened there?"

"What?"

"You flinched while staring at the journal. Want to talk about that? Was it a memory?"

I shook my head. "Must've been the omelet I had for breakfast." I tossed the journal to the couch cushion beside me and lifted my right arm to rest against the back of the loveseat.

Dr. Kearns stared at me, tenting his fingers.

"Why'd you become a head shrink?"

His busy eyebrows rose. "Head shrink?"

"Yeah, why would you go through undergrad and then four years of medical school and come out the other side and settle for being a damn psychiatrist instead of a real doctor?" I cocked my head to the side, awaiting his answer.

"Is that what you think? That the only *real* doctors are the ones who work in the emergency department, cut people open, or treat wounds?"

I shrugged. "If the shoe fits. You had to learn all of the biology and anatomy in undergrad and med school, plus rotations which incorporates working in a hospital and getting your hands dirty. And now, you what? Sit and talk to crazy fucks all day?"

He leaned forward. "Crazy fucks?"

I shrugged again.

"Is that how you classify yourself, Jacob?"

My anger grew. I hated the way he said my first name. But I answered his question. "Yeah. I'm crazy. Wouldn't be here if I wasn't." I'd known I was crazy for some time now. I knew there was no way someone could grow up the way I had, with the mother I had, and be considered normal, in any capacity.

"And what do you consider crazy?"

I pushed out a harsh breath. "Do you always answer a question with a question?"

"Do you?"

Grunting, I tossed my head back against the wall because it was either do that or hit something with the level of frustration I was starting to feel.

"Jacob, we can go round and round for the next twenty-six days, you leave out of here and nothing has changed. You'll still be the same. Angry and using fighting and working to deal with your problems. And that's *if* you still have a job."

My gut clenched at the reminder that my job was seriously on the line.

"Fighting and working aren't the only things in my life."

"And then there's Grace."

Her name alone had my chest filling with something light. That is, until Dr. Kearns said, "And how long do you think she's going to stick around through your constant ups and downs? How long do *you* want to put her through that?"

My hand tightened into a fist and that hot feeling I always get when my anger begins to boil to a rage started in the pit of my belly. I leaned forward and through clenched teeth I told Dr. Kearns, "Don't mention her again."

To his credit, Dr. Kearns didn't even blink in the face of my anger.

Instead, he eased back in his chair, lowered his hands, and said, "It's that anger, right there, that will end up driving her away if you don't find a way to deal with it, Jacob."

His words were like a needle to the balloon that was my animosity. I felt it deflating with the acknowledgement of the truth. I couldn't expect Grace to linger around a fuck up who only knew how to fight, get angry, and throw tantrums when shit hit the fan. She deserved more than that. Hell, *I* deserved more than that. Or, did I?

Either way, Dr. Kearns was essentially telling me that I had a choice to make. And I had better make it fast because in a little over three weeks I would be released from this place and could either be no better off than when I first got here, or maybe just slightly better, but at least on the road to improving.

"Next session, how about you have that list of coping mechanisms for me, and we'll discuss it."

My eyes darted up to the clock on the wall. Fifty-five minutes had passed just like that. During my stay at Willow Springs, I was to meet with Dr. Kearns twice a day, five times a week.

"Fine," I responded, standing and grabbing the journal from the couch before exiting. Yeah, I was still pissed that the twists and turns of my life had brought me to this place. But maybe, just fucking maybe, this was worth a shot.

CHAPTER 25

Grace

"I'm sorry, but what proof do you have that Jacob even attacked Suzanne?" I questioned the three attorneys who sat across from me. I was in one of the executive conference rooms of the hospital, sitting opposite the hospital's team of lawyers, who all stared at me intently while the middle one asked questions.

"Nurse Young, we cannot discuss with you what we've found in our investigation into this matter, thus far."

I looked to the male lawyer who said that. I hated the way his hands were clasped tightly in front of him, his dark suit, and the way his dark hair was slicked down without a one out of place. I narrowed my gaze on him, angry at all three because they were acting like none of this was that big a deal. Or, more so, acting as if they'd already drawn their conclusions on the matter.

"And have you even done a thorough investigation? Did Jac– Dr. Reynolds give you his side of the story?"

I turned my attention to the Asian female lawyer who cleared her throat and squirmed in her seat slightly. "Nurse Young, again, we cannot divulge the investigation to you—"

"Are you sure? Because Suzanne is running around the hospital telling anyone who will listen her version of events. And that includes patients. By the way, isn't it against hospital policy for staff to tell patients things like that? At the very least, it should be, right? Nurses venting to patients about their work problems isn't a great look for the hospital."

"We had not heard about that issue. Our department will again reiterate to Nurse Greene the importance of discretion."

I lifted an eyebrow. "Again? So you mean this isn't her first time speaking out of turn? Sounds to me like something isn't quite right with Nurse Greene."

"Nurse Young, this interview isn't about Nurse Greene. It's about us getting to the bottom of Dr. Reynolds' behavior to the rest of the staff."

"And why would that even matter in the issue between him and Nurse Greene?"

"It could speak to a pattern of behavior with Dr. Reynolds. Now—"

"A pattern of behavior?" I moved forward in my seat. "Have you checked with human resources?"

The three lawyers looked between one another, but I kept going.

"I'm sure people in your positions have surely taken the time to check with HR to see if there have ever been any complaints made about Dr. Reynolds on or before this incident. Have there?"

The other female lawyer who'd spoken very little during this meeting pinched her lips.

"I'll take that as a no. And what about patient complaints? Lawsuits?"

Same reaction.

"Right. Dr. Reynolds may not be the friendliest doctor in the surgical unit but he's professional and courteous when he needs to be. He's never been inappropriate to staff to the level in which they have even gone to HR to complain about him. Granted," I held up my hand when the male attorney started to talk, "I understand none of that negates the seriousness of the current issue at hand. And yes, there are supposedly witnesses to what happened in his office, but how do you know they have the full story? Aren't you taught in law school or somewhere that eyewitnesses can be the least reliable?"

That's what some of the Crime TV shows I'd watched over the years reported.

There was no response, but some very frustrated expressions.

"Nurse Young, this is not a matter for you to argue. This is not a court of law, you are not on the witness stand, and Dr. Reynolds is not being prosecuted."

"Yet."

I shot daggers at the male attorney who just had to add that *yet* in.

"And if he is, that will be out of our hands. It is our job to ensure the safety of the staff and patients at Memorial Hospital. If a doctor, *any* doctor is a threat to that safety, we need to be aware of it and let them go. Unless you have more to add on that matter, we ask that you simply stick to answering the questions asked of you."

I huffed and clenched my teeth but didn't verbally respond. She was right, I didn't have anything else to add. I wasn't there in the room when the incident took place between Jacob and Suzanne, nor did I have any proof that Suzanne was lying. Or at the very least, exaggerating what happened.

Hell, maybe I was just digging for more information on her because I didn't want it to be true. I didn't want to believe that Jacob could be capable of putting his hands on a woman in that manner. But I'd seen him after he left the hospital that day. He wasn't himself. Yes, he could be surly at times and withdrawn, but he'd gone past that point. He was angry and hostile and reactive to the point that he actually injured himself because he was so out of control.

I kept remembering back to watching him at the Underground, in the ring. Something in him snapped and he began kicking, punching, and fighting as if someone was trying to steal his very life. Joshua Townsend, and another man I heard named Damon, had tried to pull him off the new guy but he wouldn't stop. That was when I ran into the ring and began yelling his name, to get him to calm down. He'd looked at me, his eyes cleared for the length of time it took me to inhale a breath. Then someone was pulling me out of the ring, telling me it wasn't safe.

That was when Jacob yelled for them to get their hands off of me, and he was out of it again. He slammed his fist into a guy who tried to stop him and then another, but the second guy ducked, causing Jacob to punch one of the concrete cylinders that was attached to the roof. I heard the cracking of the bone in his hand and my knees nearly buckled, but Jacob didn't stop. He just kept swinging and punching whatever stood in his way.

"Nurse Young."

I shook my head, lifting my gaze to meet the three pairs of eyes that stared back at me.

"We have been told that you and Dr. Reynolds' relationship goes beyond just co-workers. Is that the case?"

I frowned at the man who asked, especially the way he was asking, as if he had played his *gotcha* card and won.

"There's no hospital policy against co-workers dating, is there?"

Again, the woman who still hadn't said much cleared her throat and the man's eyes darted over to her. She was warning him to tread lightly.

Yeah, Arturo, be careful, I thought.

"No, there isn't, but your romantic relationship with Dr. Reynolds might lead one to believe that your opinion of his behavior at work, or with other staff, might be biased."

"In that case, yes. It's true. Dr. Reynolds and I are more than mere co-workers, and you're right. It does make me biased in my assessment of this situation. However, I will say that even before Dr. Reynolds and I began our relationship, I could see that he was an especially skilled surgeon and doctor. He's attentive, hard working, and doesn't let things like petty hospital gossip get in the way of performing his job to the utmost of his abilities. With that said, I think we're done here." I stood from my chair and glared down on the three other people in the room.

Arturo was the first to stand. "Nurse Young." He nodded.

I didn't bother waiting for the other two women; I pivoted on my heels and marched out of the room, my concern for Jacob's career even greater than it had been prior to this interview.

* * *

Jacob

"When's the last time you spoke with Luke?"

I flinched at the question. I knew Dr. Kearns was going to hone in on my last statement about my brother.

"Two months ago."

"And how did that go?"

"We got into a fight."

Dr. Kearns raised an eyebrow. "Oh?"

"He didn't want to see me after his match."

"You went to one of his fights?"

"Grace surprised me with tickets to his match. She'd seen the recordings I saved of his fights. She thought I was just a fan."

"You never told her that Luke was actually your brother, beforehand?"

I shook my head.

"Why?"

Of course he would want to know why. Any sane person would. "We hadn't spoken in years. He goes by a different last name. I didn't know she bought VIP tickets to get his autograph afterwards. I didn't think it would come up."

"So the younger brother you loved, one of the *only* people on this planet you admitted to loving since you were a young boy, the one you protected by taking his beatings when your mother forced you to fight, you didn't think it would be necessary to tell Grace he's your brother? Why?"

I knew the answers to his questions but I hesitated because they would lead to more questions. After a week and a half of these sessions, I'd learned Dr. Kearns' style. He asked leading questions, and just when I thought I knew where we were headed, and I could head him off at the pass, he'd latch onto something seemingly minuscule that would open up something huge. My relationship, or lack thereof, with my brother was that something big.

"I'm not—" I broke off and stared off to the corner of the room.

"Why not, Jacob?"

"I'm not his brother … not in any meaningful sense of the word, all right?" My voice raised instinctively because I still hated being pushed into territory I'd tried to forget about for years.

"Define that for me."

I knew what he was requesting. What did I mean by *meaningful sense.*

"I'm older than Luke by two years. I'm supposed to be the big brother, the protector. But I spent most of my damn childhood beating the hell out of him for the most minuscule infractions."

"At the behest of your mother."

I rolled my eyes. "That doesn't matter."

"It doesn't?"

I shook my head. "I should've known better."

"And your mother shouldn't have?"

Of fucking course she should've! my brain yelled.

"I suppose."

"And you said …" he paused, flipping through his notepad, "if you didn't fight Luke or vice versa, she would physically abuse you herself, correct?"

I nodded, gritting my teeth.

"Can you walk me through a scenario where that happened?" His voice softened up as he asked that question. He knew he was treading into seriously ugly territory. It was the voice of a doctor asking a patient to do something they knew the patient didn't want to.

Do you want to get better or not? An image of Grace onstage, singing, flashed through my mind at my brain's own question.

"I'm listening whenever you're ready, Jacob."

I sighed. "I'm not closing my eyes for this."

"You don't have to."

I pushed out a heavy breath. "Fine. I was in eighth grade and Luke was in sixth. It was the day we came home with our report cards. I could tell in school earlier that day that Luke was dreading seeing his grades. I passed him in the hall a couple of times and he avoided making eye contact with me and I just knew. My mother picked us up from school that day. She always did on the days we got our report cards."

I shook my head and stared out the window.

"My father was out of town on another business trip. As soon as we got in the house, she held out her hand, demanding we place the report cards in her palm. She looked over mine first and frowned but didn't say anything. I'd gotten straight A's and excellent remarks from all my teachers. I always did. School came natural to me, even without her constant pushing for excellence and the violence that came if I fell short. But Luke …

"School wasn't as easy for him. He wasn't dumb … he just didn't enjoy it as much. It was harder for him to focus. He was naturally gifted at being more social than I was. But she did her best to beat that out of him."

Thinking about the reports I'd read about Luke's antisocial behavior throughout his career, I frowned. And most recently, he got into a fight with a news reporter who simply asked him a question right after his fight.

"He had a few A's and a B and a couple of C's one in science and the other in history. Most parents would've been satisfied with that, right?" I looked to Dr. Kearns but didn't wait for his confirmation. "But not Anna Reynolds. At first, she began cursing at Luke, calling him an idiot and an embarrassment to the Reynolds name."

"I knew I should've aborted you when I had the chance! But your father, no, he convinced me to keep you. Now where is he? Gone! Working. While I'm left to deal with this mess. You are a disgrace to the legacy we are trying to build. You know that's why he works so much. Look at me while I'm talking to you!" she yelled in a fury.

"She lunged at Luke, slapping him across the face and then pulling his hair. When he tried to shield himself from being hit, she hit him harder, punching him in the ribs. Then she insisted I finish the task because she was tired."

"Not in the face, though. I don't need your teachers calling me asking me what the hell happened. I'll already have to explain his face as it is. I got carried away."

"No." I refused for the first time as I stared down at my brother. I could already see the red welt forming on his cheek.

"What did you say to me?" She was outraged but I couldn't stomach it any longer.

"I said no … and that resulted in the worst beating she ever gave me. I ended up with a cracked rib after she hit me with a frying pan. I walked around for weeks in pain. And when my father asked what happened once he returned home from our trip, I told him the truth. I told him his wife beat the shit out of me for not beating the hell out of Luke just because he'd gotten a couple of C's on his report card."

"And how did your father respond?"

I blinked at the interruption of Dr. Kearns' voice. I was so caught up in the memory I forgot he was even there. I'd forgotten where I was. I blinked, turning to face him, returning to the present and Willow Springs Treatment Center.

"What?"

"What was your father's reaction when you told him what happened?"

I scowled. "He told me I was overreacting. That my mother was just disciplining Luke for not living up to his full potential and I'd gotten in the way of that. I never even told him that my fucking rib was cracked, among other things."

"What was that?"

I blinked and lifted my gaze to Dr. Kearns. "What was what?"

"The last part of your statement. What do you mean *among other things?"*

My lips tightened and I stood, peering up at the clock on the wall. "I think our fifty-five minutes are up, Doc."

"Jacob," he called as I was halfway out the door. "Maybe it'll be good for you to do some writing in that journal, after your meditation session."

"Maybe," I grunted before I kept going, closing the door behind me.

I had an hour to have dinner and then to the meditation class they taught. Dr. Kearns believed it was one of the things here that I could incorporate into my coping strategies, as he put it. Mindful meditation or whatever the fuck it was. So far, it only served to piss me off. Who had time to sit and listen to their own breathing for an hour?

Besides, whenever I tried to do it, all that ended up happening was flashbacks to the memories I was trying my damndest to forget. Of course, Dr. Kearns said that was good, that the memories not being suppressed were a good thing. And that eventually, they would stop coming on as acutely. But I had to be open to them at first.

I sighed and opted to go out for another walk around the trails instead of having dinner. I'd just grab one of the protein shakes they had available afterwards. It was cold as fuck outside due to it being winter and all, but I wasn't in the mood to sit still and eat and then have to put up with meditation after that. And as a last minute thought, I grabbed the notebook and pen from off the chair in the corner of the room.

CHAPTER 26

*G*race
"Journey, how are you?" I answered the phone excited as I pushed my way through my front door. I was just coming home after a swim, after getting off of a twelve hour shift. I was tired but I needed to swim to make me even more tired so that I'd sleep that night. That was the only way I could sleep lately. And yes, it had everything to do with the fact that it'd been almost two full weeks since I heard Jacob's voice, or any word from him at all.

"I'm okay."

I frowned because her response sounded weak at best. I shouldered out of my coat and hung it up on the rack next to the door before switching the phone from my right to my left ear.

"What's wrong?"

Journey sighed on the other end. "I hate being different."

"Because of your bipolar?" I didn't want to sugarcoat things with Journey. I chose to be honest and open about her illness and I still got the impression I was one of the only people she could fully be open with. My father and step-mother had come around to acknowledging Journey's illness but she still came to me when she needed a dose of realness.

"Yes, because I'm sick and I always will be."

"Journey, where's this coming from?" I pressed the button to put the phone on speaker and placed it on the bureau in my bedroom, so I could strip out of the sweatpants and T-shirt I put on after my swim.

"Josie got engaged last week."

I nodded, recognizing the name of one of her close friends from back home.

"Her fiancé, Darwin, is great. He just completed his first year as an associate at one of the top law firms in the city. He's handsome and comes from a great family."

"Okay, sounds like you should be happy for Josie."

"I am. That's the problem. Who's going to want me when I'm this screwed up?"

My shoulders sagged at the sadness in her voice. I moved across my bedroom, completely naked, and grabbed my phone. When I turned around, I came face-to-face with my body on display in the full-length mirror. I looked over my body, my eyes finally settling on the right side of my chest where my scarred breast remained. I scanned the scar I'd avoided for so many years. And then I remembered Jacob's lips caressing my scar so tenderly that it made my insides quake.

He seemed to relish that part of my body more than any other. Repulsion had never been evident in his eyes when he stared at my body. And nor was the trained look of a plastic surgeon either. He didn't view me through the lens of a doctor, inspecting the body of a patient. He was a man fixating on the body of his lover.

"Journey, I thought the same thing, too," I said after a long pause.

"Why?" She sounded so confused that it made me giggle as I took a seat on the edge of my bed.

"You know I never got reconstructive surgery after my mastectomy, right?"

"You didn't?"

I could just envision her face scrunched up on the other end of the phone as she tried to figure out why not. I had never talked to her much about my recovery process.

"I just assumed you did. Most women do, right?"

"Yeah, many do. Probably most, but I chose not to. I was tired of being a patient and wanted to heal as quickly as possible. I wanted to get back to caring for others instead of the opposite way around. Also well … I don't really know. I just didn't want the surgery."

"Okay."

"Somewhere along the line I started to believe that it made me different from other women. That men wouldn't value me or wouldn't fully love me because of it. And because I was never really one for relationships or want to get married and have kids, that was fine with me. Then I met someone who changed those beliefs for me."

"That Jacob guy?"

I laughed again because my sister's voice spiked with the curiosity of a younger sister happy that her big sister was opening up to her.

"Yes, Jacob. Anyway, when he finally saw my scars he didn't run screaming in the other direction. He kissed them."

My sister sighed. "Really?"

"Yeah, really. Not once did he ever make me feel like my body was grotesque, or that I was some sort of charity case. He even showed up to my doctor's appointment and held my hand as I waited for the results of my latest scans."

"Wait, you had more scans? Does that mean—"

"No." I shook my head even though she couldn't see me. "It's something most cancer patients in remission have to endure. Each year I go to my oncologist to get tests and make sure I'm still doing well. After five years of a clean bill of health, chances of my survival go up incredibly. This was my fifth year."

"And?"

"It's all good. Scans looked great."

She pushed out an exasperated breath.

"But back to the point. I told you all of that to say, that while I wasn't one for romance and love and all that stuff you believe in, even I was able to find a guy—a great guy, who accepted me flaws and all."

"Being a cancer survivor isn't a flaw."

"And neither is being a person living with a mental illness. We all come with our own hang ups, flaws, illnesses, trauma, or whatever. But you are a highly talented artist who's going to be huge one day. You're a kind soul who loves animals, and most importantly, you're my little Journey."

She giggled because that'd been my nickname for her ever since she was an infant.

"I told you to stop calling me that," she said through laughter.

"And since when do I listen to you?"

"Since never."

"I love you."

"Love you, too, Grace." She paused. "You know, Victory had a lot of problems and in my eyes wasn't all that great a mother, but she did a couple of things right."

"What's that?"

"She gave me the best older sister I could've ever wanted and she named us appropriately. You're every bit as courteous, good-natured, and refined as your name."

A smile a mile wide blossomed on my face.

"I think that's the best compliment I've ever gotten."

"You deserve it and more."

I dipped my head, continuing to smile because my chest filled with love for my little sister.

"You're going to be all right, Journey," I said a little while later.

"We both are. I know you miss Jacob. I can hear it in your voice. Is he still away for work?"

A pang of guilt rang through my belly at the white lie I'd told her. But I didn't think it would be fair to Jacob to tell anyone who didn't know him where he was at the moment. That would just lead to more questions, many of which I didn't have the answers to.

"Yeah, he's still away. But he'll be back in a few weeks."

"Good. He must be really important to be gone for work for so long."

"Hmhm. How're you doing with your medications? Any side-effects?" I asked, changing the subject.

"Not so much anymore ..." she answered, thankfully, not picking up on my mood change.

We talked for a few more minutes about Journey's different medications and the treatment plan she was continuing to work through with her doctors. I sent up a silent prayer, thankful that my sister had been brave enough to seek out the help she needed and that she had the means to do so.

And of course, my thoughts wandered to the other person in my life who was in need of help. I still wasn't sure whether or not I made the right decision in calling Dr. Kearns. Jacob had agreed to the in-patient treatment but that didn't mean he liked it or wasn't pissed at me for facilitating it in the first place.

"I'll call you in a couple of days, sis," Journey said as we ended our call.

"Love you."

"Same."

I hung up the phone and stared at it, wondering what Jacob was doing right then. And just when I was about to turn my phone over on my nightstand and crawl into bed, the screen lit up with an unfamiliar number. Usually, I didn't answer numbers I don't know but something niggled at me to pick it up.

"Hello?"

"Hey, baby."

My eyelids closed at the deep sound of his voice.

"Jacob."

* * *

Jacob

All the oxygen was sucked out of the room when she said my name. I pressed my back into the wall behind me to steady myself even though I was seated comfortably on the bed. It'd been a long two weeks since I last heard her voice.

"It's late," I stated as if I wasn't the one who called her.

"I just got in from work and then Journey called. How are you? Are you okay?"

Ordinarily, someone asking me those questions would tick me off, but the inflection of worry in Grace's voice only made me long to soothe her anxieties.

"I'm f—" I started to say I was fine but that wasn't the complete truth and I was working to be more truthful with the people who mattered to me the most. "It's ... difficult."

"Willow Springs? Do you not like it? Is the staff not—"

"No, they're fine. Dr. Kearns is fine. It's all the other shit that's ... hard. The shit in my head."

"Oh."

"But that's what I'm here for, I guess." Sighing, I pressed the button to turn the phone's speaker on and placed it on my lap to run my hand through my hair in frustration. I hated how pathetic I sounded.

"I didn't recognize this number."

"I bought a temporary phone."

"From where?"

"There's a little store not too far from Willow Springs. I pass it most mornings on my daily runs around the grounds here. One of the trails leads to a road which leads to a town. Anyway, they sell phones. And since they confiscated mine once I arrived here ..." I shrugged even though she couldn't see me.

"So you're not supposed to be calling me?"

I chuckled because she caught me. "No, but it's not like I'd let a little thing like rules stop me from contacting you."

Her giggle on the other end of the phone caused my heart to stop beating for a full second.

"I need to tell you something."

"What's that?"

There was that worry back in her voice.

"I can't have kids."

There was a gasp followed by silence. "You mean you don't want to have kids."

"Yes. I mean, I don't want to have kids so much that I made sure I couldn't have kids."

"Jacob, what are you saying?"

"I'm telling you that when I was twenty-five years old, I had a vasectomy because I never want to bring children into this world."

A part of me wanted to apologize to her because as much as I abhorred the idea of having my own children, I could absolutely see her as a doting and loving mother. Nothing at all, like the one I'd had. And that still didn't make me want children.

"Jacob?" she called after a long pause.

"Yes?"

"I don't want children, either."

"You're not just saying that, are you?" My shoulders sagged in relief but I still had to ask.

"No. I've told you I have an IUD."

"Yeah, but I thought that was just for birth control until you were ready to have kids."

"I'll never be ready to have kids. I don't want to have kids. Never have."

I shook my head, still trying to wrap my mind around the idea of a woman as caring, loving, and yes, gracious, as she was, not wanting to be a mother.

"I've cared for people since I can remember. I believe it's what I was born to do on this Earth, but being a mother isn't the only way I can care for others. I have my career and family. That's enough for me."

My body filled with the alleviation of the burden of wondering whether Grace and I would truly work if she wanted kids and I didn't. But the words coming from her were a balm to that worry. And the firmness at which she stated them, assured me that she wasn't just trying to appease me. She meant it.

"Sing for me."

"Are you serious?"

"As hell. I haven't heard your voice in fourteen days and ..." I pressed a button on the phone to check the time, "twelve hours, and it's been even longer since I've heard you sing."

There was laughter on the other end of the phone. "You're going to get in trouble if you stay on the phone too long."

"Well worth it. I want to hear you sing."

She pushed out a heavy breath and I knew I'd already won this little battle.

"Any special requests?"

"Yeah, that song with my name in it. The one you sung to me before."

"Oh, 'Jacob's Song'. Okay."

She inhaled, and this time I could tell it was preparation for the notes that would spill from her lips.

I relaxed even more with each passing word. Though the phone was on speaker, I held it up to my ear so I wouldn't miss one syllable. Closing my eyes, I pictured her laying next to me, singing directly to me as her soft hand stroked my face. Just like the first time when she'd sung this song to me. In less than a verse of the song, I was back in her bedroom, just the two of us, free of the bullshit that separated us—my bullshit.

When she stopped singing my eyes popped open and my lips formed a deep frown upon realizing that I was still at Willow Springs and Grace was back at her home.

"Thank you."

"My pleasure," she whispered.

"I miss you. More than you know."

"I miss you, too."

I appreciated that she didn't ask about when I was released from this place. She didn't try to make plans for the future or ask me what, if anything, would change between us once I was discharged. Because I didn't have all of the answers. There was still a ton of heavy shit I needed to work through, and according to Dr. Kearns, would still be working through long after these thirty days passed.

"Jacob?"

"Yeah?"

"I don't know if this is the right time to tell you this but … your father and his company had to pull out of their contract with the hospital. There hasn't been an official announcement but he's been gone for the last week. There are rumors saying he had to go back to Washington for family reasons …" Her voice trailed off and I pictured her biting her lower lip with worry. Her thoughts ping-ponging between whether or not she should've told me this or kept the information to herself.

"Anna's dying," I finally stated.

"Anna?"

"My mother." My jaw flexed with rigidity at those two words. "Cancer. He told me the first day he was there."

"I don't know what to say."

"Nothing to say. The world will be a better place without her in it." I paused before asking my next question. "You want to know why I'm an atheist?"

"Because you're a scientist."

I actually chuckled. "My atheism started even before I went to med school or practiced medicine."

"All the hypocrites you went to church with, you said."

"But even more than them, the hypocrite who gave birth to me. She named me Jacob and my brother Luke, for Christ's sake. We're named after characters in the Bible and she diligently sat in the first few rows of the church every Sunday and yet behind closed doors she was a real live monster. The devil incarnate. How can I be a believer with that type of upbringing?"

"I don't know, Jacob. No one's forcing you to be a believer."

"I know." I ran my hand through my hair again.

"My mother would force me to read the Bible to her. On days when she couldn't get out of bed and she wasn't in the mood to hear me sing, she made me read passage after passage to her. And then there were periods during her manic episodes where she would yell and scream at Journey and I the different passages and tell us we were sinners because we failed to obey her correctly. She'd become volatile over things like me spilling juice on the counter. She even hit me with her Bible a few times."

"But you still believe, right?"

"I do. I don't blame God for what my mother did or how she treated us. She was sick and never got the right treatment for her condition. But because of what I learned from her growing up, it's made me a better nurse and a better sister to Journey who doesn't have to suffer the way our mother did."

I shook my head because she made it sound so easy. It almost made total sense.

"But you don't have to believe in anything, Jacob."

"I know."

"Good."

I pushed out a breath and my eyelids drooped. I hated how tired I felt. It still stunned me how tired I became from doing all this emotional work throughout the day. In my day-to-day life I could perform an eight hour surgery, do rounds, paperwork, and then still make it to the Underground to go through rounds in the ring. But here at Willow Springs it felt like these two sessions per day with some group meditation, and other bullshit sessions like art, were wiping me out.

"That's because you're new to this."

I blinked, not even realizing I'd been saying my thoughts out loud.

"Feeling actual feelings, especially ones that have been buried for years is exhausting. Go get some rest."

I didn't want to hang up the phone, but I knew she was right.

"Okay. I'll talk to you soon." *Love you.* Those were the final two words that lingered in my mind as I hung up the phone, although I didn't say them. It didn't feel like the timing was right to admit the depths of my feelings for Grace. I still had more work to do to get there.

CHAPTER 27

*G*race

"You're leaving early today?" Charles questioned as I stepped into the nurses' station and headed to the computer to input some patient information.

I turned and smiled over my shoulder, nodding. "Three isn't *that* early," I reminded him. "I've been here since seven this morning."

I'd taken an earlier shift than usual because I had a very important errand I needed to run after work.

"Guess I'm just used to you working these twelve hour shifts, lately."

I nodded as I continued to type. "Yeah, me too. Feels weird leaving so early but I have to take care of some family stuff," I lied.

"I hear you. I'm helping my parents move into their smaller home this weekend and am already dreading it. Family is …"

"A pain."

We both laughed.

I saved the information I'd been putting into the computer and logged out. Standing, I smiled over at Charles. "You enjoy the rest of your shift. I'll see you in a couple of days."

I had the next day off and then Charles had a couple of days off so we wouldn't see each other for a few.

I tossed him a nod over my shoulder as he said good-bye and I put my long, black coat on, strapping the belt closed, and grabbed my purse from underneath the desk. I had an hour and a half drive ahead of me and I was hoping to make it to my destination at just the right time to meet up with the person I intended.

I didn't even bother to stop for food or anything on my way. I was headed to another city outside of Williamsport, and the first stop I made once I reached the city was the police station whose address I had written down on the notebook in my purse. Checking the time, I realized I still had ten minutes before the desk I needed to get the information I'd requested closed.

Slamming my door shut and clutching my coat close to my chest due to the cold, I hurried inside the main door of the station and scanned the entrance for the records desk. I made a beeline and was happy to see no one else there waiting.

"Hi, I'm Grace Young and I put in an online request for information." I smiled at the older gentleman dressed in his police uniform.

He frowned slightly as he looked from me to the computer but then his eyebrows lifted. "Here you are. Damn computer hasn't been working right all day. Now ten minutes before I'm scheduled to leave it decides to cooperate." He let out a hefty chuckle.

I smiled. "Technology. Can't live with it, can't live without it."

He snorted. "Okay, let's see here. You put in a request for a … Suzanne Greene, correct?"

I nodded.

"And …" He paused, and I held my breath. "No, it looks like you requested just a basic criminal background so we don't require a signed statement from Suzanne granting you permission to have this information. It's open to the public."

I released the breath I'd been holding, grateful that I was able to get what I came for.

"Printing it out now. The total will be five dollars."

I lifted an eyebrow.

"There's over fifty pages here but I won't charge you for the last three."

"Thank you." The copies were only ten cents a page according to the police station's website. The fact that there were more than fifty pages led me to believe there was a great deal of information in these reports.

"Have a good day," I said to the officer as I grabbed the envelope full of the papers he'd given me and headed back to my car. Right there in the parking lot of the police station, I sat in my car and pulled out the documents and began reading.

"Dr. Cameron LaRoche …" I read out loud. A physician at Bloomfield Medical Center back in 2016, the time of this report. According to what I was reading, Dr. LaRoche had filed numerous complaints against Suzanne, which escalated to accusations of stalking. He even pursued criminal charges against her but eventually dropped it. And that wasn't the only stalking accusation I read in Suzanne's file. There were two other physicians at the same hospital who accused her of harassing them, and their wives, one even went so far as to say that Suzanne has tried to blackmail one of the doctors when he outright refused her advances.

Pulling out my phone, I did a quick Google search for Dr. Cameron LaRoche and was elated to find that he no longer worked at the hospital where he met Suzanne, but now had his own practice. He, too, was a plastic surgeon. Putting the address of his practice in my phone, I saw that it was only a fifteen minute drive from the police station to his office.

Less than fifteen minutes later, I found myself pulling into the parking lot of a nice looking office building. Shutting off my car, I grabbed the envelope with the police reports in it as well as my purse, and climbed out. I paused at the main entrance to locate the correct office, as there were more than one doctors' office in the building. A few minutes later, I exited the elevator on the third floor and was happy to see that the lights to the office I was searching for were on.

Pushing the door open, I saw there was no receptionist at the front desk but the little bell overhead that sounded when the door opened must've alerted someone of my presence. A second later, I heard footsteps from down the hall moving in my direction.

"Cheri, is that—" the man who started to ask stopped when his eyes landed on me. A wrinkle appeared in his forehead. He was average height with dark, curly hair. A slightly better than average looking guy. And he was exactly who I was looking for, unless he was some imposter wearing Dr. LaRoche's white coat.

"Hi, I'm Grace Young," I started with my hand outstretched, moving toward him. "And you're Dr. LaRoche, correct?"

He nodded. "I'm sorry, did I have a consult?" He started for the desk, reaching for the clipboard that sat there.

"No. My apologies for coming into your office like this but I'm doing … um, some research on a very important matter and your name came up."

He frowned and his eyes scanned me up and down. He must've noticed the scrubs I wore because his next question was, "Are you a medical or nursing student?"

I shook my head. "I'm a nurse at Memorial Hospital in Williamsport."

"And your research led you out here to Bloomfield?"

"Yes."

"What's the topic of your research?"

"Suzanne Greene."

Dr. LaRoche's eyes widened and his eyebrows nearly touched his forehead but I didn't get to fully explain myself because the office door opened behind me.

"Cam, I've been waiting in the—"

I turned, looking over my shoulder to see a beautiful woman with blonde hair entering the office. She stopped as she peered between Dr. LaRoche and I.

"And you are?" Her voice was immediately terse and defensive.

I looked from Dr. LaRoche to this woman.

"Grace Young."

"Cheri, Grace just came in asking about Suzanne Greene."

The woman's mouth curled in obvious anger.

"Grace, this is my wife, Cheri," Dr. LaRoche stated, moving around me to his wife's side.

"What the hell are you asking questions about that witch for?"

I sighed. "Good, you have the same impression of her as I do."

That seemed to take some of the wind out of Mrs. LaRoche's defensiveness.

"Look, Dr. and Mrs. LaRoche, I didn't come here to start trouble. Trust me when I say I'd rather not have to be here at all, but Suzanne is causing trouble for someone I care deeply about, and I'm not convinced she's telling the whole truth. I stopped by the police station before I came here." I pulled out the envelope and the papers inside. "There are over fifty pages in here and complaints made by three different doctors at Bloomfield Hospital. But the most detailed report is yours, Dr. LaRoche," I looked him in the eyes. "You started to pursue criminal charges against her but dropped them ..." I let that hang in the air.

Dr. LaRoche looked from me and then to his wife. He had a guilty expression on his face. Mrs. LaRoche rolled her eyes, her shoulders slumping. "We might as well tell her. If Suzanne's up to her dirty tricks again, then it's best she knows."

I let out a relieved breath.

The LaRoches were courteous enough to order Chinese takeout, while we sat in their conference room. Turned out, Mrs. LaRoche was the office manager of Dr. LaRoche's medical office. The couple seemed to work well together but as they told me about how Suzanne's manipulations had nearly destroyed their marriage and Dr. LaRoche's career, I grew hot with anger.

"I want to make it clear, that I never had an affair with that woman," Dr. LaRoche stated firmly, as I stood, preparing to leave after two hours of talking. "I was tempted ..." he quickly looked to his wife, guilt-ridden, but then turned back to me, "... but I never did. However, Suzanne was relentless. The way she rallied the staff against me, waited outside of my home, even spying on our children while we were at their different sporting activities. She cornered me in my office more than once, threatening to tell Cheri we were having an affair. She's sick. That was when I filed a report. I secretly taped her on my phone and took it to the police and to HR."

"Thank you, Dr. and Mrs. LaRoche, for telling me all of this." I shook hands with them, feeling both thankful and pissed as hell at Suzanne.

Dr. LaRoche hadn't been the only doctor she pursued so aggressively either, according to him. There was a pattern of Suzanne going after prominent doctors at the hospital she worked at, and if they didn't immediately fall into bed with her, they would coincidentally find themselves in trouble with the human resources department, or getting the cold shoulder from staff due to Suzanne spreading rumors.

The entire time I drove back to Williamsport I tried to figure out the best way to take Suzanne down. I just knew, intuitively, that she tried to do the same thing to Jacob. The only problem standing in the way of HR believing me were the eyewitness reports and the fact that Jacob still wasn't talking about the incident.

CHAPTER 28

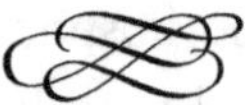

*J*acob

"Let's talk about work, Jacob."

I snorted. "You mean the fact that I might not have a job or career to go back to?" My eyes immediately went to the cast on my right hand.

"No," Dr. Kearns corrected. "I mean let's finally talk about the incident that led to all of that happening in the first place."

I popped up out of the couch and began pacing, my body tightening all over.

"Jacob, listen to me …"

I didn't say anything, but my eyes crossed the room to Dr. Kearns.

"There is nothing in this room that can hurt you. What we're discussing happened in the past. It's not happening *now*. Do you hear what I'm saying?"

I pushed out a breath and replayed his words in my head before nodding.

"Let's start with that day. Walk me through it."

"I was in my office, waiting on a consult. A nurse who I knew had been flirting with me for weeks walked in. At first I thought it was Grace but it wasn't. Anyway, she said something, and I told her to leave since whatever she'd said wasn't about work. She didn't leave, but instead became more insistent and then she reached– Next thing I remember is holding her by the neck against my file cabinet, and in walks the doctor and patient I was waiting on for a consult."

"Let's go back a moment. You said she reached … reached for what?"

I pinned him with my gaze, my jaw hardening as I clenched my teeth. "What do you think?"

"I don't know, Jacob. Your arm? Your shoulder?"

"My cock! She grabbed me where I don't let anyone touch me. Not even …"

"Not even …"

"Grace."

"And that triggered you?"

I hated that fucking word. *Triggered.* But there was no other explanation for what happened.

"Yes."

"Why?"

"Because I don't like being touched."

"Why? I mean, aside from the fact that what Suzanne did was a clear violation and a sexual assault."

I scowled. "Sexual assault? You make me sound like a fucking pansy."

"You're not but that's what it was, Jacob. You instructed her to leave your office and she pushed back by grabbing you intimately, against your will."

My stomach turned at his words and I began pacing.

"And her doing so triggered a memory you'd long since tried to forget, didn't it?"

"Hands," I replied.

"Hands, what?"

"Grabbing me, underneath the blanket. That's what I remembered."

"Grabbing you the same place Suzanne grabbed you?"

"Yes."

"Whose hands, Jacob?"

I swallowed the bile down, but the nausea persisted as I said, "My mother's."

I crumbled to the couch, my knees going weak as the memories came back full force. Squeezing my eyes shut, I kept talking, telling Dr. Kearns the nights she would enter my room, complaining about my father being absent yet again, before crawling into bed with me.

"Open your eyes, Jacob."

I shook my head.

"Remember what Leslie taught you about mindfulness. Open your eyes and count to ten."

My eyelids parted and I first noticed the brown carpeting on the floor. I raised my gaze to my hands, one in a cast and one tightly clenched in a fist. I uncurled my hand and released a breath. Remembering where I was. I wasn't a child back in Washington, in the dark and feeling disgusted with the hand that was touching me.

"Jacob." Dr. Kearns' voice.

I lifted my gaze to meet his, realizing that I just shared something that I'd never told another soul in my life.

"Can you tell me what you're feeling right now?"

"I don't know."

"What sensations are you experiencing right now?"

"Tingling in my hands and I feel ill. My stomach feels sick. Like I just got off of one of those fucking spin wheel things at the park."

"What else?"

Dr. Kearns kept prodding, and for some reason I didn't clam up. As awful as everything felt to relive, there was something about finally telling it to an unbiased observer. I knew that whatever I said would never leave this room, if I didn't want it to, and even while a part of my mind yelled at me to stop talking, to keep hiding, I kept going because I needed to. I needed this release more than my next breath.

* * *

GRACE

I felt accomplished as I left the executive suites of the hospital. Nothing had been decided but at least I felt like I was able to give Jacob a fair defense in his absence. And by the looks Suzanne was throwing my way as I passed her in the hallway, she knew her gig was up. At least, I hoped it was. That bitch had stepped over the line too many times and I just knew she'd done the same with Jacob. All he had to do was go in there and tell his side of the story, and with the background information I presented on Suzanne, he was sure to be able to keep his job.

"What did you do?" Suzanne demanded as I tried to step onto the elevator.

I whirled around and got in Suzanne's face as she held her arm over the elevator's doorway.

"You know *exactly* what I did. I told them the damn truth. The *real* reason you changed jobs from Bloomfield. You weren't looking for a fresh start in Williamsport, you were forced out of your old job after numerous complaints about your inappropriate behavior toward more than one doctor at the hospital. I also showed them your numerous police reports."

Her eyes narrowed to slits. "You bitch."

"That's right. I'm *that* bitch when you mess with my man. Jacob didn't want you and your precious little ego couldn't take the hit to your pride, yet again. So you decided to what?" I goaded. "Made it look like he hurt you? You set him up? You—"

"I just invited him to get a taste of what he really wanted."

"And how'd you do that?"

"I stepped into his office and let him feel me—"

"And was that before or after he told you to leave?"

"Everyone knows these doctors play hard to get. So what, he told me to leave, he didn't mean it."

I stepped back and glared at her. "He asked you to leave and then you made another advance?"

"He wanted me to touch him. I felt how aroused he was through his pants."

My eyes widened. "You grabbed his dick, in his office."

"He wanted me to."

"And that was when he pinned you against his file cabinet? To get you off of him?"

"He was just playing hard to get. If that doctor and her patient hadn't walked in—"

"You're disgusting." I pushed past Suzanne because I didn't need to hear anything else she had to say. Especially not when I pulled out my cell phone and checked it to make sure everything she just said had been recorded. I smiled, feeling satisfied as I downloaded the file and emailed it to myself and the person in the legal department and human resources, who I just spoke with. I informed them I would be in their offices early the next morning to relay exactly what I heard Suzanne admit to, before I turned the corner and pushed through the door that led to the stairwell.

I felt so good, I didn't need to take the elevator down anymore. I floated down the eight flights of stairs down to the garage parking where my car was parked.

I hummed to myself the entire way home, feeling relieved that Suzanne was finally being exposed for the conniving trash she was. But as I pulled into my driveway, my humming immediately stopped —because I couldn't actually pull into my driveway. There was already another vehicle there. A white Range Rover.

My heart began racing. For some reason, I checked the date on my phone. I parked at the curb in front of my house and before I could even push my door open, it was being pulled open from the outside. Jacob barely gave me time to turn the car all the way off before he was pulling me by the arm, out of my car and into his arms.

Wrapping my arms around his neck, I buried my face into that space where his neck met his shoulder. I inhaled deeper than I ever had in my life, enjoying his scent.

Jacob pulled back first but only to cover my lips with his. My body instantly reacted to his and my lips opened, allowing his tongue entrance. I groaned against his lips, my eyes squeezing shut and the juncture between my legs growing moist with each second. I'd missed him so much I spent my time working double shifts and trying to dig up dirt on Suzanne all in attempts to distract me from how much I missed him.

"Let me look at you," he said against my lips after breaking off from the kiss. His hands cupped the sides of my neck and those grey eyes of his scanned my face as if making sure to see that nothing had changed in the past twenty-nine days.

Speaking of …

"What are you doing here? You weren't supposed to leave Willow Springs until tomorrow." I'd written it down in my calendar and had a countdown on my phone. But who was counting, right?

"Time off for good behavior."

I smirked and ran my hands up his chest, pulling him impossibly closer to me by the coat he wore.

"No, really, are you okay? Did something happen—"

He cut me off by kissing me again. But it was just a quick peck.

"A lot happened. We'll get to that. But right now I don't want to talk about Willow Springs." His eyes narrowed and darkened in that way that made my body hum with desire.

Seconds later, we were stumbling through my front door, tearing at one another's clothing. And while winter was generally my favorite season of the year, I resented it so much due to the extra layer of clothing both Jacob and I had to peel through to get to one another's bodies.

"I missed the hell out of you," Jacob growled as we entered my bedroom, half-naked and just before planting another spine-tingling kiss on my lips.

I soaked it all up, having missed him equally as much. I worked my hands to his waist and lifted the T-shirt he'd worn underneath the sweater that I was pretty certain had been discarded somewhere in my hallway. Once his top half was uncovered, my hands went to my own waist, undoing the drawstring of my scrubs, but then Jacob stopped me.

"Wait." He pulled back and stepped away from me.

I immediately felt cold at his withdrawal. I watched as he moved across the bedroom and flicked on the light, illuminating the entire room.

"I don't want to rush this."

Now he tells me. After he's gotten me all primed and ready.

"Jacob." His name came out more of a whine and a moan than the warning I intended it to be.

He chuckled as his hands went to my scrubs, pulling them down my legs. He let his hands follow the same trail, tracing my skin. Once he reached my ankles, he assisted me by pulling my feet free of the thick-soled, trail running shoes I wore to work. Once I was freed of my pants, socks, and sneakers, he let his hands glide up my legs again, and for the first time, I remembered that his right hand was still in a cast. I didn't have a chance to ask about his hand because his lips covered mine.

"Spread your legs," he ordered, his voice low and deep.

I stepped my legs apart, and no sooner than I did, his free hand made its way down my stomach and slipped inside of the boy shorts I wore. My breathing hitched and my head fell backwards at the feel of his strong fingers massaging my clit.

"Jacob," I whispered his name.

"Show me how much you missed me, Grace."

I tightened my hold on his shoulders and again buried my face into the crook of his neck, panted deeply when his fingers pushed inside of me. His thumb continued making circles around my clitoris while his two fingers worked my insides. I began moving my hips, needing more than his fingers alone could provide.

"You want my cock inside of you, don't you?"

I nodded. "Yesss."

"Then come for me, Grace."

I swallowed and my body began trembling with the orgasm that was just out of reach. Jacob must've sense it because he removed one finger from inside my canal and used it and his thumb to pinch my clit, sending me over.

"Oh, oh, oh!" I chanted, my hips gyrating and thighs squeezing tightly, clamping his hand right where it was.

"Shit!" I cursed once my body rode out the last tremors of my orgasm. "I never come like that when I do that myself," I giggled against his chest.

Jacob pulled his head back. "You touched my pussy when I wasn't here."

I smiled, my face still leaning against his chest. "Yeah. What're you going to do about it?"

It probably wasn't a good idea for me to tease him like that. But I didn't even have time to second guess my words before I found myself on all fours of my bed, head pushed down against my pillows, ass in the air as Jacob pounded into me, taking me from behind.

I couldn't catch my breath. He was like a man possessed and I was his willing possession. At least my pussy was, because she was singing his praises as he pulled out, only to thrust himself back in.

"Too … damn … good!" Jacob grunted between each stroke.

I would've agreed with him, but I found it too difficult to even form words. All that came from my mouth was a series of moans and gibberish that even I couldn't understand.

Not until I came a second time, did Jacob move his hand and pulled me up so that my back now rested against his chest. His left hand moved around my front, bracketing my body to his and coming to rest against the scar on my chest. He lovingly caressed my scar, and this time he buried his face into the crook of my neck. I reached around with my right hand, lifting it to his hair and burying my fingers there.

"I love you," I whispered, unable to hold the words in any longer. It wasn't the first time I said those three words to him, but it was the first time since that day.

Jacob's hold on me tightened and his hips pushed against my backside again. I inhaled sharply as he repeated the same movement over and over, building yet another orgasm again.

"Sing for me, Grace." He licked the side of my neck.

My head dropped to his shoulder and my lips parted on a loud moan, my third orgasm overtaking my body. This time my moans mixed with Jacob's groans as his body surrendered to the moment. I could feel his seed spilling into me, and it heightened my orgasm even more. I felt closer to him than to anyone I'd ever felt in my whole life.

* * *

Jacob

She was the first person I wanted to see upon my release. I got out a day early because I needed to stop by and get my hand checked out. That, and I was ready to get back to her. To my life.

"You're wearing a different cast."

A smile touched my lips as Grace's hand fell to mine, lifting my hand with the air cast on it.

"It's healing better than expected."

She turned to her side, facing me, and pulled my hand to her lips, kissing it. Her eyelids dropped. I knew she had a ton of questions swirling around in her head, but she didn't know where to begin.

"I'm still going to be a client of Dr. Kearns'," I began, to make it easier on her.

"That's a good thing, right?"

I nodded. "I guess. He's a pain in the ass with all his questions, but … he knows what he's doing."

She grinned. "I was scared you'd hate me for calling him."

I frowned. "Hating you couldn't even cross my mind. I hated myself. Loathed the fact that I lost control and scared you."

"You didn't scare me, Jacob. I was never scared of you—"

"I know. You were scared for me. Which I still hated."

"But you needed help." Her warm hand stroked down the side of my face, soothing me.

I nodded. "I see that now." I pushed out a heavy breath, still debating whether or not it was necessary for me to share what I wanted to say next. I'd bickered with myself the entire way over here. I needed to see Grace, to be with her like this, but I also needed to tell her something. And I had no idea how it would change the way she saw me.

"There are two people in this world I hate …"

She stared at me intently, waiting for what I was going to say.

"The woman who raised me. My mother. Second to her is my father, but she's number one. The fights and physical abuse were bad enough, but it was the other stuff that fundamentally changed me."

Grace inched closer, her hand moving to my shoulder, stroking it, making it easier for me to talk.

"What other stuff?"

I blinked my eyes closed for a few breaths before opening them. "The first time I was thirteen years old. I was in bed, sleeping, but the door opening startled me awake. I was always a light sleeper. She called my name before closing the door behind her. She asked if I was awake. I'd never heard her sound like that. She sounded, I don't know, soothing or something. She moved closer to my bed and climbed in. That was the first time she'd ever done that. Even as a young kid she never curled into bed with me for bedtime to read or anything like that. I was immediately suspicious and frightened. But when her hand slipped underneath the blanket and into my pajama bottoms I froze.

"I didn't know or understand what was happening. At first, she just rubbed my stomach and thighs. But then she commented on how much bigger I'd grown since she bathed me as a little boy. Then she went on to complain about how my father was never around, and that a woman had needs. That was when she began stroking me. It wasn't right. I knew that even then. This wasn't something that should be happening between a mother and son. But my body responded. My mother was the first woman I ever got an erection from."

I nearly choked on that last sentence. It still wasn't easy to say out loud. Dr. Kearns told me that it wouldn't be, probably ever, but holding it in would be even worse. Lying or avoiding it as I'd done for years wouldn't serve me.

"It's why I don't sleep with blankets or sheets. She would always use them to cover us. Always."

"A-And why you don't like being touched."

I nodded. "She always used her hands. She derived a sick satisfaction from making me come with her hand."

I went silent for a few minutes, letting what I just revealed penetrate the air around us. I couldn't look at Grace because I didn't want to see anything but the love she had for me there. I still wasn't sure if what I'd told her would change that.

"There it is," I finally said. "My biggest shame."

Grace's stroking of my cheek halted and she grabbed my face between both of her hands.

"Jacob, I love you, but if you ever say anything like that again, I'll murder you myself. That is *not* your shame. There is only one person who should be ashamed in this, and that person isn't you. Do you hear me?" And for good measure, she shook my face. "No mother, no *human* should ever do that to a child!"

"I get it," I stated, taking her hand into mine and kissing the inside of her palm.

There was a long silence and I flipped over on my back, placing my casted hand underneath my head. Grace paused to look down on me, her eyes asking a question her mouth wouldn't voice. I extended my free arm and she eased into my side, laying her head on my chest.

"Dr. Kearns gave me a journal." I snorted, still feeling awkward about having the damn thing.

"Do you use it?"

I nodded. "I minored in English in undergrad."

"I didn't know that."

"I rarely tell anyone. I always liked writing, but I never did anything with it besides take some classes. Anyway, I was writing in it a few days ago and I talked with Dr. Kearns some of what I wrote. It had to do with my career."

"What about it?"

I pushed out a breath, not knowing if what I was about to reveal would make any sense.

"From the time I was young I was pushed into becoming a doctor. It was a given that Luke and I were going to medical school. Even after I graduated high school early and left for college at sixteen, I felt freer but still under my mother's hold. I majored in biology because I hadn't even considered anything else. And then I went to medical school and residency. But initially what I thought was just because I'd been forced to go into medicine, somewhere along the line I found that I enjoyed it. I love being a doctor and I'm fucking good at it. And I attributed my success to her. Which was also why I fought."

Lifting her head, Grace gave me a confused look. "What does your fighting have to do with you loving your career?"

"I associated my success as a doctor with my mother. According to Dr. Kearns I subconsciously tried to destroy it through fighting, at least partially. He thinks it's why I get into the ring knowing the risk of injury."

"But your mother has nothing to do with your success."

I shook my head. "She pounded succeeding and being the best, and looking the best, into us, literally and figuratively. I studied for hours on end even after I left home because that's what'd been drilled into me. When other med students were complaining about having to memorize everything and procedures and terms, for me it felt like it came second-nature because I'd been made to do it for so long. I'm as good as I am because of her."

Again, Grace raised her head and took my face into her palms. "In spite of her. You are who you are in spite of that evil bitch."

Lifting my head, I pressed a kiss to her lips, hoping that I could believe her words one day.

<h1 style="text-align:center">CHAPTER 29</h1>

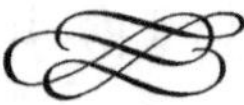

*J*acob

"Your hand is looking good, Jacob," Dr. Jeffries stated as he looked it over after having taken down the X-ray images. "How's it feeling?"

I squeezed my right hand into a fist and extended it a couple of times, feeling out the movement.

"Stiff," I grunted.

He chuckled which caused me to frown. "That's to be expected for a little while. I'm going to schedule you for some physical therapy starting next week and I want you to wear that air cast for a couple more weeks, but after that I expect you won't need it for most of the day. I'm thinking you'll be back to a hundred percent in at least another month."

My frown deepened. "I won't be able to operate for another month?"

"Depends on the operation. I wouldn't do anything too technical to start out with."

"Of course you wouldn't. You're an ortho surgeon. You guys don't know anything but breaking bones."

He laughed. "Good to see you're still keeping that sense of humor while on leave. But seriously, I want you to at least get a week or two of physical therapy under your belt before stepping back in the OR. We'll take it from there."

I nodded and slipped my hand back in the air cast, securing it at the wrist. I took the information for the physical therapist Dr. Jeffries recommended to call right after this meeting and schedule my first appointment.

"Hey, how'd it go?" Grace questioned as soon as I exited the office.

I looked over her in those electric scrubs and my body hummed to see what was underneath.

"Looks good, so far. I've got to start PT. Should be back in the OR soon." *If I still have a job,* my brain decided to remind me.

It'd been two weeks since I was released from Willow Springs and just about six weeks since the incident that sent me spiraling in the first place. I was still on suspension from the hospital while they investigated, although they called it leave, now, citing my injury as the cause.

"Do you want me to walk up with you?"

Leaning down, I brushed my lips across Grace's just because they looked so damn enticing. I couldn't even begin to comprehend the way my chest felt like it was splitting open whenever I looked at her, and as painful as that might've sounded, it was actually the best feeling in the world.

"Don't you have to look after patients?"

I tugged at her chin when she bit her bottom lip.

"I can do both."

I shook my head. "You might be the only one in this relationship with a job after this meeting. Better that you try to keep it."

It was meant to bring out a laugh, but Grace's lips turned downward. "Don't joke like that."

I pressed my lips to her forehead. "Whatever happens, it'll be fine."

She looked reluctant to let me walk away and that damn feeling in my chest started again. I kissed her forehead once more, and headed in the direction of the elevators that would carry me to the executive suites of the hospital.

Buttoning the black jacket of the suit I'd worn for the occasion, I stepped off the elevator and stopped short when the first person I laid eyes on was Nurse Greene. I narrowed my gaze on her, unfazed by the redness that outlined her eyes, as if she'd been crying.

Her face morphed into a scowl when she saw me. "I hope you're happy now," she cried.

I frowned but didn't give her the satisfaction of a response as I strode past her. I couldn't give a shit what she was upset about or even if she walked directly off a cliff. I was restraining my anger only because I was there to save my career. The last thing I needed was for another blow up at that woman, causing me to be fired on the spot. And yes, I could easily find a new position in another hospital, or hell, start my own practice, but I wanted to make that choice for myself, not have it made for me.

"Dr. Reynolds," one of the male attorneys in the conference room I just entered greeted. "Please, come in and have a seat."

My eyes darted to the lone chair across from the four people sitting on the opposite side. Two of whom I knew as attorneys for the hospital, and the other two were representatives from the human resources department.

I nodded and entered, undoing the button of my suit jacket to take a seat.

"Dr. Reynolds, first we'd like to take the time to ask how your hand is healing?"

I looked down at my hand and flexed it as much as I could in the cast. "Dr. Jeffries says it's healing well. I'll be starting PT as soon as I can make the appointment and he believes I can be back in the OR within another couple of weeks."

The quartet look between one another and nodded, pleased.

I lifted an eyebrow. "But we're not here to talk about my hand."

The male lawyer, Arturo, as he'd introduced on our prior meeting, cleared his throat. "No, we're not. Unfortunately, you have been the subject of an investigation brought on by the accusations of Nurse Greene. It has been brought to our attention that Nurse Greene initially did not give us the full story of what took place in your office, on that day."

I inhaled deeply, ready for him to ask me to explain my side of the story. I'd worked out what I would say in such an event. Even though I'd told the story to Dr. Kearns, I wasn't ready to share it with anyone else. Hell, I'd even given Grace the simplest overview of what happened. It wasn't exactly what happened with that woman in my office, that got to me, so much. It was what retelling it brought up. A past that I still was working on getting comfortable with.

"We have been made aware that Nurse Greene assaulted you, causing you to defend yourself in the process. That is what Dr. Lyons and her patient walked in on. We have confirmed this with Nurse Greene, who has been dismissed as an employee of Memorial Hospital, effective immediately."

I blinked and then looked between the four people sitting across from me. They all nodded their heads in agreement with what Arturo had just said.

I cocked my head to the side. "What does that mean for my job?"

"Well," the woman, Sharon, I think her name was, from HR began, "it means that your leave can end as soon as your physician clears you, and we at Memorial Hospital would love it if you would come back to work."

I narrowed my gaze on Sharon. "Just like that?" I was suspicious.

For weeks, in the back of my head, I wondered if I'd have a job to come back to. I even debated just turning in my resignation because the last thing I wanted to do was sit in front of a panel and explain to them why I'd gone off on Suzanne Greene the way I had. I didn't care if they saw me as the psycho doctor who couldn't control his temper, so long as I didn't have to reveal my darkest secrets to a panel of strangers.

"Some things regarding Nurse Greene were brought to our attention. Specifically, regarding her behavior toward you," Arturo answered.

"And she just volunteered that information?" I was being sarcastic because of course she hadn't.

"In a manner of speaking."

I looked to the other woman from the HR department.

"Dr. Reynolds," she began, leaning forward. "We want to make it clear that Memorial Hospital acted on the information that was presented to us at the time. It is always our intention to protect our patients and hospital staff at all times. Given what eyewitnesses saw and the story Nurse Greene gave us, we thought it best to place you on suspension directly after."

"Also, because you didn't give us much of a defense on your part."

I cut my gaze to Arturo, who visibly sunk back in his seat.

"But now that we have the full story, we understand what happened and that you were acting in a manner of self-preservation. We would like to welcome you back to your role as one of our best plastic surgeons, just as soon as you are able."

Again, I scanned the room, looking between the four. I knew there was more to this story but that they weren't going to reveal their sources. Suzanne would've never just walked in here and taken blame for what happened. But I wasn't going to push the issue. I'd missed being in the OR almost as much as I'd missed Grace those almost thirty days I was gone. And even if I couldn't operate just yet, I still could catch up on some work, review patient charts, and assist in the OR in other ways.

"Thank you." I rose.

I glanced down at Arturo as he stood and extended his hand for me to shake. I had half a mind to ignore it, but I reached across the table, taking his, and then did the same with the other three women before exiting.

My mind still wondered how everything had transpired so quickly. I hadn't given a word of my side of the story and yet I didn't need to.

"Hey, between you and me, you've got one hell of a woman in your corner."

I stopped short right before punching the down button on the elevator, and turned to face Arturo.

"What?"

"Grace."

"Nurse Young," I corrected with my head angled to the side.

He inclined his head. "Nurse Young. She really went to bat for you. Good job picking that one." He moved in to pat my arm.

"Don't touch me," I warned just before his hand made contact.

He backed away and I pivoted on my heels and headed down the hall to the staircase, instead of the elevator.

* * *

GRACE

"I need to speak with you."

My eyes widened in surprise when I whirled around from facing the nurses' station and saw Jacob barreling down on me a serious expression on his face. He took me by the arm, and I complied as he kept walking down the hallway. I figured we were headed toward his office.

I worried my bottom lip wondering what could be the matter. As far as I knew, the hospital had every intention of reinstating Jacob and leaving his HR record unblemished. But the expression on his face indicated that maybe that hadn't happened.

"What happened? Did they say you could come back?" I questioned as we entered the office and he abruptly closed the door behind us. Thankfully, the doctor he shared an office with was out on vacation.

"Yes, but you knew that already, didn't you?"

I wrinkled my forehead, not at the question, but at the angry tone in his voice. "That's a good thing, right?"

"That I still have my job or that you knew?"

My shoulders sank. "Your job."

"So you're admitting to knowing that I was going to keep my job. And that Suzanne had been fired?"

I swallowed because yes, I knew. I provided the hospital with the ammunition to do both.

"Jacob, why is this upsetting you? I thought you *wanted* to keep your job. You love being a surgeon."

"Of course I do."

273

"So why do you sound angry?"

He didn't answer immediately. Just stared at me for a few unspoken heartbeats before he folded his arms over his chest.

I ignored the way my body heated up because he looked good in his suit. He looked good in anything really.

"You never answered my first question. What did you do?"

"I just dug up a little information on Suzanne."

"What type of information, Grace?"

Rolling my eyes, I told Jacob all about how Suzanne had a history of harassing and even stalking doctors. As I told him about the confrontation I had with Suzanne, in which she admitted to what she did in the office, and that I recorded it, his expression didn't change.

"After all of that, the hospital must've seen fit to dismiss Suzanne and absolve you of any wrongdoing."

Jacob unfolded his arms and moved them to his waist, staring at me intently.

"Jacob …" I moved closer, feeling uneasy at the way he was looking at me.

"How many times are you going to try to keep saving me, Grace?"

Wrinkling my forehead, I tilted my head. "What's that supposed to mean?"

"Just what I said. I don't need you to keep rushing in and saving me. I don't need you to be my personal hero."

My back went straight. I felt like I'd just been gut punched but he hadn't touched me. His words were the only force he needed. Those and the way his eyes began to cloud over in that stormy way he looked at everyone else. I could almost feel him shutting me out.

"J—" I started but his phone buzzed.

I was silent as he pulled it out of his pocket and checked the text message. His eyebrows spiked and his lips pinched. I couldn't read the face he was making. He stared at his phone screen for a long while, as if reading the message over and over again would allow him to make sense of it.

"I need to go," he finally stated, moving past me to grab his coat off the rack in the corner of the room.

"Jacob," I called. "Where are you going?"

He turned his head to look at me over his shoulder. "Back home," was all he said before exiting the office without even looking back.

And what had been the start of what I believed would be a great day, had gone so wrong, so quickly.

CHAPTER 30

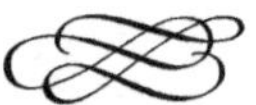

*J*acob

"Jacob, you know you don't have to go to this if you don't want to," Dr. Kearns reminded me yet again.

"Why the hell do you keep telling me that? I know." I gritted my teeth and paced the hotel room I'd been staying in for the past three days.

"I'm just making sure you're aware that you have options. No one is—"

"Forcing me. I get to make the decision. I'm aware, Doc, we've been over this." I stopped pacing and stared out the window of the hotel. From this fifteenth floor, I had a great view of the Space Needle in the heart of Seattle.

"But you're still going."

"Yes." He hadn't phrased it as a question, but I still felt the need to say the yes out loud, more as a confirmation to myself.

"And you have your journal and your coping strategies with you?"

I rolled my eyes. "We've only gone over them a hundred times since I've been here."

"Yes, we have, but this is a big deal, Jacob. What you're doing takes a lot of courage, and I don't often encourage my clients do this so early in their recovery process. But—"

"I'm not turning back."

He sighed. "I'm well aware. I will be available if you need to call throughout the day."

"You said that already, too."

"I'm telling you again. And what about Grace? You still haven't told her where you are?"

"No." Scowling, I shook my head, hating that I felt like a coward for not telling her. I also thought back to the last time I saw her face. The way I rejected her when all she did was do her best to help me. I knew that was all she had tried to do but I was someone who didn't need to be taken care of by others because the people who were supposed to take care of me early on in life had failed. Dr. Kearns helped me to see why being cared for felt so wrong, even when it felt so damn right.

"Thanks, Dr. Kearns. I'll call if I need to." I hung up, knowing that I probably wouldn't be speaking to Dr. Kearns again until I was back in Williamsport.

An hour later, I was heading out of the hotel and into the rental car I picked up for this occasion. I had an hour long drive from Seattle back to the town I grew up in. On the way there, I thought of Grace.

I'd called her once since I'd been in Washington to tell her that I was out of town for a few days. I didn't give more details than that, although she wanted to know more. I told her I would be away for a few days and that I wouldn't be able to speak with her. I heard the rejection in her voice along with the lingering questions. But I didn't have answers to give. Not yet, anyway. I was still searching for them myself.

I hoped this spur of the moment trip would provide some.

I pulled up to the house on Lakeshore Drive. The very one I grew up in. It looked smaller, less intimidating than the last time I was there, more than fifteen years ago. But there hadn't been many changes since. It was still lined with white siding, the door a candy red color that my mother loved, and black window panels. It was the cookie cutter home that fit in with the rest of the upper middle class family homes on this block. And I couldn't stand the sight of it.

I watched as a few people trickled in and out of the house, dressed in all black. Some carried flowers and what appeared to be pans of food. The solemn expressions on all of their faces turned my stomach. I turned the key in the car's ignition and drove off without getting out.

* * *

"Dust thou art, and unto dust thou shalt return."

The pastor's words floated through the open windows of the rental car, colliding with my ears. My hands fisted in my lap as I watched a line form to toss flowers onto the off-white casket. I felt nothing as the casket was lowered into the ground. But I did feel a stirring of emotion when I watched my father bend over at the waist, in tears, as a few family members hugged him in his grief.

Fuck all of them.

I felt hatred. I'd said that the number one person I hated in this life was my mother, but as I stood there, watching my father cry over her casket, I realized that was a lie. I hated him just as much.

I sat in that car for a long time as people filed out, getting into their own vehicles or one of the limos that would take them back to the home I was just at, to eat, console one another, and share fond memories of the life lost. I sure as hell wouldn't be joining in on any of that.

About forty-five minutes after I pulled up, the only person who remained at my mother's burial site was my father. His back was to me as he sat in a chair slumped over with his face buried in his hands.

I climbed out of the car, dug my hands into my pockets, and strode in the direction of the two people who gave me life. One dead, one very much alive, but after this final conversation would be just as dead to me.

I moved closer until, pausing at my father's side and glaring down at him. He didn't even notice me at first. I took a few more steps until I was at burial site. Looking down, I glared at my mother's casket.

"J-Jacob," my father's strangled voice gasped.

Slowly, I turned to him, glaring. He looked fucking pathetic.

"You came," he said, standing, moving toward me.

"Don't."

He halted in his tracks.

I glanced back over my shoulder at the casket below before turning back to my father.

"I just came to make sure she was actually dead."

His facial expression turned even gloomier. He shook his head.

"What a h-horrible thing to say about the w-woman who—"

"The woman who what? Tortured me? Beat the hell out of me? Taunted me by telling me how useless and worthless I was because I got an A- instead of an A+? That's the woman who I should be grieving over?"

"She wasn't perfect but she wanted the best for you."

I moved closer to my father. "No, she was pure evil and only wanted what was best for *her*. And you did fuck all to stop her. You left us with her to build your fucking career."

"Stop this!" my father demanded. "We were great parents to you. No one is perfect but we gave you everything you needed and more!" His voice raised and his face grew red with anger.

"You honestly believe that?" I shook my head. "No, you don't believe that shit for one second." I moved closer. "You knew what she was. Didn't you?" I was in his face, daring him to lie to me.

"Jacob, she was your mother. I-I—"

"And you were our father! It was your job to protect us and you fed us to the wolves by leaving us with her every chance you got. Did you know?" I growled angrily, my fists tightening at my sides.

"Know what?"

I held myself back from punching him right then and there, but just barely. "Did you know what that sick cunt did when you weren't around? All those long nights when you were working late or out of town. How she would sneak into my room and underneath my bed sheets because she was *lonely.* How I never said anything to anyone about it or complained and pushed her away out of fear she would do it to Luke instead. So I took it to spare him. Did you fucking know?" I growled.

My father's eyes widened in horror and his grief turned to one of shame. He shook his head in denial. "Th-that's impossible," he stuttered. "Sh-she would n-never—"

"She did. And after three years I couldn't take it, which was why I graduated high school early and left home."

"And never looked back."

"Oh, but I did come back. I came back repeatedly, to warn her that if she even so much as thought of doing the same thing to Luke, I'd kill her myself!"

"Is that why?" a deep male voice growled, behind my father.

He and I both turned, my eyebrows lifting at the sight of my younger brother. My shoulders slumped upon staring in his eyes because I knew he'd heard the truth. A truth I never wanted him to know.

"Luke," that was from my father.

Luke hardly spared our father a glance before his gaze turned to me. "Is that why she barely paid me any attention once you left?"

I didn't say anything because there was nothing to say. The answer was obvious.

Luke didn't wait for an answer either. He moved passed my father and I, toward our mother's casket.

Turning, I watched as he stared down into the grave. Then, in typical Luke fashion, he bid our mother farewell by spitting in her grave.

He turned to face our father. "I also came to make sure the cunt was actually dead." His eyes moved to me, and for a split second I swore I saw them soften just a smidgen before he pivoted on his heels and headed in the direction he came without another word.

I wanted to follow him but I still had to get something off my chest. I looked back to my father.

"This'll be the last time you and I ever speak. Because you and your dead wife won't get a second more of my life. I have a career, a life, and more importantly a woman back home who loves the hell out of me, and if she can put up with me, I'm going to marry her and live our lives in peace. And you won't ever be a part of that. You enjoy what's left of your useless life."

I gave my father one final scowl before brushing past him and walking back to my rental. I was done with this state, this town, and all of my relatives in it. Except for one.

I took one final look around to see if Luke was still in sight but he was long gone. I figured he would be. I didn't know what I'd say to him, if he was still around.

The entire drive back I only had two regrets. One was that it'd be hours before I could hold Grace in my arms, if she would still have me. I knew I fucked up by what I said and then rushing out on her as soon as I got that text from a family member saying my mother died. My second regret was that Luke had overheard my ugly secrets, the ones I'd kept from him for so long.

But as I strolled into the lobby of the hotel I was ready to check out of, I found my kid brother, now two inches taller than me, leaned against the counter. The T-shirt, leather jacket, and jeans he wore were a far cry from the prep school outfits our mother forced us to wear years earlier.

"I've been waiting for you," he said.

"So you have," I retorted, slipping my hand in my pocket.

He glanced off somewhere in the distance. "I'm gonna need a beer for this conversation."

I nodded. "There's a bar on the corner." I figured Luke wouldn't be in the mood to sit at the bar of this five-star hotel. The other bar I referred to was more of a dive bar, and by its appearance, more in tune with the style my brother had taken over the years since we'd last spoken.

"Let's do it."

Inclining my head, I turned to follow Luke out the door.

I ended up staying in Seattle for one night longer than I planned.

* * *

Grace

I checked my phone once again to see I had no missed calls and no new text messages. My heart sank.

"Hey, Grace, you ready?" Jackson questioned as he entered the back changing room where I'd been warming my voice up and getting ready to hit the stage.

Nodding, I cleared my throat. "Yeah, I'll be out in a second."

"'Kay. See ya out there."

I pushed out the breath I'd just been holding once Jackson left, and stared at my black phone screen. Jacob was supposed to come back the day before but late the previous night I received a text saying he'd be back in town today. And to make matters worse, he still hadn't even told me where he was. Or why he left. Our last real conversation was the one that took place in his office. Where he got upset for reasons I still didn't quite understand.

Maybe I did overstep, I thought. I couldn't help it. I always went above and beyond for the people I cared about. And for the people I loved? There was no limit to what I would do to help. Maybe that was the problem. I had stepped on his pride while trying to help.

I stood from the chair I was sitting in and fluffed my curls, checking over the half up-half down hairstyle I wore, mainly because I'd hoped Jacob would be here to see me sing. He loved when I wore my hair down and I enjoyed the way he always ran his fingers through my curls whenever we kissed and made love.

Sighing, I smoothed down the puffy black skirt I wore and strutted down the hall toward the front of the lounge where the stage was. I smiled at the band and waved at the audience members as they clapped for me.

"Hey, everyone." I did my best to sound cheery as I looked over the crowd. I couldn't quite make out everyone's face but I knew Jacob wasn't among them. I could always feel his presence whenever he was near. "I, uh, it's been a couple of weeks since I've been here and I was going to start off with something fast-paced but I've changed my mind."

Again, I scanned the audience with my gaze.

"This song is kind of reflective of how I'm feeling tonight, so here goes." I stepped away from the microphone and gave the band the name of the song I planned to sing. Thankfully, they knew it well.

Moving back to the microphone, I inhaled before parting my lips and beginning the words to Nao's "Another Lifetime".

Once I was halfway through the first line of the song, the soft sounds of the keyboard started playing.

I sang the song with my entire heart because right then it was how I felt. Like a lover who had found the love of her life but for whatever reason it wouldn't work out.

The words of the song seemed to float from my mouth, surrounding me and holding me up as I sang about waiting for the love of my life in the next lifetime to see if it would work out then.

By the time I completed the song, I felt spent.

"Thank you." I bowed to the audience and headed to the back room even though I had more time in my set. I needed to get off the stage to gather myself before going out again.

I took a seat in front of the bureau and dug through my purse, searching for my phone yet again.

"Hey, Grace, you know you still have more time," Jackson entered, reminding me.

Turning, I nodded. "Yeah, I just need a minute."

"Okay. Hey, um, me and some of the guys are going out to another lounge tonight to scope it out and have a few drinks. Would you like to come?"

"She's taken."

My breath hitched when my eyes moved over Jackson's shoulder to see Jacob drilling holes into the back of Jackson's head.

"Jacob."

My calling his name brought those grey irises to me. I watched as the stormy look cleared and they seemed to sparkle, that stare he always gave me. He didn't say a word as he stepped around Jackson, and none too graciously, pulled the door closed in Jackson's face, leaving just he and I.

"That wasn't very nice."

He shrugged. "So?"

"Did you just get back?"

"Came straight from the airport here. I was in Seattle."

"Why would you—"

"My mother died. That day in my office. The text message was from a cousin of mine saying she died. I went to make sure it was true. I watched her funeral from afar and then confronted my father."

"How did that go?"

"I didn't hit him or beat him up if that's what you're asking."

I grinned because a piece of me did wonder if he had.

"I would've gone with you," I blurted out.

He moved closer, reaching down to push a few curls behind my ear before running a finger down my cheek. My eyes floated closed at the ripples of sensation that small touch caused in my body.

"I know you would've. But I needed to do this alone. I don't want that part of my life to ever touch you, us, what we have." His finger traced my bottom lip. "That was a great song."

"You heard me sing?"

He nodded. "You were perfect up there, as usual. There's just one problem with it …" He trailed off while he dug his right hand into the pocket of his dark jeans. Pulling out a small black box, he flipped it open. "I don't want to wait another lifetime. How about this one?"

My eyes fell to the hand he held out, the square cut diamond ring sparkling. I couldn't take my eyes off the ring as he knelt down in front of me.

"Grace, I'm sorry about the way I ran off the other day. And all the stuff I said just before that. I know you inside and out. You will always find a way to help others, especially those you love. Which is just one of the many reasons I love you more than I ever thought I was capable of. I know I'm not an easy man to love and I still have a lot of shit to work through from my past, but I'll do it and more, just to be a better man for you. The man you deserve. Will you marry m—"

"Yes!" I exclaimed, throwing my arms around his neck and almost knocking him over.

His deep chuckle caused another ripple effect in my body.

"I love you," I gushed and took his face into mine, kissing him.

Jacob, never one to relinquish control so easily, took over the kiss, burying his free hand in my hair, holding my head in place.

He soon pulled back, releasing me and removing the ring from the box to place it on my left ring finger.

"Luke said this one would look good on you."

I stared up at Jacob. "Luke?"

He nodded and swallowed before answering. "He was at the funeral, too; for the same reason I was. He helped me pick out your ring."

He must've seen the quizzical expression on my face because he leaned down, placed a kiss to my forehead, and said, "It's a long story, baby. I'll tell you all about it later. But right now, I'm taking you back to your place so you can sing for me until we pass out from exhaustion."

I giggled as I watched Jacob gather my belongings, help me into my coat, and grab my hand to follow him out to his car to do exactly what he said.

I ended up singing at the top of my lungs all night long.

EPILOGUE

3 Months Later
   Grace

"I can't see anything," I whined, holding my hands out in front of me, trying to feel around to make sure I wasn't about to walk into a wall.

"That's the point, baby," my husband murmured in my ear before kissing the crook of my neck from behind me.

I tried desperately to ignore the shiver that ran through me, still annoyed by the silk scarf tied around my eyes, obstructing my view of the world around me.

"You did agree to this," he reminded me.

I frowned. "I know but I don't like this. Where are we? Where are we going?"

His deep chuckle caused my frown to deepen. "Just a few more steps."

I heard the distinct sound of a door being pushed open and then we were inside somewhere. But it was quiet, too quiet. I turned and angled my head but it was no use, I couldn't hear anything distinctive around me to clue me in on where we were. And of course, I still couldn't see.

"Just a couple more steps."

I let Jacob guide me a few more feet into the room or building. The heeled booties I wore sounded against a hardwood floor.

"Okay," he finally stated, holding me in place. From behind me he reached around and slowly lifted the scarf from my eyes.

I blinked a couple of times to let my vision clear, and then slowly looked around the huge, empty room. As I'd assumed, the floors were a shiny hardwood, the walls were a light blue color that I really liked, and off to the right I could see a long hallway that led to more rooms.

"Those'll be the exam rooms, my office, your office, and the manager's office, once we hire one. I'll also have the room completed for in-patient procedures within six months of our opening."

I blinked and turned to Jacob, whose grey eyes settled on me. He was reading me, to see if I was taking in what he just explained.

"Are you serious?" A smile crested on my face.

He nodded, grinning that damn smile that always caused my stomach to flip flop.

"You're opening your own practice? This is your space?"

"No, baby, this is *our* space. *Our* practice. Because I'm going to need a nurse anesthetist to help me."

I frowned. "Babe, I still have like thirty months to go to complete my degree."

He shrugged, his eyes sparkling. "I'm not going anywhere." He pulled me to him by the flowy top I wore, bringing his hands around my waist. "And neither are you, Mrs. Reynolds."

I turned my head up to meet his lips. The kiss lasted longer than expected, as it often did.

Giggling, I pulled away when Jacob's hand moved to my backside, cupping it. "Not in our new office."

"What the hell do you think I brought you here for?" he growled, pulling me to him again.

"No!" I giggled. "You have to show me around."

He sighed and pulled back. "I guess you're right." Taking my hand into his, he began the tour of the rest of the space.

"Our offices will be right next to each other. You can come in here and study during your down time. I will keep my privileges at Memorial, of course, for when I need to operate there."

I nodded, stroking his arm up and down as I listened to Jacob describe all the features he planned to have in our private practice. He'd been able to afford the down payment on this space with the money that came as a result of him selling his condo. He'd moved into my home a few weeks before we were married.

"I love you," I finally stated after watching his profile for a few minutes.

He paused his explanation, turning to me, inching closer with that prowling gleam in his eyes.

My heart rate sped up.

"How has it only been two months since I made you mine?" he questioned, wrapping his arms around me.

Grinning, I placed my hands on his shoulders, looking down at the diamond and white gold bands on my left hand. The same band that matched the one on his left ring finger.

"*I* can't believe you got me to marry you only thirty days after you proposed."

"Thirty days was too long." He frowned.

"It was the quickest we could get our families together," I reminded him.

"I could've sent Luke a damn postcard."

I shook my head laughing. "You would've regretted him not being there."

Jacob and Luke's relationship had taken a turn for the better, obviously. The two still very much had separate lives but Luke was at our wedding and seemed genuinely happy for his brother, even if his attitude was a little off-putting at first. I got the impression he wasn't trying to be an asshole, that was just his nature.

"I feel for whatever woman he ends up with."

Jacob grunted. "Somehow I suspect we should have more pity for Luke because whatever woman finally lands him, will have him wrapped around her finger."

I laughed. "You think so?"

"I know so. Look at how damned twisted you have me."

I giggled. "Pretty sure it's the other way around."

"You're confused, baby. You've probably had me wrapped around your finger since that first day I laid eyes on you. I fell in love when I watched your performance in the OR."

I rolled my eyes. "If you say so, charmer. Hey, speaking of the OR, did you hear what happened to Suzanne?"

Jacob frowned.

"I know, I know. But the work rumor mill is good for some things. Like, keeping me informed of the fact that she was actually *arrested* last month. Turns out, while she was trying to seduce you, she was also blackmailing a doctor at Central who she *was* actually having an affair with. The doctor was married, but once she tried to blackmail him into giving her money and a job at Central, he went to the police. And he's pressing charges."

"Couldn't have happened to a better person."

Smiling, I leaned into the kiss he offered. When I pulled back, I took another look around the office.

"This is going to be great, baby."

Jacob pulled me into his side as we strolled to the front door. "We just need to sign the paperwork to make it official and it's ours."

I raised up on tiptoes to give him a kiss to the cheek. "Now, let me take you home and cook for you to show you how proud I am of you."

"Only if you promise to sing for me afterwards."

I grinned. "I promise."

* * *

ABOUT THE AUTHOR

Looking for updates on future releases? I can be found around the web at the following locations:

Newsletter: Tiffany Patterson Writes Newsletter

FaceBook private group: Tiffany's Passions Between the Pages

Website: TiffanyPattersonWrites.com

FaceBook Page: Author Tiffany Patterson

Email: TiffanyPattersonWrites@gmail.com

<u>More books by Tiffany Patterson</u>

ALSO BY TIFFANY PATTERSON

The Black Burlesque Series

Black Pearl

Black Dahlia

Black Butterfly

Forever Series

7 Degrees of Alpha (Collection)

Forever

Safe Space Series

Safe Space (Book 1)

Safe Space (Book 2)

THE TOWNSEND BROTHERS SERIES

AARON'S PATIENCE

Meant to Be
For Keeps
Until My Last Breath

Tiffany Patterson Website Exclusives
Locked Doors

www.ingramcontent.com/pod-product-compliance
Lightning Source LLC
Chambersburg PA
CBHW060906210726

48293CB00006B/1985